A CASE OF GRACE

Patricia Massey Kile
Nancy Roberts-Brown

A Case Of Grace

Text © Patricia Massey Kile, 2024

Cover design by BEAUTeBOOK

The authors assert the moral right under the Copyright, Designs and Patents Act of 1988 to be identified as the authors of this work.

The stories in this book are works of fiction. Any resemblance between fictional characters created by the author and actual persons, living or dead, is purely coincidental.

All Rights reserved. With the exception of brief excerpts as part of a published review, no part of this publication may be reproduced, stored in a retrieval system, or transmitted, in any form or by any means without the prior written consent of the author, nor be otherwise circulated in any form of binding or cover other than that in which it is published and without a similar condition being imposed on the subsequent purchaser.

Thank you for buying an authorized edition of this book and for complying with copyright laws. Copyright encourages diverse voices, protects free speech, and helps sustain a vibrant culture.

Also available in eBook

Contents

To Justin and Merritt

ALWAYS A GIFT
Little
Free
Library®
NEVER FOR SALE

PROLOGUE

She turned into the parking lot at Del Rey State Park and thought about where to wait for him. The lot was empty, the patrol having chased out any late-stayers when the park closed at ten. So it was easy to see he wasn't there yet. She guessed it didn't matter where she parked except, maybe near the exit for a quick getaway? Or maybe away from the exit so they wouldn't be seen?

She pulled into a spot somewhere in the middle and lowered the window. God she was nervous. She could hear and smell the ocean. Its massive, mysterious presence only added to her anxiety. Where was he? Was he going to stand her up? She'd specified this time and place. Counting the minutes, she chewed a hangnail and now it began to bleed.

She nearly jumped out of her skin when the passenger door opened. Then he slipped in next to her. He must have parked somewhere else.

"Hey, how's it going?" That snarky smile, too often a prelude to demanding something.

"Never mind how I am—you're late. I thought you weren't coming."

"Well I'm here now, so no worries."

"Did you bring the money?"

"Hey, getting right down to business are we? No time for a little friendly conversation?" The snarky smile again. His hand squeezing her shoulder.

"I want to do what we came here for and be on my way. Where's the money?"

He pulled the bank envelope out of his inside jacket pocket. "All right, here you go. Before you take the time to count it, there's just ten thousand there. It's all I could come up with on short notice. I'll get you the rest next week."

She counted the thick wad of hundred-dollar bills as fast as she could without tripping herself up. "Okay, ten thousand. But the other forty thousand by next Friday at the latest. Let me know when you've got it."

"Absolutely. The ten k's intended to be a good faith pledge." He squeezed her shoulder again. "As I told you earlier, I agree I owe you this—I'm not holding out." She relaxed a little, took a deep breath. This was going to turn out all right.

He reached into his pocket again. "Just to prove it, I brought you a little bonus." She could see there were two pills in the baggie. "One for you, one for me. These are something new and wonderful—give you amazing clarity. You don't have to worry about driving home—you won't be impaired. But oh my God, will you feel amazing for the next couple of hours, longer if you're lucky."

He fingered the pills, then popped one into his mouth and took a sip from his water bottle. He held out the other pill and the bottle.

She hesitated. Why would he of all people have these? "I don't know," she said. "I'm trying to stay clean–get clean."

"Absolutely non-habit forming, That's the beauty of these wonder pills. I wouldn't offer you one otherwise. And I wouldn't take it myself." Well, she thought, he was a man of many secrets—this made one more. She took the pill from him, popped it into her mouth, and took a sip of water. *Here's to amazing*, she thought.

"So what do you plan to do with the money? Invest it?" he asked with a hint of snark. "I can give you some advice if you want it."

She thought about the question, not knowing whether she should tell him anything. And not able to focus on an answer. What business of his was it anyway?

Five minutes later, when she had slumped over the steering wheel, he pulled on a pair of plastic gloves and reached into her purse. He took the envelope with the money and tucked it back into his jacket. Then he removed a pill bottle from his jacket pocket and tossed it onto the floor of the car, taking care to leave it where it could be seen. He used a paper towel to wipe the door handle and anything else in the car he might have touched. Then he hiked back to his car and drove home, thinking about how easy it had been. But also about what a mistake he'd made getting involved with her in the first place.

Recovering Screw-up

July

Contrary to what you see on television, the life of a private investigator is not always exciting. Unlike Magnum, I spend a fair amount of time on ordinary office tasks, which is what I was doing on that Thursday afternoon. Catching up on email—I had a lot to catch up on—and some filing. I hated the latter, which was why I had a lot of it, but it was just me, so I had to do it. The filing was mostly electronic, and I'd been careless about where and how I'd saved my documents. I made the usual resolve to be more organized, knowing how likely that was.

Summers on the Oregon coast are usually mild, but that July day was unusually warm. Between the boredom and the heat I'd spent a big part of the afternoon dozing at the dining table that doubled as my desk. I was determined to keep going until I finished those two tasks, so it was about six when I shoved the last piece of paper into a colored folder and renamed the last electronic file. I hadn't stopped to eat lunch so I was starving. I thought about what there was in my refrigerator to eat. I kept a ready supply of frozen meals, cheap and easy—but after finishing all that work I felt I deserved something better.

I'd been living on rabbit food and water for several months and now I wanted a burger and fries and a beer. There were two taverns in town that served food—one on the main drag that was teeming with loud young people and tourists and another a little further out that appeared to be quieter. I hadn't been to either one—I'd just seen and heard them from the street. No way I was going to the loud one.

I put on a clean pair of joggers and a reasonably clean tee shirt and picked up my car keys. But then it occurred to me that if I was going to ingest all those carbs and calories maybe

I needed some exercise. The tavern was a bit of a trek from my condo. I keep an old ten-speed bike chained up in my carport, so I unchained it and rode the couple of miles to the Pub & Grub tavern.

Pedaling along with nothing on my mind but the thought of grease and hops, I was totally unaware that the events of the evening would ultimately change my life–or at least reshape my career. My first murder investigation. I hadn't set out to be that kind of private investigator. For that matter, I didn't originally set out to be a PI at all, but here I am. Nor did I ever plan to live in a little burg like Gearhart, Oregon—city boy that I am, having lived all my life in Seattle—but again, here I am.

I sat at the bar of the Pub & Grub and ordered a dark beer and a burger and fries, then sat drinking my beer and looking around at my fellow patrons while I waited for my food. Not many people. A few older twosomes at tables around the periphery and a group of people maybe near my age at one of the long tables in the middle, drinking beer and laughing at each other's attempts with the darts. One of the women caught my eye and smiled.

About that time, the bartender brought my food. I ordered another beer and started to eat. Someone sat down next to me, and I looked up to see it was the smiling woman. She was nice enough looking–blond, which is my personal preference–and looked to be somewhere around my age. So, I smiled back, and she said, "I don't suppose you play darts." I said that I hadn't for some time, but I guessed it was like riding a bicycle. I didn't tell her I'd ridden my childhood bike to the tavern.

"Madelyn Jacobs," the blond smiler introduced herself. "My friends call me Maddie." I could see she wasn't going to take no for an answer to her darts question. "Henry Case," I said. "My friends call me Henry." She laughed. "There's an empty seat at our table, over there by me." I thanked the laundry gods that I'd put on those reasonably clean clothes.

12

The next thing I knew I was demonstrating my left-handed dart-throwing prowess, ordering another beer, and finishing my burger and fries while I talked with Maddie and the others. They were, as she described them, part of a group of about a dozen people who met at the Pub & Grub to socialize and drink beer. They were working people, mostly single. There were some members of the group in the tavern almost every night. Weekends there were more. Kind of like the TV show "Cheers." Somebody asked me about myself... Did I live on the coast permanently? Where did I work? Was I single? Despite my reticence to talk about myself or to get involved with "the locals," I found myself doing just that, answering their somewhat personal questions in detail. Must have been the beer, or maybe it was the loneliness getting to me.

About eleven, the party broke up. When I got up to leave, someone said, "Hey, Henry, we're here every night. You're welcome to join us again. But I'm not going to play darts against you." I laughed and said that I hoped to see them again. I probably wouldn't, but it was the thing to say.

Riding home in the dark, I thought with some regret about all the talking I'd done. I've always believed that the life of a private investigator should be just that—private. I like to play it low key, stay below the radar. I don't make a secret of what I do; I just don't advertise it. People are always curious, assuming it involves a lot of crime. Most of the crime I investigate is insurance fraud—not sexy or TV-worthy. People also want to get me involved in their own stuff—and I'm not interested in giving it away. Most of their situations don't turn out to be something for a PI anyway. And then of course there's the confidentiality consideration.

The version of my life story I had told my new dart-playing buddies was the least interesting, basically the sanitized Cliff's Notes version, the devil being in the details of our respective lives. What I shared was that I'd been a private investigator for nearly ten years, that I was from Seattle, divorced, with an ex-wife and daughter in Seattle. I'd moved to the Oregon Coast, I said, to take advantage of the condo that my ex and I still jointly owned–no need to let a perfectly good place with a spectacular ocean view and beach access go to waste.

"So I guess you're a Husky?" someone had asked, referring to the University of Washington in Seattle. I allowed as how I'd spent some time at that fine institution. I hadn't felt the need to tell them that it had been several grueling years of law school that followed five grueling, but frequently shit-faced, undergrad years at Princeton. That always makes people wonder why I'm doing what I'm doing. So–never mind.

Our little dart-throwing group included folks who'd done time at Washington State, U of Oregon, and Oregon State. So, in addition to a "Dawg," we had a Cougar, two Ducks, and a Beaver–a regular zoo of sorts.

It had been a fun evening. I'd been living in Gearhart for about three months at that point, and it had been a while since I'd seen any socialization that didn't involve staring at a screen. That was good in that it meant I'd been catching up on my work and improving my financial position, but I have to admit life was getting a little lonely. So, I was both pleased and surprised to find a group of people somewhere near my own age who seemed happy to take me in.

When I say I was surprised, I don't mean I'm a total loser or anything. I'm not. In fact, I'm a pretty average guy overall, probably above average, and in an average group, I'd look okay or maybe even pretty good. But the family I'd grown up in and the elite private schools I'd attended were filled with beautiful people who excelled—and by comparison I was never at the top of the heap. So I was still surprised when I caught the eye and the interest of a nice-looking woman like Maddie Jacobs and when people liked me enough to invite me back.

As I say, I'm really not a loser. I usually look okay. My physical appearance is average I guess—average height and build, brown hair, and blue eyes—just your average Euro-American guy. My indulgent lifestyle in the last couple of years had expanded my waistline and made sweatpants my most comfortable option–but I was working on fixing that, pedaling my way to health on my ten-speed and eating light, the burger and beer break notwithstanding.

Not that I'm a wallflower either. I'm outgoing and social enough. Growing up. I was well-liked by people around me. Maybe I wasn't as funny or brilliant in a conversation as some guys. but I did have a good sense of humor—one of the first things people mentioned in describing me. I wasn't exactly athletic; In high school, I made the football and basketball teams but spent more time on the bench than on the field or court. I kept my head and hands down in class discussions, but I tried hard otherwise, and teachers liked my politeness and humor when it didn't get out of control. Girls weren't exactly all over me, but I could get dates for homecoming and other big events.

In my adult life, my friends have been mostly people I went to school with. I haven't dated much since my divorce, although I have a few women friends. My clients seem to like me, although a lot of our interactions are virtual or remote.

So, it had been a better evening than I'd expected, and I was glad I'd gone. I never expect to light up the room when I walk in, so I was happy to be accepted so readily. Maybe I'd go back. But not too soon, since I had to keep my nose to the wheel and my shoulder to the grindstone–or however that saying goes.

Fallen Angel

September

Buttering a slice of whole wheat toast, I gaze out of the large kitchen window. The storm raging outside is no match for the one buffeting my life. In truth, I've been tossed by storms my entire life. But this one is worse than any of the others. Suspected of murder! Murder! Oh my God. Was it only three years ago that I was a priest serving a parish in Central Seattle?

When I moved to Gearhart I had high hopes of settling into the peaceful lifestyle I'd always imagined for myself. Who knew that being one of the few Blacks around here could risk my well-being. Even my freedom. Racism here is every bit as bad as it is in the big city. Maybe worse. And now I'm screwed. So screwed. And terrified. How could I have gotten into so much trouble in the few short months I'd been here?

* * *

It was just last May, only four months ago, when my sister Val and her wife Liz picked me up at the Monroe Correctional Facility near Seattle. I'd been reluctant to accept their invitation to live with them in Gearhart - I'd always been a city boy - but it was my best offer. Actually, my only offer. My stomach was in knots most of the trip. Scared, curious, relieved to be free for the first time in two years. Worried about being one of the few Blacks in town. Praying I hadn't made a mistake.

We talked a lot during the long ride to Gearhart. "I can't tell you how much I appreciate you inviting me to live with you for a while," I told them. "For obvious reasons I didn't want to return to Seattle, but I didn't know what else to do."

"We're blood, Merritt." Val smiled at me. "That's what

family's for."

"I'm kinda nervous about the Second Chance Program. That director, Eric somebody-or-other who interviewed me seemed nice enough, but somehow he gave me the creeps. It's hard to tell much over the phone. But he hired me, so I guess I can't complain."

"I hear you, Merritt, but when I saw the Second Chance flier on the bulletin board at Providence, it looked like it could be a good opportunity for you. I'll guess we'll just wait and see."

"Yeah. Wait and see, I guess." I suddenly felt the weight of my situation. "What a come-down. I used to be a priest! And now..." I absently watched the scenery flash past the car window before continuing. "Don't get me wrong, I really do appreciate the opportunity. But sometimes it's so damn hard to forgive myself for getting myself into this mess to begin with. What was I thinking? Or not thinking. Damn it! I used to be a priest! A much beloved and respected priest."

Repeating those words over and over again did little to help me actually believe they had at one time been true. So much water over the dam. I disappointed so many people. My going to prison just about killed Gran-Mo. She was so proud of me when I became a priest. Mom and Dad, too. As the only son in our family, it was always their hope that would happen. They even named me Merritt - Merritt Grace - in the hope that I would follow a course that befitted a name with spiritual suggestion. They were all so very happy and proud of me when I was ordained. Hopefully someday they'll be proud of me again.

I took a breath, glanced up at Val and Liz, and managed a smile. "Sorry for the pity party, I really am grateful for the two of you, and for Second Chance."

Liz looked up. "Tell me more about Second Chance. I heard Val mention it, but I didn't pay much attention at the time."

"From what I understand, it's a program run by the state of Oregon to give ex-felons and other ne'er-do-wells like me a second chance at employment. Pacific Behavioral Health, my new employer, apparently gets several of its employees through the program. That's about all I can tell you right now."

"I'm sure Val told me a million times, but please remind me, Merritt, what you'll be doing for them."

"I'll be an addictions counselor. I got certified as a Substance Abuse Specialist through a program they had at Monroe, University Beyond Bars."

Val piped in. "That was a fabulous opportunity for you after all you'd been through. Possibly a new career path. I bet you'll be great at the job. You'll have plenty of clients. I know from the hospital there's a whole lot of addiction around Gearhart."

"Yeah. Well, I guess I'll find out." I wished I was convinced this was a good move for me. Would I ever serve as a priest again? Did I even want to? Was I even worthy of being a priest? If nothing else, the time in Gearhart would give me the time and space to heal from the trauma of the past few years and consider my future.

We drove in silence for quite a while, each lost in our own thoughts. I was pretty nervous, not quite believing I was free, scared about what I was getting into, and wondering whether I deserved any chances at all. Finally, when we turned onto Highway 101, I forgot the self-doubts and got excited when I caught glimpses of the ocean. I hadn't been to the beach since I helped Val and Liz move here a few years ago. "Oh man, Val. This is amazing. From a prison cell to a house at the ocean. How did I get so lucky?"

"I guess maybe you forgot where our house is, Bro. We don't exactly have a cushy ocean view." I ignored her, erasing any memory of seeing the house several years ago, and continuing to dream about my new beach home. That is, until Val turned left - away from the ocean – by the Dairy Queen at the main intersection in Gearhart, and then turned right on Railroad Street. The east side of 101 had a somewhat rural feel, with

19

several old trees and a dotting of small homes gracing well-kept lots. Not exactly "beach house glamorous", but still attractive. So I was surprised when Val pulled up at an old house at the end of the road. For some reason I had little memory of ever seeing it before. Its unkempt yard and faded yellow and green exterior did not fit in with the rest of the neighborhood.

"Welcome home, Merritt!" Val turned around and gave me a large smile. "Wait 'til you see the inside! We've done a lot of work since we moved here four years ago." I felt disoriented. Just yesterday I'd been behind bars. "Well, well good then. I can't wait to see what you've done." Once again I wondered just what I had gotten myself into or whether I deserved it.

"I'll give you a hand with your things while Val parks the car." Liz was welcoming but more cautious than Val. Since she and Val didn't live in Seattle, we hadn't had much opportunity to get to know each other. Liz and Val made an interesting couple. Liz is white, a bit stocky, just short of pretty with cropped brown hair and blue eyes. Her best feature is a smile that lights up her face. Val resembles me. Dark chocolate skin, medium height, slender, kinky hair, brown eyes, high cheek-bones, bright smile. Val's vivacious personality complements Liz's more natural reserve. Personalitywise I'm closer to Liz. At least just then I was feeling very reserved. And unsettled. Shame about my past bubbled up again. The past few years had really knocked me off my center.

"Thanks, Liz. As you can see, I don't have much. Just this duffle bag of clothes and bathroom stuff, my laptop, some photos, a few books and papers. That's basically it."

"Well, I don't s'pose you had much use for household supplies in prison. You know, Merritt, if you ever want to talk about that, or anything else, or..." She saw my face darken. "I'm sorry. Maybe I'm getting in a little too deep here."

"No problem, Liz. Maybe we can talk over dinner."

After my shock at the shabby exterior of the house, I couldn't believe my eyes when we walked in the front door. Liz and Val had totally transformed the inside. It was warm, colorful, and homey. My head was spinning. "So who's the decorator?"

"We both are. I guess the official term is 'early attic.' Goodwill and estate sales provided most of the furniture. Val made those." She gestured toward three quilts hanging on the walls.

"Really? I didn't know Val did that. They're beautiful."

"She started a couple years ago. Since I'm at the kite shop all day and she works at the hospital at night, she has a lot of time on her hands. She actually surprised herself when she discovered a new talent. She also hand painted the pillows on those wicker rockers."

"Seriously impressed. Who knew?" Several exotic plants flourished on a stand beneath a large window. "Who has the green thumb?"

"Those are mine. A hobby. My other passion, of course, is kites. Getting the job managing Above it All a couple of years ago was a dream come true. I barely earn enough for my share of the rent, but I get a great discount on fabulous kites."

I looked around. Three large kites hung suspended from the high ceiling in the main living area. "That rainbow striped box kite above the sofa comes along with me and Val whenever we march in the Pride Parade in Portland. Of course, we can't fly it while we're marching, but it's large and impressive and gets a lot of attention."

Floating just above the cluster of plants was a graceful red, orange and yellow kite. "Nice butterfly! Perfect place for it."

"Thanks. We like it."

The kite that really grabbed my attention was an impressive black and red dragon. At least eight feet long, it hovered above the large oak table in the dining area. "Whoa!

You eat with this dragon every night?"

"Not every night. Only when we have company. We usually eat in the kitchen. But isn't that a great table? We lucked out when we found it at the Goodwill. I don't think they knew its real value. It's perfect for when we have folks over for dinner and games. Everyone loves the dragon flying overhead, providing good luck, I guess."

"You and Val created this incredible space on a shoe-string. It's really nice!" It certainly beat where I'd been for the past two years.

Val walked in through the back door, which opened into a large, cheery kitchen. "Well, Merritt, what do you think?"

"I love it. You'd never know from the outside. I can't believe all the two of you have done!"

"We haven't done much with the kitchen yet–the appliances are all seriously out of date–but they still do the job. And we love this window!" The three of us took a minute to gaze through the large picture window that opened out onto the back yard. In spite of the fogginess of the old glass, it almost felt like stepping into a forest.

"Amazing. You'd never know from the street that this place is so beautiful inside."

"I know. The outside is pretty awful–but the cost involved in fixing it up is prohibitive–much more than the DIY investments and artistic flair that contributed to our sweet interior."

"Are you and Val buying the house? Is there a landlord who should be fixing things up?"

"We decided to buy. The landlord put it on the market after we'd been here for a year–he was almost giving it away–so the purchase price was in our reach. Hopefully one of these days we'll be in a financial position to fix up the outside, and with our work schedules we haven't been able to do much landscaping. It would suit us for sure, and we'd fit better into the neighborhood. We're already that strange mixed-race, lesbian couple."

"How is that for you two–being a mixed-race, lesbian couple here in this town, that is?"

"We do what we can to stay under the radar. It's clear we're mixed race. Can't do much to hide that. And we haven't come out as a couple except to some close friends. We haven't really gotten to know the neighbors, and where we work people just think of us as single women."

"Are gays accepted here at all?" My interest was more than academic.

"Yes and no. As I said, we pretty much stay under the radar, just to avoid any ugliness we might encounter.

"Why do you live here then?"

"We love the beach. We like our jobs. As I said, we have some great friends who know and love us for who we are, and we get to live in a beautiful house we can afford. Not bad, all things considered."

"I really appreciate you letting me stay here! It's a far cry from Seattle, but I've got you two as family and mentors. I think it will be OK."

"Merritt. You're always welcome here. You've been through hell. We're only glad we can help."

"Well. Thanks. And, you know, I'm really excited to be living with family again. It's been a long time. Since I was in high school at O'Dea."

"You can take the attic room. The ceiling is pretty low, and the room isn't finished, but there's quite a bit of space. The bed is comfortable enough, I guess. We found a chest of drawers at the Goodwill. We still need to find you a desk and a bookshelf."

"I guess you're forgetting I spent my last two years in a ten-by-ten cell with bars. It will be perfect." The feeling of shame resurfaced. "It's more than I deserve."

"What you deserve is a second chance, and we're happy to

help provide that." Val offered me a warm smile. "All you have to do now is make yourself at home. I have to be at the hospital in a couple hours, so I need to take a little nap before then. There's some homemade minestrone in the fridge. You'll find that Liz is an amazing cook. We're both vegetarian, but it's OK if you want to bring meat into the house. Just don't fill the place with the smell of bacon cooking. It makes me gag!"

"I'll keep that in mind."

After Val left for the hospital, Liz and I settled into a cozy nook in the kitchen. Steaming bowls of minestrone and sourdough bread were on the table. Val was right. Liz is a great cook. And, as I was to soon learn, a good listener. After just a few minutes of small talk, she dove right in.

"Merritt, I really love your sister and I welcome you into our home. And I'd love to get to know you better. Do you mind telling me a little bit about yourself?"

Wow. Where to begin. My story had as many twists and turns as a labyrinth, and they weren't all pretty. "Well, sure. Okay. What would you like to know?"

"Well, for one thing, if you're willing to talk about it–how did you happen to become a priest? That's such a far cry from anything I've had any experience with."

"That's an easy one for me to talk about, Liz." I sat quietly for a moment, reflecting on her question. "For as long as I can remember, I wanted to be a priest. I loved being an altar boy, helping Father Clement serve the Mass. I felt the presence of God in the church, and I knew I wanted my life's work to be in service to Him. At the Church of the Holy Sacrament, where our family went, there was none of the sexual abuse that was rampant in other parishes. Thank God. Father Clement was a friend, a confidant, a teacher, a mentor, and a spiritual guide. His influence on me was nothing but positive–which is why I feel so badly about letting him down. He deserved better from me."

Liz steered my story in another direction. "You and Val grew up in Seattle, right? She's talked a lot about you and your family."

"That's right. Growing up in the Central Area, we felt at home in a largely Black neighborhood. We were a close-knit family. We always attended mass together at least once a week. You probably know that our family was Val and her twin Vicky, two years older than me, our mom and dad, and our grandmother. We called her Gran-Mo. Dad had a plumbing supply business. Mom was a secretary at St. Therese's, the Catholic school we went to. Gran-Mo stayed home and kept a close eye on us." I paused for a minute as the memories flowed. "I didn't fit in with the other boys my age in the neighborhood. They went to public school, and they all seemed tough. At least to me. I was a skinny little kid, and they bullied me. So instead of running around and getting into trouble with them, I hung out with Gran-Mo, drawing, writing poetry, and learning to cook."

"So you're a cook?"

"Well, not so much now. But I'd love for you to teach me some of your tricks. That minestrone you made was amazing!"

"Sure. We'll have plenty of time for that." She looked into my eyes and nodded, encouraging me to continue.

"After I graduated from St. Therese's, I began at O'Dea, an all-male Catholic high school. Maybe Val told you that she and Vicky went to Holy Names, the female counterpart to O'Dea."

"I'm not sure, but anyway..."

"O'Dea was close to St. James Cathedral, the mother church of the Archdiocese of Seattle. It's a magnificent facility. Nothing like some of the cathedrals in Europe I guess, but far grander than our family's parish church. I loved it there. I actually began my day there with Mass every morning before heading over to O'Dea."

"Wow. What a way to begin the day. Pretty damned impressive!"

"I don't know about impressive. It just meant a lot to me at the time."

"I think Val and I were at St. James once or twice for a concert. Never for mass. But yes, I totally agree. It's a fabulous place. And the acoustics are amazing. I remember hearing the Medieval Women's Chorus singing there one time. I was in heaven."

"I know what you mean, Liz. I was really lucky to go there every morning."

"How was O'Dea for you?"

"Actually, I was a good student. Maybe even a nerd. I loved to study. I really enjoyed being in their Faith in Action program that provided service to the community."

Liz smiled. "Yes. Community service was important to me while I was in school, too. Actually, it still is. Val and I don't have a lot of money, but we try to find ways to serve our neighbors in need."

"Well, right now I guess I'm your brother-in-law in need. And don't think for a minute I don't appreciate you."

"We always get more than we give. You know that yourself from your own service involvement."

We were quiet for a moment as I thought back on those high school years.

"Yeah. Those were good years. Even as a nerd I made a lot of good friends–mostly guys I knew in the drama program. I was in a play once–School of Rock. Acting is definitely not my strong suit, but it was a lot of fun."

"Sounds just about perfect."

"Perfect? Maybe close. Except for one small detail."

Liz glanced up at me. "Small detail?"

"Well, maybe a fairly big detail." I gulped. How much did Liz know about me? But, surely this would not make any difference to her of all people. Taking a deep breath I plowed in. "It was while I was there that I realized I was attracted to boys." I glanced at Liz to see how she was responding. She was still quietly listening, nodding, encouraging me to continue. "That was horrifying to me. I wanted to be a priest, for God's sake. I knew all too well what the church thought about homosexuals. Child molesters R Us."

"I was lucky in that regard–not having the church to contend with. My first time kissing a girl was in the high school girl's bathroom. Cindy Ellis. It was a little disorienting, but I can still remember that Oh My God! feeling. Exciting, a little bit scary. But not horrifying, not at all."

"I should be so lucky. As I said, I was in high school when I first began to think that I might be gay. For a while it was just looking and lusting. Then came the night that was. His name was Jose. Killer good looks. A year ahead of me in school. Way more sophisticated than I could ever dream about being. I'll spare you the gory details, but suffice it to say, at the end of a night with him–let's say I had no doubt about who I was. And I was terrified. Afraid that who I was would keep me from my dream of being a priest. I resolved then and there to bury that part of myself, and to never, ever come out to anyone. Anyone."

"Oh, Merritt. I'm so sorry. It's hard enough to be gay in this world, but then add the church's censure on top. Plus you wanted to be a priest. It's a miracle you survived to tell the story."

"Well, as you know, the story hasn't all been pretty. Not even close. You and Val are so great together. I know it's hard, but you've carved out a good life for yourselves here. Something to hope for, I guess. Right now I can't even dream about a happily ever after ending. If there even is one for me."

"You're still young, Merritt. I know there have been some rough patches, but I'm sure there were good times, too. You've been a priest, for God's sake. Serving your own parish. That's nothing to sneeze at."

"You're right. There were some really good years. After graduating from O'Dea I went to Seattle U. I majored in

Theology and Religious Studies. I wanted to convince myself I wasn't gay, so I made it a point of getting close to a girl named Miranda, one of the only Black girls in the school."

"How'd that go?"

"Not well, as you can imagine. One more thing I hate myself for. Miranda was cute, intelligent, and funny. We were in several of the same classes, and we both loved community service. We dated, had some great times together. We even had sex a few times."

"I get it. I really do. But I'm guessing there's not a happy ending here."

"Uh, no. It sounds crazy now, but I never even talked with Miranda about the future, or about my hope to be a priest. When she began hinting about marriage I finally realized how deceitful I'd been to her. I broke things off with her. I hate myself for how I'd treated her, how I'd used her."

"Life can be so damn complicated. I'm sorry for both of you that things turned out that way. I know you never intentionally meant to hurt her. Do you ever see her?"

"No. I'm the last person she'd want to see. I think I heard somewhere that she'd gotten married. I hope so. I hope she's happy. She's a wonderful girl. And still, it was clear to me that I wanted to be a priest, and even if that never happened, I could never marry a woman."

"No, I guess not."

"After I ended things with her, I convinced myself that all my future relationships, with men or with women, would be purely platonic. And that worked for a while. I went to St. Patrick's Seminary in Menlo Park, California. The change of scenery was a good diversion–it's beautiful there–and my experience there was all I could have hoped for. I made deep friendships with students and faculty alike. I did well in my studies and followed the Catholic Social Teachings, which call us into service to the poor. I finally felt like I was on the right path."

"You were clear about your calling your whole life. You're lucky in that. I for sure wasn't called into managing a kite shop–although I do have a passion for kites. But it's hardly the same. I envy your conviction."

"Which is why I feel so damned guilty and confused now. I really lost my way. But to finish my story–I just about lost it when Trayvon Martin was murdered and George Zimmerman got off scot-free. I took a deep dive head first into racial activism. That, plus my academics and my community service, kept me plenty busy, and kept my sexual feelings at bay."

Liz smiled at me. "I think Freud called that sublimation."

"Well, whatever it's called, it worked for a while. As soon as I finished seminary I took my final vows and was ordained. Father Merritt Grace. God! I loved the sound of that. I was assigned to serve the Church of the Holy Family in Seattle's Central Area. The parishioners were people I could really relate to–racially mixed, low income. It felt like a perfect match with my calling, and I convinced myself that the rewards of the priesthood would trump my desire for sex."

"So, how'd that go?"

"At first, it felt like a dream come true. I loved my congregation and thrived on serving them–listening to their stories, hearing their confessions. Many of them told me how easy it was to confide in me. They shared my passion for protesting racial injustice and several came with me when we visited the immigrant detention center in Tacoma. A few of them had undocumented relatives there. I guess some of them were undocumented themselves, I never asked. And, right there at the center of everything, I still loved the mystical experience of God's presence during the Mass."

"It sounds wonderful."

"It was. Until it wasn't. After a few months the rewards I got from being a priest no longer kept the wolf away from the door. I became obsessed with thoughts of men. Sex with men, to put a fine point on it. Believe it or not, that time with Jose was my only time. Somehow I'd managed to put those thoughts away through college and seminary. But then, just as my dream seemed to be coming true, I was living in a nightmare."

"Oh, Merritt. I'm so sorry. You know, I could never understand why the church requires its priests to be celibate. Sexuality is a healthy part of human life." Liz's voice rose. "And what about all those blankety-blank priests who sexually abuse little boys. My God. Wouldn't it be better if those men could enjoy a healthy sexual relationship with a loving adult partner–male or female?"

"So it would seem, I guess. But here I am–a priest who not only wants sex, but sex with a man. Twice damned. At least by the church."

"Well, you know my feelings about same-sex relationships. Val and I have a great marriage, and I have no belief whatsoever that I'm headed for hell because of who I happen to love."

"No, I don't believe that either. But within the church my life became a living hell."

"Did anyone in your church know you were gay?

"Not that I know of. I never talked about it. I think I look pretty straight. My little secret. One that I even keep from myself whenever possible."

"At quite a cost. You can only lie to yourself for so long. What did you do when you started thinking those thoughts?"

"I prayed. I used willpower. I tried to distract myself with my work. But nothing worked. I was constantly obsessing about sex. I even lusted after men in my parish. Oh God, shoot me now!"

"Merritt. Stop! You were in an impossible bind!"

"I felt like I was losing my mind. Something had to give. I guess I should have talked with someone–a priest, a therapist, someone... But no such luck. I decided I could have it both ways, as long as I was discreet. I wrote a bunch of rules for myself. No one can know. No commitments. No emotional connections. Just sex. Safe sex. Wake up in my own bed. By myself!"

"That's quite a set of rules."

"It was actually OK at first. I started cruising gay bars. I'd never even been to one before. I was so fucking naive. My mind was blown. Gorgeous, sexy men, all looking for a good time. It was terrifying! And amazing! At first I hid out in the shadows, but before long I was partying along with the best of them."

"I bet you're a good dancer. I have two left feet, but Val is awesome."

"As a matter of fact, yes, I am a pretty good dancer, if I do say so myself. I got a lot of attention. Turned a few heads. Found plenty of chances to hook up."

"How long did that work for you?"

"A few weeks, I guess. If that. I scrupulously followed my rules. Faceless fucks, as they say. I'm sorry, Liz. But that's what it was. And I hated it. Hated it! I'd primed the pump and I wanted more. More relating. More love. I was a serious basket case."

"Oh, Merritt. My God. Why does it have to be so fucking hard? Sometimes I just hate the church! I'm sorry, but it's true. What you have to go through, just to be yourself. I can't imagine you could function well as a priest through all of that."

"I dunno. I guess I couldn't. Basically going through the motions by day, faceless fucking by night. One morning after yet another sleepless night, I realized I was at the end of my rope. I had to get help or, well... I don't even want to think about what I was thinking."

"Were you suicidal?"

"I dunno. I know suicide is a sin. Doom me to hell. But Liz,

I was in such a deep hole."

"Thank God you made a different choice! What did you do??"

"I threw on some clothes and drove over to the Church of the Holy Family."

"That's a safe place for you?"

"Yes, I always trusted Father Clement. I don't know why it took me so long to turn to him. Embarrassed and ashamed, I guess. Thank God he was at the church. First thing in the morning. He was surprised to see me–especially in the appalling condition I was in, and he dropped everything to talk with me."

"I'm glad you found the courage to go there."

"I think God guided me there. And as I said, I always trusted Father Clement."

"Thank God for that."

"After I poured out my story to him, he wrapped me in a giant hug. I felt so loved and accepted. Then he took my confession. I walked out of the confessional a new man. A huge weight off my shoulders."

"I've never been to confession. It's always felt like some kind of magical, artsy-fartsy, abracadabra kind of thing. You confess and you come out pure as the driven snow. I'm sorry, Merritt. I know I'm talking smack about your beliefs. And it sounds like it meant a lot to you. Please forgive me."

"It's okay, Liz. I can understand your feelings. Since I grew up in the church, going to confession was always something I looked forward to. Get things off your chest, pray for forgiveness, do the penance the priest gives you... After your sincere participation in the holy sacrament, your sins are forgiven. Ready to start afresh."

"I can see the appeal. But I still have trouble with the church making you feel guilty simply because of who you are. But if going to confession helps, well, I guess I can't argue with that."

"It's not just the church, Liz. It's society at large. And, I guess if I'm honest with myself, it's also me. It's so hard to accept myself, Liz. That I am gay."

"You've never really had a chance to explore being gay in a healthy way, have you?"

"Not really. I was never free from guilt while I was at school and in the church, and I pretty much kept to myself at Monroe– passing as straight was the safest option there."

"Does anyone in your family know? Other than Val, I mean."

"No. I haven't come out to my parents. Or my grandmother. My dear, sweet Gran-Mo. I wasn't about to tell them while I was in seminary or then in my church. I could barely tell myself. And for most of that time it was a moot point. Until those last awful months of my priesthood I wasn't seeing anyone, much less having sex with anyone. Except for Miranda, a few times when I was at Seattle U. There was no reason to tell them while I was at Monroe. They were already so crushed when I wound up there. It just about broke Gran-mo's heart. Both that I wound up in prison–but especially that I had to leave the church. She was so proud when I became a priest. I'm afraid it could send her over the edge if she knew the truth about my sexuality. I just can't risk it. And I hate that! Oh God! How can I be such a fucking disaster to all the important people in my life?"

"I can see how you feel that way now, Merritt. You've been through so much, and you made some bad decisions. But you've paid your dues, and you're ready to make a new start. I'm not trying to give you advice, but I think you might be surprised at your family's response if you came out to them. They're good people, Merritt."

"Yeah. I know. I know. It's not like they haven't already been through this with Val. How has that been for the two of you?"

"It took your parents awhile, but they've come to accept me

as their daughter-in-law. It wasn't easy for them. As good Catholics, they believe that homosexuality is a sin. But somewhere in the back of their minds–I can't believe they totally accept that. Look at Father Clement's acceptance of you. He's been a rock for you through all of this."

"Do you know if my parents ever talked with him about you and Val?"

"I don't know. The church has nothing to do with our relationship, and we never discussed it with them. As you know, we were married by a Justice of the Peace."

"I remember. My parents were there. I know they wish you had a church wedding. But the two of you were so happy, and I know they wanted to be happy for you, too. God bless them, they somehow found a way to make peace with your relationship. I appreciate them for that. It was hard enough that their daughter was marrying a white woman and not being married in the church. One of these days I may tell them the truth about their only son. But before that, I need to come to terms with myself. Liz–I honestly don't know who I am right now. And the biggest feelings I carry around with me are shame and guilt."

"Merritt–I understand that–and I hope that your time in Gearhart will help you find your way through that and accept yourself for the amazing and beautiful man that you are."

"Thanks Liz, I really appreciate your support. It's good to be able to talk with you about these things, Besides Father Clement, I don't think I've discussed this with anyone besides you and Val."

"I'm always happy to listen, Merritt."

"Have you ever felt guilty about being a lesbian?"

"No. Not really, I guess. I spent some time feeling abnormal, different from most folks. But no, never guilty. I didn't have the church breathing down my neck like you did."

"That's strange, isn't it? How the church can make me feel

so guilty and then so forgiven, all at the same time."

"So just what were you confessing? Being gay? Breaking your vow of celibacy? Faceless sex?"

"You know, I can't be totally sure. It all seemed to be mixed up together. But after my confession, after Father Clement told me my sins were forgiven, it felt like a new day for me. I prayed for God to get me back on the straight and narrow, so to speak."

Liz smiled. "So to speak."

"It actually worked for a while. Back to my parish, serving my congregation, being a full-time priest."

"Too good to be true?"

"Too good to be true. Otherwise, I guess I wouldn't be here now. I definitely wouldn't have wound up in prison. But I'm really tired now, and that's another story for another day. And thank you Liz, you're a great listener. What I've told you tonight is just the tip of the iceberg."

"Whenever you're ready, Merritt. Now, good night."

"Good night, Liz."

* * *

And now, after four months of living in Gearhart, I prayed that I wouldn't spend the rest of my days behind bars again.

CHAPTER 3: HENRY
Getting to Gearhart

April

I'd been in the investigating business for six years when I relocated from Seattle to Gearhart. How I got to Gearhart is a story in itself. And I owe it all to my dear sister, Julia, and my ex-wife, Janis.

* * *

I thought my life in Seattle was going okay. Justin Case Investigations LLC was making me a not terrific but adequate living. My specialty was insurance fraud, and there seemed to be plenty of folks out to defraud their insurance companies. My ex-wife Janis was married to my ex-best friend Steve and living the life she'd always wanted. Our daughter Jenny was ten and doing well at my old alma mater, The Bush School. Jenny and I spent plenty of time together. Janis and I had a friendly relationship that even included lunch once in a while to talk about how Jenny was doing.

Things were going okay, but not every aspect of my life was perfect. After that many years, I could do insurance fraud in my sleep. That's the good thing about a specialty. But doing the same thing all the time, especially something that can be as routine as insurance fraud, is, well, boring. Which is the not so good thing about a specialty. I loved puzzles, but I was accustomed to solving those puzzles by now, so most of the rush was gone.

Even though my income was adequate, my expenditures were outpacing it by quite a bit. To offset the routine of my work life, I found excitement in hanging out with a group of other single people—mostly friends from school and people I met through them. These were professional types, living a rather hedonistic lifestyle, and most of them had sufficient assets to fund the lives they'd grown accustomed to—or maybe their credit cards were maxed out, too. Several were divorced and helping to pay for an ex-spouse's good life as well. Ex-best friend Steve made a shitload of money, so at least I wasn't paying alimony to Janice.

I felt out of my league socially and financially. I wasn't used to that, since I'd grown up in a family with money. But you don't exactly get rich working as a PI. I'd known that from the beginning. My father had died several years before, and I have a little trust from his estate which supplements my lifestyle, but it's not huge. And so it was that my life gradually slipped out of control and into a kind of financial chaos. Before I knew it, I was living in a bigger apartment, overspending on clothes I didn't need, taking trips I pretended I could afford with my wealthier friends, and driving a sports car that was out of my price range. Overeating, drinking too much, and letting myself go. And every week promising myself that I'd get things under control—next week.

Meanwhile, my sister Julia had graduated from law school, passed the bar, and had a junior partnership at Campbell, Case, and Wells, the firm where both our father and grandfathers had practiced. She was doing well, engaged to a man she'd met in law school who was now an Assistant U.S. Attorney. Julia and I went out to dinner occasionally, usually just the two of us. At one of our dinners, I made the mistake of confiding in her that my finances were out of control. I don't know why—maybe I really just wanted someone to slap me around and make me get my shit together. Which is pretty much what happened.

I knew that Julia and Janis were tight, but it hadn't occurred to me that Julia would share my confession with Janis, blood being thicker than water. I knew soon enough. Janis called me the next week and suggested we get together for lunch. We did that periodically, so I didn't think anything of the invitation. As soon as we'd ordered, she hit me with it. What the hell was I thinking? My life was a mess. I'd made the choice to be a PI and make less money, so I needed to learn to live with that. And all the weight I'd gained, was that from drinking every night with the fast crowd I hung out with? And all the debt I'd racked up— how was I going to get that under control? I had responsibilities as a parent. Jenny adored me—thought I walked on water. For her sake, I needed to grow up, get my life together, take care of my health. There was part of me that wanted to be pissed off, to tell her how I lived my life wasn't any of her business. But as I said, I think I'd been wanting someone to tell me to stop doing what I was doing—and here she was—and, I knew she cared about me, she always would because I was her daughter's father.

Marrying Janis was the one thing I had done that my parents considered a mark of success. She and I had known each other in high school and were both living in Seattle after college. She was working in an interior design firm and I was in law school. She was the youngest child of a prominent cardiac surgeon, spoiled but sweet-natured (at that time). I guess our respective credentials and gene pools impressed each other's parents. My father could think of her father as his social and professional equal. My mother liked Janis's career choice, as she saw it as just a step above "homemaker." And Janis was beautiful, kind of a junior version of my mother herself, with big brown eyes and thick, honey-blonde hair. I later learned that they were both "suicide blondes"—dyed by their own hands. I'm sure my mother thought Janice's genes would upgrade her grandchildren's physical appearance. She had begun to mention my slightly receding hairline and my slightly expanding waistline—clearly worried that I might be letting myself go and that I'd never find anyone decent to marry me.

But Janis's parents seemed just as excited about me, which inspired me to propose to her after just six months of dating. She said yes immediately. Later, when I asked myself if we had loved each other, I realized that had never been much of a consideration. Janis looked good—in and out of her clothes—but as I discovered later, that has little to do with love or with making a relationship last. We came from the same world. We weren't going to rock any boats by choosing each other. We had identical visions, or so I thought, of what our future would look like. And we had the approval of each other's families. And maybe in the world we came from that was the most important thing. Or, as it turned out, maybe not. At any rate, we had a big celebration and said our "I do's." And then we did—until we didn't anymore.

We were married for seven years, and at the time of this critical lunch conversation we'd been divorced for four years. The one really good thing we had going for us in all those years was parenting Jenny. Even after the divorce, our shared custody was totally civil.

Before we were married, we had talked about waiting until we were established in our careers to have kids. But it wasn't more than a few months into our marriage before Janis told me, somewhat sheepishly, that we had our first child on the way. She had no idea how it had happened. I wasn't sure what to say, but I could see she was happy. Her family was Catholic, so maybe she wasn't really taking those birth control pills. Both our parents were happy; hers were ecstatic and mine were pleased despite what they knew would be the hardships of working, studying, and parenting all at once. Jenny would be the first grandchild on both sides, which meant everyone would come to dote on her.

Being parents, which required us to put someone else's needs before our own, had helped us both grow up. Janis's dad offered to pay her share of our living expenses so she wouldn't have to work before or after the baby was born, but Janis refused. She liked her job and she wanted to keep it. But more importantly, she wanted us to be independent from our parents, to stand on our own two feet. It was probably the first time I saw my wife as a real adult. I thought she might change her mind at some point, but she didn't. I wanted to put law school on hold for at least a year. This time it was my father who refused, and I guess that didn't surprise me considering how determined he was for me to follow in his footsteps. I'm sure he realized that if I left, even for a short time, I'd never come back—or if I did I wouldn't be able to pick up where I'd left off. So we had a rough couple of years with very little sleep. But we had Jenny. If I had been less than enthusiastic about becoming a young father that faded the first time I saw her. She was my everything.

The primary issue in our marriage, or at least the straw that broke the camel's back, was my choice of a career as a private investigator over a career as an attorney. Actually, it wasn't totally a choice. If things had been different...

I had a college buddy who was just a fount of interesting, somewhat humorous, and almost always rude and crude sayings. It seemed a little out of character for William Harrison Stanhope the Third (better known to us, his buddies, as "Billy the Turd"), who was heir to a big horse-raising enterprise in Kentucky. Billy was smart as a whip and quite the Southern gentleman, except for the witticisms. Maybe he used them just to try to prove he was an ordinary guy. Of course those little gems found their way into my limited vocabulary right away and remained there forever. And since Billy and I had stayed in touch intermittently, I got the occasional refresher course.

One of Billy's favorite sayings came to mind almost every time I reflected on the course my career and marital status had taken. "If." Back at Princeton, whenever one of us would say "if," Billy would remind us, "If your aunt had balls, she'd be your uncle." And if I'd passed the bar exam on the first, second, or even third try, I might be a practicing attorney–maybe even the case partner at Campbell, Case & Wells. And I might still be married to Janis. But I didn't and I'm not either one of those. How I missed Billy and his sayings that made me laugh—but I digress.

Jenny was six when we decided to call it quits officially. It was a surprisingly amicable parting of the ways with shared custody of Jenny. Janis thought I was a better father than husband. All things considered she was happy to be rid of me and to move on to the life she wanted, which included marrying Steve, a partner in one of the big accounting firms in Seattle—probably destined for managing partner. Steve and his wife Evie had been our best couple friends and they'd split recently. We'd been pretty good friends, Steve and I, and I was pissed that he'd do this to me. But after a few months, we were all almost as friendly as if Janis and I had never been married. Steve had kids of his own and he wasn't interested in taking my place as Jenny's father, so I didn't have to feel threatened in that department. All hunky dory.

So here was my good friend and ex-wife Janis about to get my life on the right track. "I have a suggestion," she said. "What if you gave up your apartment and lived in the condo in Gearhart? Just long enough to get things back on track. Maybe just a month even. I'm assuming you can work from anywhere. And in Gearhart there wouldn't be any distractions."

The condo in Gearhart, Oregon, had been left to Janis and me by her aunt Rachel in the first year we were married so we'd owned it jointly. We'd never stayed there. It had been rented out this whole time, and we didn't want to lose the income. When we divorced, we agreed that it should go to Janis, but we had never changed the title, so technically, I was a co-owner. Janis kept the rental income and paid the taxes and other bills. Like I said, an amicable divorce.

Janis was right, even though I hated admitting it. I could work from anywhere—so why not from a condominium in Gearhart? The boredom, that's why. When Janis said there wouldn't be any distractions, I knew she was absolutely one hundred percent right. So how to keep from getting suckered into this great idea?

"What about the renter?" I asked.

"He's getting married and moving to Portland."

"If I only stay a month, where would I live after that?"

"Someplace cheaper than where you are now. Or maybe you'll want to stay longer than a month."

"You've been to Gearhart. How many months would you want to live there?"

She laughed. "Maybe the town has hidden charms. Maybe they really need a PI."

"What about seeing Jenny? It's a five-hour drive."

"You could come back to Seattle for some weekends. Jenny could visit you at least once, if we could figure out how to get her there. FaceTime, text, email. And honestly, Henry, you'll want some time without distractions." Easy for her to say.

"I have a lease on my apartment, but it's up in six weeks. I was just getting ready to renew."

"Don't. For your own good. Take this deal. I'm not even asking you to pay rent on the condo. At least not for a month. That'll give you a leg up on getting your debt paid off. If you did decide to stay longer we can negotiate something."

I breathed a sigh of relief. "Okay. For one month. If I go bonkers, I'll come back earlier."

"You won't go bonkers. You'll be glad you've done this."

The northern Oregon coast, where Gearhart is located, is a popular getaway destination for Seattleites, even though it's a five-hour drive. The attractions are sandy beaches, gorgeous vistas, and sweet little beach towns with good food and expensive lodging. Tourist favorites town-wise include

43

Cannon Beach, Seaside, and Astoria, where there are more tourist attractions and accommodations. There are other little towns in between, including Gearhart, that aren't as well-known or popular. Of course we'd inherited a condo in one of those.

Janis and I had gone to Cannon Beach when she was pregnant with Jenny. I only remember driving through Gearhart because she had suddenly remembered that her aunt owned a place there. It looked like a nothing town. It wasn't until after we inherited the condo that we explored the town enough to know that west of the highway, on the water of course, were some very nice homes and condos, including the place we now owned. There was a nice park, golf courses and tennis courts, and a kind of cute little downtown area. But even with those things, it was quiet and unexciting. I immediately began to think of spending a month there as a kind of prison sentence. I wouldn't be going to Gearhart to play golf or tennis, just to get my shit together. I didn't plan to be there that long.

The end of March I moved out of my expensive apartment and put my stuff in storage. I drove down to Gearhart and moved into the condo the first Friday in April. It was Good Friday, and I remember thinking "what's so damn good about it anyway?" Maybe Jesus felt the same way. And maybe lightning will strike me for having these thoughts. But as usual, I digress.

Jenny was busy with school and soccer and excited about everything else in her life, so she wasn't as sad about my going as I was about leaving her. I'd sold my sports car and bought an older SUV with cash, and the whole way down the coast I wished I was driving my sweet little Porsche with the top down. I felt generally morose, wondering what the hell I'd let myself in for.

The SUV was stuffed with my computer setup and boxes of work files, some clothes appropriate for working at home, a couple of bags of non-perishable groceries, and my flat-screen

TV. The condo was furnished, but there was no TV. Janis had called to remind me of that—and to suggest that maybe I'd be better off without one anyway, since I'd be working twenty-four/seven. No way I was going to be without a TV. I had my old ten-speed bike that had been molding away in my parents' basement on a bike rack on the back. Good for helping get in shape, but definitely not a substitute for a TV.

I drove into Gearhart a little before sunset. The town looked like it had the last time we were there. Not much charm unless you drove off the main highway toward the water. On my way in I stopped for some additional groceries and headed for the Seaview West condominiums. Seaview West is west of the highway, the "good" side, just to the north of the Seaview East condominiums. That made no sense that I could see–shouldn't they be Seaview North and Seaview South? But what the hell—maybe there was a reason for it—and with only a month to stay here, did I really care?

Each building appeared to have about a dozen units, each unit with an outside entrance. They looked fairly nice from the outside, and most of the cars parked in front were newer and expensive—always a good sign regarding the neighbors. Inside, "our" unit was a little drab and dated, although in relatively good shape. Janis had contacted the rental agent and arranged for it to be thoroughly cleaned after the renter moved out. It smelled vaguely of antiseptic cleaning products and weed, which made me wonder momentarily if perhaps Mr. Renter had left me a little surprise in one of the drawers. I reminded myself that I was going to be a good boy for the next month—no exceptions.

My first reaction to my new short-term home was vague disappointment until I thought to open the shades in the living room. The entire outside wall was windows that looked out on the ocean. The master bedroom had a similar view. A decent trade-off for the tasteless décor.

The second bedroom didn't have a view, but it wasn't going to be occupied. Unless of course Jenny came to visit. But I probably wouldn't be here that long. Mr. Renter had left a fairly decent treadmill and a set of hand weights in there. Probably because he never used them. Maybe I would. Probably I wouldn't.

I unloaded my meager belongings from the SUV and set up my office on the dining area table so I'd be ready to hit the ground running the next day. I connected the TV to the cable and tested the channels. Someone had paid the cable bill, thank God. It occurred to me that I'd probably want another TV for the bedroom and a subscription to Netflix, but this would do for now. I watched some news, ate a bowl of cereal, sent Jenny a text telling her I'd arrived safely and to have a good week—and went to bed. I hadn't slept so well in years—which was ironic, considering how ambivalent I was about the month ahead of me.

CHAPTER 4: MERRITT
Life in the Little City

May

My first night in Gearhart, my first night in freedom, I barely slept. Part of the time I was anxious about starting a new life and wondering what I'd gotten myself into. And when I wasn't thinking about that I was obsessed with feelings of guilt about the pain I'd caused my family and shame for breaking my vows and desecrating my church. My talk with Liz had been good—she was a great listener—but it also triggered so many old and troubling memories.

After I finally dozed off I slept late—until almost 9:00. Centering myself with a morning prayer, I brushed my teeth, scrambled into some clothes and trotted downstairs. Liz and Val were at the breakfast table, just finishing up. "Would you like some scrambled eggs, Merritt?" Val stood poised at the stove ready to cook, so how could I say no?

"Sure. Thanks. And some black coffee if you have it." I was determined to shake off my malaise and make the most of my day.

"We always have coffee here, Merritt. It's a speciality of the house."

Taking my first sip, I had to agree. "Thanks for a good talk last night, Liz. It was helpful, if a bit painful, to take that little trip down memory lane and you're such a good listener. So—what are the two of you up to today?"

"Well, I have to work at the kite shop. I actually need to leave pretty soon now. I'm not sure what Val's planning for the day."

"I'm sorry, Bro, but I'm afraid I'm gone most of the day myself." Val looked chagrined. "I hate for both of us to leave you alone on your first day here, but I've got a required training at the hospital."

"Would you like to borrow my car, Merritt? You're welcome to use it whenever you need it as long as you drop me off at the kite shop." Liz's spontaneous generosity deeply touched me.

"That would be great, Liz. Are you sure it's OK? I wouldn't mind taking a look around Gearhart as long as you're both gone today."

"For sure. Out here in the sticks it's almost necessary to have a car. There's a bus you can take to your job in Seaside, but it only runs once an hour or so, and it only goes up and down the highway. So at some point you'll probably want to get yourself a car. And in the meantime, whenever I don't need mine, as long as I can get to and from the kite shop, it's yours to use."

"Have I mentioned that I really appreciate both of you more than I can say?" Only about a million times, but never enough. "Thanks, Liz, I'll take good care of your car."

Driving around Gearhart, I discovered that the main section of town was a far cry from Val and Liz's neighborhood. It reeked of wealth. Mansions lined the beach for blocks on end. The streets were wide and tree-lined, and luxury cars graced the driveways of most of the houses.

I parked near some tennis courts, hopped out, and stopped to read a notice posted on the fence inside of the courts. As I was reading, I was approached by a middle-aged couple who'd just arrived, tennis rackets and balls in hand. "Can we help you?"

"I'm just reading the regulations on the use of these courts."

"I don't remember seeing you around here."

"Actually I'm new in town."

"Do you live around here?"

"This notice says the courts are open to everyone. Nothing about needing to live here to use them."

"Are you visiting someone who lives in this neighborhood?"

"I'm not sure that's any of your business."

"Well, if you're not playing, you'd best move on now."

I fought the urge to stand my ground. I for sure didn't want to ask for trouble on my first day in town. They stared at me as I got in the car and slowly drove off. Once again, I asked myself if I'd made a mistake in coming here. Does Val deal with this shit every day? Well, I wouldn't let this one encounter spoil my day. It occurred to me that if I'd been wearing my clerical collar, no one would have found me threatening. Clerical privilege. I guess that little perk was a thing of the past.

I headed north, following the beach. Beyond the mansions were the Seaview Condos. They looked nice—but facing the ocean as they do they were likely way beyond my means. What do people do around here, anyway, to have so much money?

The Gearhart Golf Links was just beyond the Seaview Condos. A large sign proclaimed that it's the oldest golf course west of the Mississippi. Really? You never know. Or care. I guess it's important to someone. I pictured a lot of black-tie affairs taking place at their clubhouse. Don't think I'll be invited to many.

It was almost time for lunch, so I drove back to the center of town. The main street was a mix of high-end shops and galleries as well as establishments that catered to the common folk. Nothing quite hit my fancy. Continuing my exploration, about half mile up the road I spied the Gearhart Pub & Grub. Nondescript, but the parking lot was full. A good sign. I decided to try it out. A group of people about my age were gathered at a table in the center, talking and laughing. They got quiet when I walked in, likely surprised to see a Black man. Oh God. Here we go again. A few of them smiled and greeted me as I made my way to a booth in the back. I wondered what they'd think if they knew I'd marched with Black Lives Matter. Whatever. I nodded, ordered a burger, fries and an ice tea, and ate my lunch in silence.

After lunch I went back to the house. By then Val was back

home, and I told her about my morning, including the couple at the tennis courts. She wasn't surprised. "Damn. I'm sorry that happened to you on your first day. I guess it's just part of life here in Gearhart. But as you know, racism is all too alive and all too well just about everywhere. I'm not sure it's much different here from anywhere else. It's a rare day I don't get some kind of slight. For the most part I just ignore it."

"It was bad enough in Seattle where I didn't feel so totally conspicuous—and alone. This town is so bloody white. I'm not sure this is going to work out for me."

"There are a lot of good people here, Merritt. Liz and I have several close friends who accept and love us for who we are. I hope you'll give it a chance. There's a lot for you here—a place for you to be with family, to heal, to contribute to the community, to find yourself again. You are a good, wise and loving man, Merritt Grace."

"A man who fucked up royally."

"Yes—and you've paid your price. Now it's time for a new start. I have faith that you can make it work. Liz and I always have your back. You know that."

I didn't sleep well again that night, and the next day I was filled with anxiety. I decided to spend some quiet time at the ocean. Borrowing Liz's car again, I headed for Del Rey State Park, a few miles north of town. I left the car in the parking area and scrambled over some driftwood to get down to the beach. It was just about deserted. I took in the scene—the beach, the logs, the rolling waves, the scent and feel of salty air—and took a deep breath. The ocean called out to me. I took off my sandals, rolled up my pant legs, and waded a few steps into the water. It was too cold to think about swimming, but I relished the feel of sand beneath my feet and the lapping of the waves against my ankles.

As I walked along the beach, my mind was flooded with memories. I guess my talk with Liz the other night had primed

50

the pump. Just three days into my new-found freedom, I found myself thinking back on all that had happened to me at Monroe.

* * *

The day I reported there I was pretty scared but resigned to my fate and prepared to serve my time as best I could. Hopefully that would help me become someone I could again like and respect. In keeping with my agreement with the Archbishop, I hadn't yet talked with anyone about the mess I was in. It was especially hard not telling my parents or Gran-Mo—they were members of another parish, so for a time they knew nothing about my situation. I knew it would devastate them when they learned the truth. That said, they'd find out soon enough, and I wanted my church to have time to adjust to a new priest before I shared my story with anyone. Besides—I felt so much shame that I really didn't want to face my family. I'd get in touch with them, and a few other friends, in a couple of weeks.

I spent my first few days learning the ropes—finding my way around, attending orientation, getting to know the other inmates. Many of them were friendly enough. Turns out I knew a couple of guys from my old neighborhood. They took it upon themselves to watch out for me. Thank God. Not everyone on the block was friendly, and I was just the kind of guy that gets bullied—or even worse—inside a prison. I have those brothers to thank for the fact that I never ran into any real trouble the entire time I was at Monroe.

It took me a few weeks to get used to the routine—body counts five times each day, eating when a bell rings, showering and exercising on a schedule—but it was okay enough, I guess. I was in minimum security so there was quite a bit of freedom. Within limits, of course.

For the first three months I spent nine hours a week in

Substance Abuse Treatment. It was a good program, and by the time I was finished I was pretty sure I wouldn't relapse after I got out. I was even inspired to think about addiction counseling as a new career direction. At least for a long time I wouldn't be getting back into the priesthood. That bridge was pretty badly burned even if I wanted to go back—which was still a big question for me. After what I did, I wasn't sure I could ever feel entitled to serve in that way again.

I'd been working for a few months in the prison kitchen when I heard about University Beyond Bars. It's a program that provides Monroe inmates with access to higher education. I got excited when I saw that Seattle Central College, one of the UBB partners, had a Chemical Dependency Specialist Certification program. I applied and was accepted. That turned out to be one of several providential occurrences I experienced during my incarceration. I could feel God's hand guiding me, even as I was behind bars.

The two years of my sentence passed pretty quickly. After about a month I told my parents, Gran-Mo, my sisters, and a few close friends where I was. My cover story was that I'd gone on vacation so they didn't really suspect anything when they didn't see me for a few weeks. At first they—especially my family—were just about destroyed. They'd been so proud of me when I became a priest. I was the first in our family. But at some level they weren't that surprised. I hadn't hid my drug habit as well as I thought I had, and they'd been worried about me.

They were as horrified as I was that I'd used the confessional as a venue for my drug business. Still, even though they had trouble understanding, they were all supportive. Way more supportive than I thought I deserved. Gran-Mo, my folks and my sister Vicky all lived close by in Seattle and came to visit every month or so. Val lived farther away on the Oregon Coast, but she and Liz came a couple of times when they were in town. Two close friends also visited fairly often, and Father Clement was a regular. I lived for all those visits. They kept me sane, connected with the outside world. Everyone who visited was sworn to secrecy regarding my whereabouts, and, as far as I know, no one from the Church of the Holy Family ever learned the truth.

Toward the end of my sentence I began to think about next steps. Having a felony on my record was not going to help. Talking with Father Clement, I was convinced that it was too early to return to the priesthood, if I ever could at all. Then one day Val and Liz came up to see me and told me about Second Chance. And here I am, one of the very few Blacks in Gearhart, ready for my second chance.

* * *

A large wave breaking close to my knees drew me out of my reverie. Leaving the surf and walking back to the beach, I sat on one of the logs that had been swept in by the ocean. I wondered where it had come from and I thought about where I had come from. Me and this sturdy, craggy log, somehow both brought to this place. I felt the sun on my face and began to relax. My mind drifted to my church, the parishioners I'd loved so much. Celebrating the mass, marching for justice, creating community. I wondered if those days were gone for good. With the exception of Liz and Val, no one around here knew that I am—was—a priest, and I aimed to keep it that way. At least for the time being.

Gazing into the distance, I thought about the past few years. Was that really me? Someone else must have done all those things. That said, I'd never be able to forgive myself until I looked at and accepted the truth. I took in another breath of damp, salty air, and prayed for God's forgiveness. That would be a good start.

I wiggled my toes and focused on the sand beneath my feet to ground myself. Looking out over the vast expanse of ocean, I became aware of the immensity of the planet, the grandeur of the universe. In that moment, I suddenly felt more connected to my soul, more connected to God, than I had in a long time. It felt like I'd been touched by grace. My name. Grace. Merritt Grace. I was experiencing grace. In spite of everything I've done, I merit grace. Thank you, God. Thank you. For the first time since arriving in Gearhart, I felt hopeful about this next chapter in my life.

Getting My Sh*t Together

May

The month I'd committed myself to went much faster than I'd expected—which speaks to why it was that I was still there after three months to meet the Pub & Grub folks. From the first day I focused primarily on two things—my work and my physical condition. The first morning I set my alarm for six o'clock, got up, and went for a brisk walk on the beach before I had coffee and cereal for breakfast. Then straight to work.

My first objective was to work through the backlog of emails that had built up while I was having fun, more and working less. I had thought I could finish that the first day, but by noon I could tell that so many of the emails required follow-up that I'd be lucky to get through them in a month. I kept at it though, and began making lists of what I needed to do and by when. I felt a sense of satisfaction every time I could cross something off one of the lists. Any personal texts, emails, or phone calls I put off to answer in the evening after I'd quit working for the day. My commitment was to work seven eight-hour days a week and to allow myself as few distractions as possible. The exception was any message from Jenny—those got my immediate attention and response.

I worked nine to one and two to six every day. During my hour off in the middle I exercised for at least a half hour. I either worked out with Mr. Renter's hand weights and treadmill or went for a walk on the beach or a bike ride. I ate lunch during that time, too—something small like a sandwich or a can of soup. Dinner was one of those Lean Cuisine frozen meals and a salad. I drank water all day and treated myself with a diet soda at night. I didn't buy any alcohol to drink at home, thinking I'd have a couple of beers if I ever went out.

However, I left the condo very seldom, except for my daily walks and bike rides and trips to buy groceries and other necessities.

Early on, I didn't go out to eat or to a bar or tavern. I didn't know anyone to go out with. Evenings I watched TV. If there was nothing on, which was usually the case, I read. I'd put off subscribing to Netflix to save money. I returned messages and calls from my buddies in Seattle as well as calls from my mother and sister. I had thought I would be strict about not working after six, but I found myself answering emails from clients that arrived in the evening. My work had become something of a burden in recent months—a necessity to be tolerated—but now, without the distractions I had in Seattle, I was able to really focus on it. And as a result I found it a lot more interesting and compelling.

By the fourth week things had begun to turn around and I was getting caught up. I got requests for additional projects from a couple of my clients, which were likely a result of my improved performance. Once again, I began to feel the anxiety related to being overwhelmed—but this time I was either going to say "no" or get myself some help before I reached the boiling point.

And the exercise and changes in my eating had paid off. My arms, legs, and core had hardened up and the few clothes I'd brought with me were too big. There was no scale in the condo, but I was sure I'd lost at least ten pounds. I felt less winded when my daily walk took me uphill—and I could definitely get farther faster on foot, bike, or treadmill.

I was surprised in the middle of that week by a call from Janis. It gave me the opportunity to have the conversation I'd been planning to have with her when the month was up. "So, how's it going?" she asked.

"Surprisingly well, actually. Want to make it double or nothing?"

"Double or nothing?"

"Any chance I could stay another month?"

"Wow, it must be going well. I thought you'd be climbing the walls to get out of there by now."

"I guess I should be thanking you. This must have been just what I needed."

"So, tell me."

"I'm almost caught up on my work. In fact, I've generated more work for myself. I'm starting to think again that I might need to get someone—a partner or an associate—to join me. Several more months like this and I'll be able to pay off my credit cards."

"Good for you."

"And I'm getting back in shape. Daily exercise and cutting back on what I'm eating."

"And drinking?"

"No drinking so far. Nobody to drink with."

"Again, good for you."

"Again, thanks for making this happen."

"You're welcome. And sure, if you want to stay for another month, that's fine. For that matter, I guess you could stay longer if you wanted to. Although I'd be surprised if you did want to."

"Maybe I won't. I'll just play it by ear. But I'll let you know in advance what my plans are. I'll probably drive back to Seattle at the end of the month. I need to get some things and I'd like to see Jenny. I'll stay with either Julia or my mother."

"If that doesn't work out you can stay with us."

"You're too good to me, Janis."

"Mostly for Jenny's sake, Henry," she laughed.

I liked having a cordial relationship with Janis. It certainly made life easier. Sometimes I wondered why we couldn't have made it work. Of course there was my career. But there were some very good things about our marriage. We were good in bed together for one thing. Not that that's the summum bonumof a good marriage—but we liked it. I missed it, and I'm pretty sure she did, too. After the lunch, at which she had convinced me to spend the month in Gearhart, she gave me a friendly little hug outside the downtown Seattle restaurant before we parted company. Two women walked by and one of them said, "get a room." We laughed, but when we looked up from the hug, we realized we were standing a half block from the Sheraton. The wine with lunch, the friendly hug, the woman's suggestion—not to mention the proximity of a few hundred beds—and the next thing I knew I was cheating on my former best friend with his second wife and my first wife.

Afterwards I asked Janis if she felt guilty. "A little," she said. "Mostly relaxed. And in case you're wondering, this is my first little (little?!) indiscretion since Steve and I have been married."

"But not the first time you've cheated on a husband," I reminded her.

"True. And I'm not proud of that. You're a nice person, and you didn't deserve that. I guess what goes around, comes around. But don't think I'm going to make a habit of this." I didn't think that, but she was right—what goes around, comes around. So now I could feel a little smug the next time I was around Steve, having gotten a little of my own back.

Of course what I really, really wanted to ask her ("Mirror, mirror, on the wall...) was which of her two husbands she thought was the best in bed. Of course I didn't ask. Maybe I was afraid of the answer. Steve has a lot more money than I do, and we all know "money talks." But if he was so damn good, what was the last couple of hours all about?

* * *

During that first trip back to Seattle, I wondered if I really

58

wanted to spend another month in Gearhart. I saw a couple of my old friends for dinner and drinks, and I realized how much I missed just being with people. And of course spending time with Jenny—I didn't want that to end. But a deal's a deal. And it was just for one more month I told myself.

I was gratified by how happy Jenny was to see me. I'd been afraid she would rather be with her friends than with dear old Dad, but I actually heard her telling a friend on the phone that she wouldn't be going to a movie because her Dad was in town for the weekend and she wanted to spend time with him. Before I left, she asked when she could come to Gearhart for a visit. I said I didn't think I'd be there that much longer, that maybe we could go to the Oregon Coast for a visit after I was back in Seattle for good.

I came back to the condo in Gearhart with a few things I took out of storage to make my new home a little homier—my favorite comfy chair and my work set-up—a small filing cabinet and a good lamp. It required borrowing Steve's pickup and letting him use my SUV, which would mean another weekend trip back to Seattle soon. I wouldn't mind that, even if it meant ten hours of driving, since it also meant spending a few hours with Jenny. Of course I would just have to haul all that stuff back to Seattle in a month or so.

One of the things I'd thought of on the drive back down there was how things might be different now that I was going to be there longer. I was already thinking that this could be for more than just another month. What would I do differently? How would I structure my days? Even more critical, what about my evenings? I had hardly interacted with another soul in Gearhart, except in the purchase of life's necessities, in that first month. I needed someone to hang out with, grab a burger and a beer with. That had been so clear when I was with my old friends in Seattle.

It occurred to me that it wouldn't hurt to make the

acquaintance of the local law enforcement personnel, even though that was more work-related than social. Not that I would be working with them, but still, we were colleagues of sorts, being involved in work that was somewhat similar and related.

I'd gone online to see who the local constabulary was. The police force in Gearhart was made up of three individuals: Police Chief Bert O'Donohue, Sargent Bruce Gellerman, and Officer Terry McConnell. I could tell from the photo that the latter, although the name was spelled with a "y," was female. No one with the title Detective, although maybe that wasn't necessary in a town the size of Gearhart. Under "Contact Us" there were no email addresses, just one phone number. The second morning I was back, I dialed it and asked for the chief. I figured in a town this size he might be willing to extend me the professional courtesy of an introductory conversation. I'd even buy his coffee if necessary.

Whoever answered the phone passed me along to the chief. "Hello, Mr. Case. What can I do for you?" The chief's tone was cautiously friendly, although I figured he probably wondered who I was.

"I'm a private investigator, living in Gearhart and working out of my home here for a few months. I was just hoping you could spare a little time to meet me for a cup of coffee. I don't need or want anything in particular. Just to introduce myself."

"Sure, sure. I know who you are. You've been living here for several weeks now—out in the Seaview condominiums. If I remember right, in a condo owned by a Ms. Janis Halvorsen. Used to belong to Rachel Burns." Jesus, I'd forgotten what it was like in small towns.

"Yes, well, technically I'm a co-owner. Janis is my ex-wife." Why was I getting into a pissing match with this guy already? I shut up.

"Sure, sure. I have time for coffee. If you want to come by

here we could just have coffee in my office or walk across the street to the Daily Grind."

"Is there a day and time in the next week that works for you?" I hit the calendar icon on my iPhone.

He guffawed. "Hell, any time this afternoon works for me. This is not your big city with a murder every ten minutes." He laughed again. "That's assuming you're not otherwise busy."

"No, not at all. I'll come about two, if that works."

"Works fine. See you at two."

The police station was part of city hall, it's a very small town. O'Donohue's office was in the back, but he was out front, laughing about something with his staff, when I walked in. "Hey, Mr. Case, right on time." His handshake was very firm, and I thought he looked familiar, although I couldn't think where I might have seen him before since I'd hardly gone out in the first month. He introduced me to Sargent Gellerman and Officer McConnell.

Gellerman was early middle age, a little portly and pretty serious looking. It made me think of "In the Heat of the Night." McConnell was also serious-looking. No make-up, hair pulled back in a bun, tortoise-shell glasses—a no-nonsense lady cop for sure. Both were wearing uniforms, a contrast to O'Donohue's GQ outfit. I reminded myself to drive slowly in Gearhart.

After we'd made a little polite conversation, during which I told them the bare minimum about myself, O'Donohue and I headed across the street to the Daily Grind for coffee.

Chief O'Donohue was an interesting man. Good-looking, expensive-looking clothes, pretty full of himself. Right off he told me he was running for state senate—but between us, that was just a first step to something bigger like a U.S. Senate seat or governor; he had connections. That was why he looked familiar; I'd seen his photo on campaign posters somewhere or in the news.

I wondered why someone with O'Donohue's ambitions had wound up as the top cop in a small town like Gearhart. He answered that as if he had read my mind. He'd been assistant police chief in Eugene with no chance for advancement, as the chief was years from retirement with a wife who had a good job at the University of Oregon. The job in Gearhart had come up, and the field in that part of the state was more advantageous for his political purposes.

He asked me about my politics. "You a Republican, one of us good Americans?" he asked. I'd never been too interested in politics, and neither had Janis. Both our parents were Democrats, the dominant party in liberal Seattle. We leaned to the left, too, and I guess were registered as Democrats, but we'd always preferred to characterize ourselves as Independents. "I'm more of an Independent," I said. "Well, since your door swings both ways," he smirked, "and since you're a solid citizen of Gearhart now, maybe you'll want to get involved with my senate campaign." I said I wasn't sure how solid a citizen I actually was, how long I'd be in Gearhart. Well, I could always let him know, he said. He really needed someone to help with communications. I said I wasn't sure that was my forte, but I'd give it some thought. I could tell he was disappointed in my response, which made me think maybe I should get involved.

We spent a little time talking shop, about any possible overlap in our work, which wasn't much. He didn't do much with insurance fraud, and I didn't do much with drunk and disorderly, or the myriad exciting things a small town top cop takes care of when he isn't running for office.

"So, you a U-Dub graduate?" he asked me. The University of Washington is a prestigious institution, and I guess people assume if you're from Seattle, you're a U-Dub graduate. I could have given him the short version, but for some reason—maybe because he was the law or maybe because I was lonely and needed to talk—I pretty much told him my life story.

"I graduated from the U-Dub law school. I went to Princeton for undergraduate," I told him.

"Holy shit—that's a lot of expensive education." I figured what he meant but didn't say was "for someone working as a PI."

"My father and both my grandfathers were attorneys, partners in a prestigious Seattle law firm—Campbell, Case & Wells. My father was pretty determined that I'd be an attorney, too. He got me in where he'd gone to school and then got his firm to hire me. But it just wasn't my thing. I really wanted to be an investigator. So that's what I'm doing. My sister, Julia, went to law school, and now she's a partner in the family firm. I'm sure our father's smiling down from heaven. Or maybe up." The chief laughed. Well, that was the short version. I hadn't felt the need to give him the sordid particulars—in which the devil resides—although they may be more interesting.

* * *

My father, Henry Case, Jr., and my maternal grandfather, Justin Wells, were prominent Seattle trial attorneys. My mother was what I guess you'd call a society matron—active in Seattle's arts world, mostly in fundraising, frequently featured in the society pages of the local paper back when such a thing existed. My sister Julia, three years older than I, was beautiful, popular, and an excellent student. Teachers always seemed a little surprised to discover I was her younger brother. Not because I was a total fuck-up or anything; it was just that by comparison I didn't quite measure up.

Even before my birth my parents had me enrolled in Villa Academy, the Laurelhurst neighborhood's most prestigious pre-kindergarten and elementary school. Later I moved on to

Lakeside School, an esteemed private school best known as the alma mater of the founders of Microsoft. When I graduated from Lakeside, where I failed to distinguish myself in any quarter, my father wrangled me a place in the freshman class at Princeton, his alma mater. There, with the help of tutors I managed to graduate in just over five years, again having failed to distinguish myself.

I was an average student, more street-smart than school-smart, and not particularly gifted in any other way. That made me something of a disappointment to my parents, but that didn't stop them from "pulling me through a knothole" toward the future they'd envisioned for me.

It had always been assumed that I would become an attorney like my father and be rewarded with a place at Campbell, Case & Wells. I couldn't imagine that any law school would have me., But after I graduated from Princeton my father was able to pull some strings with the Dean of the Law School at the University of Washington. He continued to cash chits with my professors, several of whom were his cronies, to keep me enrolled and passing my courses. I worked at CCW throughout my years in law school. That turned out to be one of the best pieces of my education.

* * *

Interrupting my ruminations, the chief commented, "So, considering all that education, I'd expect you to be a lawyer, working in some big office building in downtown Seattle."

"Not everyone's cut out to be a lawyer," I said. "That was my father's dream, not mine. What I wanted to do, and where my skills lie, is in the area of investigating. And I like working for myself."

I was telling the truth and nothing but the truth, but it wasn't the whole truth. But the whole truth was a lot more than I wanted to share with the chief unless we became friends. I somehow doubted that would happen, but occasionally I'm wrong. Not about people very often though.

"So, I'm curious," the chief went on, "about why you're living in our fair burg. Not that you're not entitled to live anywhere you want. A city boy like you must find it lonely, though. Or at least boring."

"Just wanted to try somewhere different," I said. "And the condo was here and available." He shrugged.

We finished our coffee, shook hands, and he left.

I got a refill on my coffee and while I was at it invested in a chocolate chip cookie, which after so long without sugar tasted pretty amazing. I sat there drinking my coffee, still thinking about what I'd told the chief about how I'd become a PI.

* * *

It hadn't been a smooth path, what with my three years of struggling with the bar exam and then dealing with my two major barriers—my now-ex-wife and my late father. The sad thing is that those two people who were so important to me were not only barriers to my chosen career—my choice had a negative impact on my relationships with them.

My marriage to Janis limped along for several years after I made the decision to switch careers. I was serving an apprenticeship with Charlie, a PI I knew from my work at the law firm. The apprenticeship was almost as much work as law school—and I was still working part-time at CCW. It wasn't just the time I was spending at work; it was the fact that I wasn't going to be a partner at CCW—or even any kind of lawyer.

And then, oddly enough, there was the little matter of my first name. I'd started using the name 'Justin', which is my actual first name, instead of 'Henry', my actual middle name. It's a long story, one that Janis didn't find amusing in the least.

I could remember vividly the morning after I'd announced to her that I was going to forever-after be a PI named Justin Case. I woke up with a blazing headache, but oddly enough I didn't have any regrets when I remembered the previous day and evening. While it had been less than twenty-four hours since the idea of being a private investigator had come to me, I was in full ownership of it, as determined to pursue it as if it had been my lifelong dream.

Janis was absent from our bed, and the house was quiet. I assumed she had taken Jenny to daycare and gone to work. I looked in the kitchen to see if she'd left me a little apology or love note, or at least some breakfast—but there was nada. Uh oh.

I could see from the clock that I was going to be late to work. More uh oh. I called the receptionist and told her I had a meeting out of the office, to give me a little time to get my head together. I was thinking that since I had already told two people about my bar exam failure and new career plans, I should tell my father before he heard it from some other source. The thought of telling him terrified me, and I knew he would try to talk me into taking the bar exam again. He might even have some work-around for getting me a passing score. If he had done those things, I might have had an entirely different life. As it turned out, he didn't—and so, as it turned out, I didn't.

* * *

A lot of water under the proverbial bridge, I thought, as I sat there in the Daily Grind in Gearhart, Oregon, finishing my coffee. When I got to the door to leave, I noticed a "For Sale" sign in the window. I went back to the barista. "This place is for sale?" I asked.

"Yep, sort of."

I asked what that meant. He told me the owner had had a couple of offers, which she had rejected. Apparently she wasn't that interested in selling. I could tell from the outside that the building was larger than just the coffee shop, but there didn't appear to be another business next door. I pointed to the door on the back wall and asked the barista what was behind it.

"Storage."

I asked if I could see the space.

"You interested in buying?" he asked.

"Probably not, but I'd like to see it," I said.

He found a key in a drawer and handed it to me. The room was a mess, but even so, I could envision the possibility of an office for myself. There was adequate square footage and windows on two walls. An outside door off the side. Not bad if I wanted an office in Gearhart, and the answer to that was probably not. "So, just in case," I said, "could I have the owner's contact information?" He wrote it on a napkin and handed it to me, and I left—wondering why I had wanted it anyway. I'd be moving back to Seattle soon enough.

Lead Us Not into Temptation

May

The next morning Liz dropped me off at Pacific Behavioral Health. My first day at my new job. I was both excited and apprehensive as I started this new phase of my life.

My job was in the Substance Abuse Treatment Program, a part of the center's Adult Services Department. I was greeted by Cindy McLaughlin, manager of the Substance Abuse Team and my new boss. She welcomed me, gave me a quick tour, showed me to my cubicle, and handed me a sheaf of paperwork to complete. I hoped that she would prove to be as welcoming and supportive as she seemed.

When I finished with the paperwork, Cindy took me in to meet with Dr. Erik Sandaas, the Medical Director. I hadn't talked with him since he'd offered me the job. When I entered his office he gave me the once-over, then invited me to sit down. I was instantly wary. Just some vibe. Where most everyone else I'd seen was casually dressed, he was tall, erect, dressed to the nines in a gray three-piece suit. With steely blue eyes and perfectly coiffed silvery hair, he radiated wealth and arrogance. Some of yesterday's euphoria began to fade.

"Well Merritt, it is Merritt, isn't it? Yes? Interesting name. We don't have too many Merritts around here. Anyway, I want to welcome you to PBH, tell you a little bit about who we are, talk about how we can all get along."

"Well, OK. I'm happy to be here, and certainly interested in knowing how we can best get along."

"As you know, you were hired under our Second Chance Program, for people like you who have barriers to your employment. Say a felony on your record, history of addiction, something like that." He glanced up at me when he said that. I sat like a rock. There was something about this man I just did not trust. "Here at PBH, we believe that everyone deserves a second chance. So you were, let's see here, in prison for drug trafficking. Is that about right?"

"Uh, yes. That's right." Didn't he already know my history?

"You need to know that Second Chance is closely monitored by the state. They expect good performance and exemplary behavior. None of whatever it was that got you into the program or you're out. Zero tolerance. The state pays two-thirds of your salary and they want to be sure they're getting their money's worth."

So that was it. He could care less about second chances. He just wanted to staff his programs at a discounted rate, courtesy of the State of Oregon. "Well, I hope to demonstrate that I'm worth the state's investment in me." *And by the way, kiss my ass.*

"I see that you're going to be working here as an Addictions Counselor. That's good. We have a lot of call for that program. But, you know, Meryl, we don't have many of your kind here. We're mostly white here in Clatsop County. Have you worked with whites before? I'm not sure you told me why you wanted to work here."

Didn't we already cover this at my interview? I struggled to be polite. "It's Merritt, sir. My sister lives in Gearhart." *And by the way, she's Black, too, you asshole.* "She's a nurse at Providence. She invited me to move here after I was released from prison. She's the one who told me about Second Chance. It looked like a good way to get a fresh start."

"Your sister. You say she's a nurse at Providence. Well, OK. That's good. That's good."

"Yes. It IS good."

"Well, Merritt, I just wanted to welcome you to Pacific Behavioral Health and tell you that I'll be happy to do anything I can to make your time with us beneficial for one and all.

You'll be reporting to Ms. McLaughlin, so you probably won't see much of me. I'll let you get back to your desk, now."

"Well, thank you so very much, Dr. Sandaas. It has been a real pleasure meeting with you, and I appreciate the opportunity to work with you at PBH. I trust that I won't disappoint you." I hoped he didn't hear the sarcasm dripping from my lips.

Cindy caught my eye as I walked back to my cubicle. I shrugged. I couldn't read her face and I was already reeling from my encounter with Sandaas. Back in my cubicle, I checked out the Adult Services brochure I'd picked up.

Here at Pacific Behavioral Healthcare, we believe everyone deserves to live well, and the breadth of services available through our adult outpatient program reflects this conviction. We offer comprehensive services in mental health, substance abuse treatment, problem gambling, pain management and more.

With Erik Sandaas in charge, I doubted that anyone like me was included in the "everyone" who deserves to live well. Well, whatever. I was not going to let him get the better of me, and I needed the job.

For the rest of the day Cindy oriented me to my work. She gave me files on ten clients and walked me through all the paperwork involved. "I'm really glad you're here, Merritt. We're crazy busy these days. More clients than we know what to do with. I'll start you with these ten and we'll work you up to about sixty."

"Each week?"

"God, no. You'll see about twenty individual clients and run a few groups each week. Not to worry. You'll be plenty busy. At least for the next few months we'll schedule weekly supervisory conferences to review your cases and paperwork. And I'm always available if you need me outside of that time."

"Sounds like a plan. Thanks Cindy."

And so my job began. The first few days were a little chaotic—meeting new clients, learning the ropes—but it didn't take long to get into the groove. I had no more contact with Dr. Sandaas—thank God—and Cindy turned out to be a supportive and helpful supervisor. A few clients seemed surprised to be working with a Black man, but for the most part they were more interested in their own problems than in my race. Only one or two asked to see a different counselor. Their loss! I found myself easily falling into the deep listening and caring that had been central to my priesthood, and even though my clients were different from me on the surface, I found it easy to relate to them. I was off to a good start.

For the first few weeks I spent most of my time getting to know my new job and locale. In spite of being a lone Black man in a white world, the racist micro-aggressions lobbed in my direction weren't much different from what I'd experienced in Seattle. Val was right about that. Every once in a while Liz and I grabbed a bite at the Pub & Grub while Val was at work. The center table regulars observed us with curiosity and smiled, but no one said anything beyond a friendly greeting.

Right from the start it was necessary for me to pay attention to my own recovery. The NA meetings I'd attended at Monroe had been very helpful and I wanted to see what I could find close to my new home. There were a couple of meetings each week at PBH. Most of my clients attended at least one of them, and since I didn't want to run into any of them at a meeting, I looked around for other options. I found a Thursday evening meeting a few blocks away from PBH, at the Helping Hands Outreach Center, that looked like it might fit the bill.

As soon as the next Thursday rolled around, after work I grabbed a bite to eat and walked to the meeting. About eighteen people, mostly around my age, were there. The format was familiar—people introducing themselves, the Serenity Prayer, celebrating recovery anniversaries, sharing stories. It's a system that works. I felt at ease as I was welcomed as a newcomer.

I wasn't yet ready to share my story with everyone. I knew that I needed to—that telling my story was important to my recovery—but I was still so embarrassed, so ashamed. Waiting for the bus to return home after one of the meetings, I was flooded with unwanted memories of how my own story began.

* * *

I had been buoyed up by my meeting with Father Clement those many years ago. By telling him all about my sex life. With men. He had been so accepting, and my confession had been liberating. For a while I felt almost normal. Like I could really beat this one, could be the kind of priest I wanted to be. But the grace of the confessional did not last long. Almost in spite of myself I began again to cruise the bar scene, go home with strangers, engage in safe sex, then rush home to catch a few hours of sleep in my own bed before my day began. beloved parish priest by day. One-night-stander by night. Shame, guilt, and anxiety eclipsed the rewards of my work. I was in deep trouble with myself. Something had to give.

Something gave all right. Just not in the right way. I first saw Rafael seated alone at the bar at Neighbors. Caramel-colored skin, black, wavy hair drawn back in a ponytail. Handsome, mustachioed face, soulful dark eyes, crooked smile, deep dimples. Well-chiseled physique. He reminded me of Jose, back at O'Dea. I should have taken that as a warning. With my energy at low ebb, and feeling anything but attractive myself, I was surprised when he caught my eye. He bought me a drink, then suggested we leave.

"You look like you could use a pick-me-up." Was it that obvious? Reclining on the king-size bed in his apartment, he took a snort of cocaine. "Here. Try some. It'll fix you up in no time."

I was instantly wary. My self image definitely did not include being a druggie. But what the hell, I've sunk this far. Why not? The angel perched on my right shoulder screamed "NO!" but the devil on my left shoulder won. "Well, maybe just once." Famous last words.

The powdery substance burned my nose, but almost instantly I felt alert, confident, and sexy. OMG. _Really sexy_. So this is what coke is all about! It was the first hit of my life. The night went by in a blur—phenomenal sex, more hits, more amazing sex. It was already morning when I stumbled home to get ready for my day. What just happened?

Having already broken two of my rules—no drugs, always wake up at home—it was all too easy to break the third. Never get involved.

I arranged to meet Rafael again and soon we were meeting three or four times a week. Each time the sex was astonishing, enhanced by a cocaine-induced euphoria. And each time, after the effects of the drug wore off, I was paralyzed by guilt and shame. I could barely do my work, but I did my best to hide it from my parishioners. I honestly don't know what they thought. All I really knew is that I lived for those nights with Rafael.

Then one night, an unwanted surprise. "Hey, Mer" – that's what Rafael called me, Mer—"Hey, Mer. It's time for you to put some skin in the game." I looked up at him, confusion written onto my face. "You need to start paying for your drug habit."

What? Pay? It had never even occurred to me. I was the stay-at-home kid, cooking with Gran-Mo instead of using drugs with the neighborhood kids. Could I be more of an idiot? FUCK! "Um... how much?"

"The street cost of what you're using each night is about $150."

"What?" I was dumbfounded. I'm not sure exactly what I thought.

"Did you expect to stay on the gravy train forever?"

So fucking naive! I never even thought about it. I suddenly saw Rafael in a sinister new light. What, actually, did I know about him? Precious little. I'd broken all my rules, compromised my values, jeopardized my priesthood and my identity to be with this man for God's sake, and I didn't have a clue who he really was. I knew as well as I knew my own name that I should get the hell out of there and never look back. But that's not what happened.

"I don't have that kind of money. You know that." I could barely squeak out the words. I craved a hit to quell the shame and terror flooding my system.

"Well, as I see it, you've got two choices. Walk now or find a way to pay. The good news is, I can help you get the kind of money you need for as long as you like." He reached out to me, smiling his crooked smile, rubbing my neck. "To keep us together for as long as you like."

"Go to hell!" Glaring at Rafael, I beat a hasty retreat. "Go to hell, asshole."

* * *

A tooting bus horn pulled me out of my memories. "You getting on, bud?" barked the driver.

"Yep. Thanks." Climbing aboard I found myself wishing, fervently wishing, that that had been my final encounter with Rafael.

Deliver Us from Evil

June

The Thursday night NA meetings quickly became an essential part of my routine. Although I didn't have much trouble staying off drugs, they reinforced my commitment to stay on the straight and narrow. Plus I was getting to know some of the regulars, especially a young woman named RaeAnne. She wasn't a knockout, but there was something about her. Tall, almost too slender, with unkempt shoulder-length dishwater blond hair, startling green eyes, and a perpetually haunted expression, everything about her said, "I need a friend."

After a couple of weeks I suggested we get a cup of coffee after the meeting. Over conversation at Dutch Brothers Coffee we discovered we were both in the Second Chance Program at PBH. She worked in the finance department as a medical billing assistant in a different part of the building from where I worked. After about an hour of conversation—which included our shared antipathy for Dr. Sandaas—I had to run to catch the bus back to Gearhart. I had enjoyed talking with RaeAnne, and on the ride home it occurred to me that perhaps I had made a new friend. It would turn out to be a more significant friendship than I could have imagined.

RaeAnne and I developed a routine of having coffee together after our meeting. We enjoyed comparing notes about our jobs, gossiping about coworkers, and guessing about who else might be in Second Chance. To avoid any misunderstanding, early on I came out to RaeAnne, asking her to keep that part of my identity to herself. She was surprised and, possibly, disappointed. But she still clearly wanted to be friends. "Oh! Well damn. OK then. Your secret's safe with me."

After a couple months of idle chatter, we began to share

more of our personal lives with one another. One night, after we were seated at our usual booth, I opened the conversation. "So, RaeAnne. You've talked at NA about your addiction, but not much about anything else. Would you tell me more about yourself?"

"Whaddya wanna know? Basically, most of my life has been hell. You sure you wanna hear about that?"

"If you want to talk, I want to listen."

"Chapter One. My loving mother was a lifelong addict. Chapter Two. I spent the first weeks of my life in the NICU withdrawing from the shit in my system when I was born. Great start, eh?"

"Not the best."

"So of course, she was totally wasted when she finally took me home. And of course, my dear father was a nice, friendly, violent kind of guy. Always beating on my mom. But did CPS show up then? Noooooo, of course not. Left me there to rot in my crib."

"Whew. RaeAnne. I'm sorry."

"Whatever. Shit happens. So anyway, a few years later Luther, my little brother, shows up. I guess I was three at the time. I was his self-appointed guardian angel. I just stood there by his crib for hours on end. Watching him like a hawk. Just me and him against the world."

"Where's Luther now?"

"I'm getting to that. Spoiler alert—not a happy ending."

"RaeAnne. You don't have to keep going... "

"No. I want to tell you the whole story. It helps to talk sometimes, you know?"

"Yes. I do know."

"So anyway, when Luther was three and I was six my loving father finally left. Three years of me and Luther hiding out whenever he was on a tear. Scared shitless he'd find us and beat us to a pulp. Helpless to protect our mother."

"CPS never showed up?"

"Nope. Not then. Some story, eh?"

"So... what happened after your dad left?"

"Well, my mom couldn't afford to pay for where we were living so she moved the three of us into this drug house. Oh my God Merritt, you would not believe that place!"

"What was it like?"

"What was it like? Good question. Number one. Filthier than any place you could ever possibly imagine. Creeps me out just remembering. Number two. God knows how many people living there. All over the place. All the time. All of them stoned out of their minds. All the time."

"God, RaeAnne, how did you and Luther survive?"

"No one paid any attention to us. I kinda continued my role as his mother. Scrounging whatever I could find for us to eat from the refrigerator, sometimes from shoplifting."

"I get it. You had to eat. Still no CPS?

"Well, they finally showed up. And, you know, it was weird. Even though our mom was too wasted to pay much attention to us, she was still, you know, our Mom. And when CPS took us away it was awful. Mom cryin' and screamin'. Me and Luther cryin' and screamin'. You get the picture."

"Yeah. I do."

"You know. She was a shitty mother. But she was our mom. And we were her kids. And we loved her, and I guess she loved us. We were all she had. But she was so far gone..."

"Yeah."

"So anyway, I held Luther on my lap the whole way to the foster home. I. Would. Not. Let. Anyone. Touch. Him. I was going to protect him, no matter what."

"Did you go to the same family?"

"Yes, thank God. I don't know what might have happened if they tried to separate us."

"Good that they found a place for both of you. Did you like

the family?"

"John and Ginger Bowen. They were OK enough I guess. For Luther anyway. They took an immediate shine to him. But they didn't like me from the start. I guess CPS told them if they wanted Luther, they'd have to take me too."

"Well..."

"No, really, it was pretty damn clear. Listen to this. My mom never got her act together. They finally terminated her rights to me and Luther. So we were free for adoption. And guess who got adopted. And guess who didn't. And guess who had to leave the beloved Bowen household after her brother was adopted." RaeAnne's voice rose higher and higher as she dissolved in tears.

"What? That's awful! How old were you?"

"I was eleven. Luther was eight. He was really torn. He loved the Bowens. They'd been his parents since he was three. But I'd been his big sister his whole life. Me. I'd been looking after him the whole time. It was really bad shit all around. But—shit happens. It was one big, gigantic shit storm."

"Yeah. I guess so. So do you see Luther now?"

"Not really. I haven't seen him in years. After being so close we drifted apart. It was hard for him, you know, feeling loyal to both of us. Tore him apart. And he finally went with the Bowens. Yeah. He went with the Bowens. I guess I understand. Ginger was his mother since he was three. She doted on him. Why couldn't she love me, too? Why not, Merritt? Why couldn't she love me, too?"

Tears were streaming down RaeAnne's face and people in the other booths were staring. "Let's get out of here, RaeAnne."

I grabbed some clean napkins from the table as I led RaeAnne outside. I held her in my arms as she wept, her tears soaking the front of my shirt. When her crying was spent I asked her where she lived.

"Just a few blocks away. The Jackson Apartments."

"How do you usually get there?"

"Walk."

"I'm walking you home tonight."

"No, I'm fine. Besides, you have a bus to catch."

"RaeAnne. I am walking you home."

By the time we reached her apartment, RaeAnne had regained her composure. "Thanks Merritt. You're a good man. Sure you wouldn't like to come in?" She seductively fiddled with the top button on her blouse.

"No, RaeAnne. No."

"I get it, Merritt. I'm sorry. I do understand. And I do want to be friends."

"OK. I want to be friends, too. And now I really have to get going." I held the door open for her as she entered her tiny, dark apartment. My heart ached for her, living there all by herself. So isolated. So lonely. It was good I'd been so clear with my boundaries. I did want to be her friend. "Thanks for trusting me, you've been carrying a lot."

"Maybe next time you'll tell me *your* story."

"Sure." We briefly hugged and I walked to the bus stop. I'd just missed the bus and the next one was over an hour away. I called Liz, who came to get me. She looked at me curiously when I got in the car, but I shook my head. "I'm fine. Just helping a friend in trouble. Thanks for coming."

* * *

For the next couple of weeks, I saw nothing of RaeAnne. She wasn't at the NA meetings and she wasn't at work either. I was really worried about her. Was she hurt by my rejection of her advances? Did telling me her story trigger her? I had no way of knowing anything for sure. I called and texted her a couple of times but nothing. I prayed I wasn't somehow responsible for whatever it was that was happening.

Three anxious weeks later I was very relieved when RaeAnne was back at NA. She avoided my eyes but spoke up at the meeting. "I'm RaeAnne and I'm an addict. I've been in recovery for three years. A few weeks ago a ton of shit heaped up on me and I started using again. I finally got it together to call Awakenings. Thank God Peggy, my old counselor, was still there. She helped me get my head screwed on again and made me come back here. So here I am."

"Welcome back, RaeAnne. We're glad to see you." There's nothing quite like the support of an entire NA group. While I was glad that RaeAnne had returned, I was still worried about her, about my potential role in her relapse, and also pissed that she'd totally ghosted me.

Later, over coffee: "I'm really sorry Merritt, I'm sorry I worried you. Talking about Luther and all—I guess it got to me."

"Well, yeah, I was definitely worried. I wish you'd gotten in touch with me! Are you sure you're OK now?"

"Well, not really. I'm pretty sure I won't use again. But damn it's hard. You know... the thing about not being adopted... I'm just so alone. I don't belong anywhere. I have no family. Any so-called friends are still using. You're my only real friend Merritt. "

"You can always count on me, RaeAnne."

"Well that's all fine and dandy but, you know... damn it Merritt, you won't be who I want you to be in my life. That makes me feel even more alone."

"You're right about that, RaeAnne. I'm sorry. I can't be your boyfriend. But you can always count on me to be a good friend."

RaeAnne smiled wanly, tears trickling down her cheeks. "And I do appreciate that Merritt. Truly I do. It's just... " For a minute she was quiet, her eyes closed. Then, looking up with a bright smile she said: "Merritt, I think it's time I hear some of *your* story."

Wow. OK. Where to begin? "So here's something you may find hard to believe!'

"OK. I'm sitting down. Shoot."

"Before I went to prison, I was a priest."

"You're shittin' me. Really?"

"Yep! It's true. All my life I wanted to be a priest, and I was. For three years. Until I fucked up."

"Wow. That *is* a shocker. Merritt Grace. A priest. Wow." She laughed. "Has anyone ever told you you've got the perfect name for a priest?"

"Once or twice maybe. And sometimes I actually believe it. That I merit grace that is."

"You're shittin' me. You can't ever wonder that. You're incredible. Kind. Good listener. Yeah—I can see you as a priest. So what happened?"

What happened? That was the question. I forced myself to recall that nightmarish time before responding to RaeAnne.

* * *

I'd been really sick—craving a hit, loathing who I'd become, furious with Rafael when he suggested I deal. Distraught, I ran to my church and found my way to a pew in the front. There I sat—I don't know how long—filled with remorse, shame, anxiety, and confusion. I tried to pray, but I had no faith that God was listening. I went home and tried to sleep, but sleep didn't come.

That netherworld persisted for several days as I pretended to go about my work. Try as I might, I was just going through the motions. All I could think about was getting high with Rafael. Even as I felt more guilt and shame than I thought possible, I craved the drug to raise my spirits.

One evening something snapped. I could not go on. After

stumbling through the 6:00 o'clock mass I changed my clothes and went to Neighbors, hoping to find Rafael. I'd been there about half an hour when he strolled in, looking as good as ever. My stomach was a knot. I prayed I didn't look too desperate.

"Well look who the cat dragged in." He gave me a knowing look, a come-hither smile. Uncle! I couldn't trust him any more than I could throw him across the room, but I could _not_ resist him. After one drink, we left and went to his apartment.

"So, you've changed your mind...?"

My belly hollow with remorse, I agreed. "So it seems."

"It's a perfect win/win. You work for me. Small-time. Nothing big, unless you want it to be. You earn enough for your own stash and we get to play—all we want." His smile suddenly seemed sinister.

God how I missed those highs, that sex. Despising my weakness—unsure of who or what I had become—I glared at Rafael. "OK, what next?"

"For $300 each, I supply you with eight-balls of coke. Each one is about 3 grams. You sell it for whatever you can get—the going rate is around $150 a gram. Do the math. With practically no effort you have plenty to take care of yourself. As I said, a win/win." That unsettling smile again. That hand caressing my neck again. "Comprendes?"

What was he saying? Non comprendo. Except I did understand. All too well. My stomach lurched and I swallowed hard to keep from throwing up.

"You know, as a priest you've got the perfect setup."

"Keep my being a priest out of this! Completely! Comprendes?" My voice rose as I shook with rage.

"Well, whatever you want, Father Grace. I'm just saying—you can distribute without ever even leaving your church. Plenty of dealers spend a lot of time running around town. Your customers will come to you, and no one will ever know."

"I don't like where you're going with this."

"Well, as I said, your choice. It's just a suggestion. If you don't mind my saying so, you look like you could use a little help."

"OK, I give. What's your suggestion?"

"Sell out of the confessional. I'll get you your first customers. You get a text—someone will come to confess. The text includes a code that alerts you that the sender is a customer. You text back with a time and your price. Once in the confessional the customer says "it's been thirteen months since my last confession." That's how you know this is your customer. You hand over the drugs, they hand over the cash. They leave—with or without a penance. That's up to the two of you." A self-satisfied grin spread over Rafael's face.

Time stood still as I was paralyzed by confusion. This was so totally different from everything I knew as right. Everything the church stood for. Everything I thought I stood for. How depraved had I become? And then, disgusted with myself, I caved. "Well, you clearly have all the bases covered." I hated myself for even saying that.

"Your choice Father. It's foolproof. Maybe this will help you think about it." He passed me a line of cocaine.

Unable to stop myself, I snorted deeply. It had been several days, and the impact was immediate. My anxiety and indecision were replaced by excitement and confidence. "Sure, Rafael, I'm in. I'll give it a try." He laughed as he pushed me back onto the bed.

* * *

Recalling those days, I could barely believe that had actually been me. "You asked what happened to me as a priest, RaeAnne." She'd shared so much of herself with me. I decided to do the same. "Do you have a few more minutes?"

RaeAnne nodded her interest. I told her the whole sordid

story, ending with the time I'd agreed with Rafael's plan. I just couldn't bring myself to talk about everything that happened after that. Not then, anyway, it was just too painful.

When I finished she just stared at me for several minutes. Then... "Holy shit, Merritt! Man oh man. Oh my God. I dunno what to say. Do you want some tea or somethin'?"

"Thanks RaeAnne, tea would be good. Maybe some soothing chamomile" I took a few minutes to settle myself while she went to the counter to get it. Took a few deep breaths.

When she returned both of us were more composed. The hot tea was soothing. "Thanks RaeAnne."

"Thanks for telling me your story Merritt. I had no idea. So—I'm guessing you were in prison for dealing?"

"Yeah."

"And you were a priest."

"Yeah."

"That's a lot to take in."

"Yeah. It's a lot to live with."

"I s'pose so. Does anyone else know?"

"I don't think so. Except Val and Liz of course. It's not how I think of myself right now. I didn't include being a priest on my Second Chance paperwork. All they know is that I was in prison for dealing drugs."

"Well, your secret's safe with me. Thanks for telling me."

"Sure. I know I can trust you."

"So, about your story—a couple of things confused me."

"Like what?"

"What was that place where you distributed?"

"The confessional."

"Confessional?"

"You don't know what that is, do you?"

"Uh, no. I've never actually been inside a church."

"Wow. OK." I let that sink in a minute. The church was so important to me. Even at my lowest point. RaeAnne was going through life without the support that was most important to me. I promised myself once again to be a good friend to her, no matter what. And then I answered her question. "Well, a confessional is like a little stall inside the church. The priest sits inside on one side and people who want to confess sit on the other. They're separated by a screen. The person who is confessing tells the priest all their sins and the priest tells the person what their penance is."

"Penance?"

"It's what you do to atone for your sins. But... let's not go there now. If you really want to know more we can talk about it later."

"OK, whatever. So, what made dealing out of the confessional so horrible?"

"The confessional is a sacred space. Dealing drugs out of a sacred space... I still can't believe I did that. I'm not sure I can ever forgive myself."

"So—you've left the church for good now?"

"I dunno. I can't think about that right now."

We were both quiet again for several minutes, feeling the intimacy, and vulnerability, of all we had shared. I was getting ready to leave when RaeAnne spoke up again. "Merritt, you've shared so much of your story with me. Do you have time to listen to a little more of mine?"

I glanced at my watch. If I left right then I'd just catch the next bus. "Sure, RaeAnn. I've got all the time you need."

"Thanks, Merritt. I really appreciate it. So anyway... after I got kicked out of the Bowen's I bounced in and out of a bunch of foster homes. It was a nightmare. And then when I was thirteen I wound up with a family I liked a lot." She paused and took a deep breath. Her voice was wispy when she continued. "After a couple of months the father started comin' to my room at night. At first, we'd just talk. Then he started giving me a massage. First on top of my clothes, then under my clothes.

One thing led to another and before long we were having sex."

"Oh man, I was afraid that's what you were going to say! How dare he. Tell me his name. He needs to be arrested."

"No, no names. I'm so fucked up. Part of me really liked it. He was tall and handsome. He said he loved me. Can you believe it? No one else has ever said that to me."

"I'm so sorry."

"Part of me knew it was wrong. He said not to tell anyone. It was our special secret. When I turned eighteen, we'd run away together."

"Damn him."

"I wanted to believe him. And, you know,... life went on. School, hanging with Luther every once in a while, late night visits, jealous when he went out with his wife... "

"Did you tell anyone? A teacher? Friends? Anyone?"

"No. I didn't have any friends. And I wasn't about to talk to any of my teachers. God no!"

"What about your social worker?"

"You've got to be kidding. She's the last person I would of talked to"

"OK."

"It was all so fucked up. I thought I was in love. I didn't want to get him in trouble. I still thought we'd run away together. How dumb can a girl get? Thank God I didn't get pregnant."

"Well, that's a blessing anyway. You must have felt so alone."

"Yes, totally alone, except for those nights with him. For a few hours I felt like I finally belonged."

"So what happened?"

"My damn foster mother got suspicious and started to spy. She caught us in the act and the next day I was out on my ass."

"How old were you then?"

"I guess I was sixteen, I'm not exactly sure. Everything is kind of foggy."

"What did you do?"

"I ran away. No way I was going to another foster home. So I just split."

"Where did you go?"

"I looked for my mom. I hadn't seen her in years. Would you believe I found her in the same drug house where she used to hang? Totally wasted. Bitch didn't even recognize me."

"So painful."

"Well, yeah, I 'spose. But I found what I needed. Methamphetamines. Speedo Bandito!"

"Had you used before?"

"Occasionally. Nothing regular. But... that first hit of meth, Hello Happyland! A new way of life. Hangin' at the house, turning tricks. Well... you heard that part of my story at NA."

"Yes. I remember."

"After a couple of years I got disgusted with myself. Can't say exactly why. Just woke up one day sick of my life. Something had to give or I'd wind up in an early grave. I called my social worker. The one that put me in that foster home."

"Did you tell her about being abused there?"

"No, no way. Part of me still loved my foster father, and even believed he still loved me. What a jerk. No, I just asked her for help."

"Did she help?"

"Yeah. She referred me to Awakenings. After I finished treatment there they referred me to Oxford House."

"Oxford House—good program. You were lucky to get in."

"Yeah. It definitely worked for me. Live there as long as you need to. Using not allowed. Self-run—no authorities telling you what to do. Everyone pays their way. I washed dishes at Denny's to earn my keep."

"How long were you there?"

"A couple of years. Long enough to get my GED and my certificate in medical billing and coding. I earned that online.

After that, Second Chance came along. I moved to Seaside and the rest is history."

"You're a survivor, RaeAnne. But I'm still wondering—in all of the treatment that you got, did you ever talk about what happened in the foster home."

"No, never. And I don't plan to. You're the only one I ever told about that."

"Well OK RaeAnne. If you ever change your mind, I'll be happy to help find a therapist who can help. I'm sure there are people at PBH, but I know you don't want to see anyone there."

"I don't want to see anyone anywhere, Merritt. But thanks."

If I ran I could just catch the next bus, so I gaveRaeAnne a hug and left. All the way home my conversation with her swirled through my brain. RaeAnne was so vulnerable, She'd been through so much. And with that, the nagging thought: was I crazy to trust her?

The Wages of Sin

August

Weeks quickly turned into months, and before long I'd been in Gearhart for nearly half a year. Liz, Val, and I easily settled into a routine of shared living, and the three of us often spent time together on weekends when none of us was working. We liked walking the beach watching for seals, whales, and waterfowl, and we especially loved kite-flying when the wind was up.

In August we drove up to Long Beach, Washington, about thirty miles north of Gearhart, for the International Kite Festival. It's the largest kite festival in North America, hosted each year by the World Kite Museum. Long Beach is the perfect setting—miles of long, straight beach and strong, steady winds.

Liz, of course, was in heaven there. She was at the festival all week, managing a booth for Above It All. Her staff manned the booth for a few hours on the weekend while she, Liz, and I displayed some of the shop's specialty kites—huge billowing wheels that reminded me of giant candy-sprinkled donuts undulating across the beach, a string of seven or eight dolphins, all suspended from a single line. And my personal favorite, a gigantic octopus. Everywhere I looked I saw kites of every imaginable shape and size filling the sky and visitors crammed on the beach and boardwalk to get a good view.

Imagine my surprise when Liz left me and Val for the kite-fighting contest. That was a new one on me. I'd read about kite fighting in *The Kite Runner*, but I thought it just took place in Afghanistan. Live and learn. Turns out kite fighting is extremely competitive—fliers set on maneuvering their kite to bring their opponent's down. Stunning skill on full display, fans cheering their favorites on, me and Val jumping up and down screaming for Liz to win. In a flash I compared that moment to the highs I used to get from cocaine. This felt so pure, so good. I sent a little prayer of gratitude up to the kite-filled skies.

Eating well also became a part of my life in Gearhart. Every other week or so Liz and Val invited a bunch of friends over for dinner and game night. They usually cooked up a fantastic vegetarian soup and home baked bread. Everybody else brought drinks, salad, and dessert. After dinner we played Scrabble, Trivial Pursuit, or poker. I favored the Trivial Pursuit nights because I was really good at it, but I wasn't so bad at poker either. It wasn't long before Liz and Val asked me to help with the cooking. I enjoyed learning vegetarian cooking (a lot more complicated than throwing a burger in a pan and applying heat), and I found a used copy of *Greens Cookbook* at the Seaside Antique Mall. I poured through that book to check out new soup recipes to try.

Liz and I continued our ritual of eating once a week at the Pub & Grub while Val was at work. We enjoyed one another's company and their food was pretty good, with enough meatless entrees to satisfy Liz. Over the weeks we got to know some of the folks in the "center table gang" as I came to call them. They were a friendly crew of mostly single young professionals who basically enjoyed being with one another instead of being at home alone. I think they thought Liz and I were a couple and we did nothing to confirm or deny. We kept things pretty much on the surface with them.

Over the next few weeks I grew concerned about RaeAnne. She seemed to be fatigued and she wasn't taking care of her appearance as well as she usually did. I hoped she hadn't relapsed again. She still went to NA meetings, so maybe not, but she begged off of our usual coffee time afterwards. "I'm sorry Merritt, I've got a lot on my mind."

I was really worried about her. "You look like you could use a break. Would you like to take a walk this weekend?"

"I'd like that. Thanks. I'll pick you up and we can go to Del Rey from there."

For a variety of reasons I didn't want to bring RaeAnne that close into my home territory. Finding the balance between being a good friend and leading her on could be tricky. "That's OK Rae. Let's meet at PBH and walk to the beach from there. It's not far."

Sunday morning was crisp and bright. I met RaeAnne where she parked her car in the PBH lot. She seemed distracted but happy to see me. "Thanks for suggesting this Merritt, it looks like a nice day for a walk."

With waves gently lapping the shoreline, for several minutes we walked in silence, each lost in our own thoughts.

After a while RaeAnne tugged on my arm. "Can we stop for a minute, Merritt?" Looking at me, her green eyes were clouded, filled with fear.

"Sure. Let's find a place to sit and talk."

We found a log large enough for the two of us and sat down. We both gazed out into the ocean for a few minutes before RaeAnne opened up.

"I'm in a shitload of trouble, Merritt."

"What's happening?"

"I'm just about broke. I can't pay my bills. I might lose my apartment."

"Whoa! Is this new?"

"Goddam landlord raised my rent. PBH pays me peanuts. Plus some other shit."

Putting two and two together I suspected she was using again. It fit the pattern. "Have you talked with Peggy about this?"

"Why would I talk to her? I don't have enough money is all. She can't help me with that!" After a minute, "let's walk again."

We walked a mile or so down the beach and back. I listened to RaeAnne, tried to problem solve with her, but she was still pretty agitated when we ended our walk.

Back at PBH she thanked me for the walk and offered to drive me to the bus stop. "It's the least I can do." She fumbled through her purse. "Shit! Shit! Shit! What else can go wrong? Now I can't find my fucking keys. I hope to God I didn't drop 'em on the beach."

"Let me have a look." I poked through every pocket in her large bag but came up with no keys. "Nada. Sorry."

"Fuck! Well one good thing anyway. There's a spare set in my desk. You got your keys? Run up and get 'em for me, would you? They're in my top drawer."

"Sure thing. I'll be just a minute."

It felt odd to be walking around in PBH on a Sunday afternoon. Except for the security guard, the building was empty. I showed him my ID and all was well. Arriving at RaeAnne's cubicle I turned on the small desk lamp and opened her top drawer. I didn't immediately see her keys but I couldn't help but notice a letter lying at the top of the drawer. Ordinarily I wouldn't have thought anything about it, but my curiosity got to me when I saw the letter was addressed to Erik Sandaas.

Dr. Erik Sandaas
Medical Director
Pacific Behavioral Health
Dear Erik,

In my job here I see a lot. Things you wish I didn't see. I happen to know you're prescribing way too many drugs to your pain management patients, and that you get a kickback on each prescription. I also know you're over-billing Medicare and Medicaid by thousands of dollars. Even though I'm only a Second Chancer I'm not stupid. And even though I'm only a Medical Billing Assistant, I did get certified. I know what I'm talking about.

The good news is—we can both be winners. I get 10% of

everything you take in—and I know just what that is—and your secret is safe with me. Ignore me and I go to the authorities. It's that easy. The choice is yours. You know me well enough to know that I mean what I say.

I'm sorry things had to come to this. I really hope this won't get in the way.

Very truly yours,

RaeAnne MacArthur

My knees buckled as I sank into RaeAnne's chair. Oh my God. RaeAnne. Blackmailing Dr. Sandaas? Did she already send that letter? And since when did she call him Erik? And what did that last sentence about not getting in the way mean?

I found the keys, replaced the letter in the drawer, and returned to the parking lot. My head was swimming and I needed time to think. I tossed the keys to RaeAnne. "Here you go, Rae. I'll pass on the ride. Thanks anyway. Bye." She glared at me with "what the fuck" written all over her face, but before she could say anything I raced to the bus stop. My God. what just happened?

First thing the next morning I confronted her. "We have to talk. Where can we have some privacy?"

"You're right about that, asshole!" She led me to an office adjacent to the main billing area. We went in and she slammed the door.

"So what was with the disappearing act yesterday?" she asked. "I shared all my deepest shit with you and poof, you're gone. Just like everybody else. I thought you were different, but no. Damn. I can't trust anybody!"

"I did appreciate our talk, RaeAnne. I'm glad that you trusted me with your problem. But then, after I went up to get your keys... "

"What?"

"When I opened your desk drawer I found the letter you wrote to Dr. Sandaas. Or, I guess I should say, to *Erik*. Are you

95

blackmailing Dr. Sandaas, RaeAnne? I know you said that you're broke, but... "

"What the hell, asshole, now you're reading my private mail?" Her normally quiet voice was rising.

"Did you send that letter, RaeAnne?"

Louder. "I might have. What's it to YOU?"

"You can't blackmail Dr. Sandaas. I'm going to have to report you."

"Some goddamn friend you are!"

"Please lower your voice, RaeAnne. Everyone in the office can hear you. I promise you, I AM your friend. And for that reason I'm telling you, if you haven't sent that letter, don't. Because if you do, I can promise you—something bad will happen!."

"So, Mister Clean Gene, you're so innocent yourself!"

"What are you talking about?" I heard my own voice rising.

"Oh, come on, FATHER GRACE. You know just what I'm talking about. You want everyone here to know your little secret? Or should I call up your old church and let them know who you really are?"

With that remark I lost it, and a shouting match was on. "RaeAnne. I told you those things in confidence. You can't... "

"What are ya gonna do? Kill me?"

"Kill you? RaeAnne, don't even say anything like that! Just keep your damn mouth shut."

"You keep quiet. I keep quiet."

It was a nightmare. We were both out of control. I had to clear my head. "I'm outta here." I was shaking as I stormed out of the conference room. Several sets of eyes followed me as I headed for the elevator.

That was the last time I saw RaeAnne. When she didn't show up for work the next day, I figured she'd relapsed again. Poor Rae. what a mess. And what about that letter? Had she sent it? Had Dr. Sandaas responded? I just didn't trust that man. And what if everything RaeAnne said about him was true? Was he really over-prescribing opioids? And defrauding the government? And what about Marjorie? She signs off on RaeAnne's work. Is she involved too? My God, what kind of a house of cards am I working in?

It was two more days before I heard anything. When I did, the news was stunning. It spread quickly throughout the agency. RaeAnne had been found dead on her car, parked at the beach. They suspected suicide.

For several minutes I sat at my desk in shock. Reliving our argument. Devastated that we'd parted in such anger, And now she was gone. Gone. Oh my God RaeAnne. I'm so sorry I let you down. I should have listened better. I could have helped. I could have lent you money. I could have... I took a deep breath to pull myself together—I had clients to see.

I was between clients when Cindy approached me at my desk. "Merritt, the police are here. They want to talk to you."

CHAPTER 9: HENRY
Fraternizing with the Enemy

August

It was a decent day weatherwise, not too hot for August, so I thought I'd ride my bike into town for some exercise, maybe get a good iced coffee at the Daily Grind and take a walk on the beach. I had plenty of work to keep me busy but I needed a change of scenery to help me clear my head. The ride from my place was easier now that I was in better shape, and that was a boost to my raging ego. I wanted to keep it that way, and I'd been eating more forbidden foods lately. Pedaling along, I promised myself I'd ride into town at least a couple of times a week.

The Grind was almost empty. I was waiting for my coffee drink when the door opened and Chief O'Donohue walked in. I almost didn't recognize him. I'd only seen him a few times before and he'd always been wearing a suit and tie, very nicely dressed, all freshly shaved and combed. Today, he was wearing casual clothes and Nikes. His hair was tousled and curly and he had a little growth of beard. He was still pretty good looking for an older guy and the casual look suited him.

He didn't seem to recognize me either at first. He ordered his coffee and then noticed me standing there. "Hey Case, how's it going? I haven't seen you to talk to since we had coffee a while ago." I said that things were good, that I had a lot going on, that I was just taking a break to get some exercise and clear my head. "Me, too," he said. He was taking a day off, doing some work from home. He'd come to the office to pick up a couple of files and wanted to grab a coffee before he headed back home. He went on about how his political campaign was going, bragging about the prominent Republicans and civic groups that were endorsing him. "So, can I count on you?" He was staring at me. I must have tuned out and completely missed what he was asking.

"Uh, sure," I said tentatively. "What can I do to help?" He said the first thing I could do was to attend the upcoming cocktail party and fundraiser at the Orca Club. His friend, Erik Sandaas, was president and had persuaded the club's board to sponsor the event. Apparently Sandaas was kind of a local VIP, a psychiatrist who was medical director of Pacific Behavioral Health in Seaside. I tried to act impressed and said okay, I could probably come, although I didn't know how much I could contribute. He was more interested in having a crowd than in how much the event raised, he said. And the fundraiser would be a great way for me to meet his other supporters and get motivated to get on board with his campaign. While I doubted that would happen, I figured if nothing else the fundraiser would be a good way to meet some other people, whatever their interests. Some of them were bound to be female.

"So just tell me when and where," I said. He looked in his jacket pocket for something to write on and came up with an envelope. He borrowed a pen from the barista and wrote the particulars on the envelope. As an afterthought, he wrote "O'Donohue fundraiser," I guess so I wouldn't forget what it was about, and handed it to me.

"Doors open at 7:00."

"See you there," I said. I stuck the envelope in my jacket pocket.

"Thanks," he said. "I was gonna drink my coffee here—care to join me?" He was a lot friendlier now that he'd suckered me into supporting his campaign.

"Sure," I said.

He got up and went to the counter and came back with a couple of their chocolate chip cookies. "Brain food," he chortled. "Hey, how'd you become a PI, anyway? I mean, I know you went to law school, which seems like it might be useful. But how'd you make the crossover?"

"I worked in my father's law firm all through law school," I began. He looked sort of impressed. "After I graduated from law school I had a place carved out in the firm and it was assumed I'd become the next Case partner." Even more impressed. "But I couldn't seem to pass the bar exam." Less impressed. "When I failed for the third time, I realized I probably wasn't meant to be an attorney—and didn't really want to be for that matter." Definitely unimpressed. "So, I had a few beers with a law school buddy and when he asked me what I'd really like to do, being a private investigator popped into my head. Great idea, but there were two problems, my wife Janis—now my ex-wife—and my father. They were both counting on me being a partner in my father's law firm."

"How'd you work that out?"

"Not so well with my wife. We have an amicable relationship now, but it was rough going for a few years. Got divorced obviously. She's remarried and happy. We share a daughter, Jenny, who's in middle school."

"And your dad?"

"That was rough going, too. Before I told him about my exam results, I contacted a PI I'd worked with at the law firm and asked if he'd mentor or apprentice me. He said he would if my dad agreed. Campbell, Case & Wells was his best client. My dad wasn't happy with me or with that idea, but eventually he agreed, and I worked with the PI—his name was Charlie—for a couple of years while I learned the ropes and got my license. Then I went out on my own."

"Did your dad come around? Accept your choice of vocation?"

"Sadly, he died while I was still working with Charlie."

"Too bad."

My bright idea had been to get my ducks in a row before I told my father about my bar exam results and new career plans. I'd get Charlie to let me work with him, at least while I was learning the ropes. I was pleased with myself for thinking of it. As usual, Charlie sounded glad to hear from me when I called to ask if we could have coffee sometime. We weren't working on anything together, but there were a couple of cases that might have needed some follow-up, and probably he was hoping for the paid time. I felt a little guilty about my reason for asking him to talk with me. So I bought his coffee and gave him the short version of my dilemma. When I asked if he could help me, take me on as an associate or just teach me the ropes and cut me loose, he scowled and asked what my dad knew about my new plans. I told him I'd be telling my dad soon, but wanted to check things out with him first.

He looked at me with a fair amount of pity. "You understand that CCW is my best client, sometimes my only client, I do so much work for them. So if I help you and your dad doesn't like it, I'll be shooting myself in the foot," I nodded. I guess I'd been naïve. He said he wanted to help me but wouldn't do it unless my father asked him to. I could see then that I was less in control of my own life than I had believed.

*

The chief went on, "I'm assuming your dad okayed the apprenticeship. He must have been supportive if he did that,"

"Kind of. I don't know that he ever got over what he saw as my great failure. But he did come around and helped get me started on an alternative career."

"What kind of stuff did you do—surveillance?"

"No, nothing that exciting. Mostly stuff Charlie didn't want to do. But it was still a great way to learn the business."

* * *

I'll be honest—there was more than one occasion when I questioned my new career choice, starting with the first week. Charlie used my employment to offload his most loathsome work. I don't mean sharpening pencils or making copies—he had an admin assistant who took care of that—but doing research and making phone calls related to what he found least exciting. And for the most part that was insurance fraud. He preferred the stuff that I had imagined doing—the sexier stuff such as surveillance, research related to extra-marital affairs, and the like. It got him out of the office while I was spending most of my time sitting in a chair in front of a computer screen.

* * *

"What does it take to get a detective license in Washington?" The chief was surreptitiously picking a piece of walnut from the cookie out of his teeth.

"Not as much as I'd expected. My background in the law gave me a leg up. The apprenticeship was the icing on the cake."

* * *

I'd been caught up short by both my law school buddy and Janis, who had asked if I knew what it took to be a PI. Since I didn't, I did a little Google research to get an idea. I found a website that provided state-by-state information and scrolled down to Washington. First of all, one had to be a U.S. citizen over eighteen years of age, free of any criminal convictions directly related to one's investigative work. They didn't really set that bar too high, did they?

The next one was harder—one had to be employed by a Washington State private investigating agency. I was three for four so far. Once you were employed as a PI, you could apply for a Washington State private investigator license, which required a minimum of thirty-six hours of training in areas related to a PI's work, a lot of which might have been covered in law school. There was an exam, which scared me shitless, but it appeared to only be required for principals of investigation firms and certified trainers.

*

"You carry a gun?"

"No, I don't really need one in my line of work. And since my daughter spends a fair amount of time at my house—or she did when I was in Seattle—I don't want a gun around. And of course, neither would my ex-wife."

* * *

Something on that website that got me to thinking was the list of license categories. There were four. At that time I didn't have to think about establishing my own agency or becoming a certified trainer—although those were goals I'd probably be pursuing in the future, assuming I actually could make this happen. My immediate choice appeared to be between being armed and unarmed. The former required a Washington State issued CWP (Concealed Weapons Permit). Hmmm. Definitely something I hadn't given much thought.

I'm not anti-gun. I'm a fan of the U.S. Constitution and all twenty-seven of its amendments, including number two, but my experience was limited. As far as I know, my parents didn't own any guns and neither of them knew how to shoot one. I'd visited my friend Jamie's family farm in Wisconsin with him a couple of times when we were in high school. I remember it was deer hunting season both times. I didn't bag a deer, but I did a fair amount of target practice with both a rifle and a handgun. Shooting a gun hadn't scared me and I had actually enjoyed the experience, although there had been no opportunity to follow up and hone my skills any further. It had been enough, now that I was remembering it, to make me think I would be okay with pursuing the CWP.

I was pretty sure, though, that Janis wouldn't want a gun in our house. And for that matter, I wouldn't want Jenny to be near a gun. Maybe I wouldn't need one. Since there was a PI license that didn't require a sidearm, clearly not every PI carried one. Not surprisingly, Charlie advised me to apply for the "unarmed" Washington State PI license. Considering that my work presented a relatively low level of danger and that I spent a lot of my time in the office, I agreed that it made the most sense. As he said, I could upgrade later if or if things changed.

*

"The work that you do now," he asked. "You travel a lot? Anything exciting or dangerous?"

"No, I do a lot of insurance fraud investigating. And a little missing persons work. I work mostly from home."

* * *

Gradually the insurance fraud work began to come together for me. I can still remember the first time I uncovered the facts leading to the discovery that a client firm's claimant had set fire to his own building. It saved the firm a buttload of money—and eventually the claimant was arrested and convicted of arson. I got such a rush from that experience I barely noticed the kudos I got from Charlie. After that I was like a dog on the hunt, looking for evidence that would lead to my having that rush again. It leveled off after a while, but not so much that I was bored, at least not for the first few years.

The other work I inherited from Charlie was what I called "Carmen San Diego" cases, after the popular children's TV show that I sometimes watched with Jenny, "Where in the World is Carmen San Diego?" Those cases were the ones where the client was looking for someone or something—and I tell you, I could write a book about them, Charlie's disdain notwithstanding. Perhaps the most interesting was looking for an heirloom wedding dress for a woman whose estranged husband had done something with it out of spite. I did find it, but sadly it had been dyed bright red

Charlie handed off the Carmen San Diego cases he was less excited about—mostly ones that required travel to some boring or inconvenient place. Even so, I liked them, partly because they got me out of the office and partly because they provided a way for Jenny to relate to my work, or at least I thought so...

*

"So did Charlie make you a partner?" he asked.

"No, he was sort of a lone wolf. And I really wanted to go out on my own. We still keep in touch and I still consider him a mentor. We refer cases to each other occasionally. "

*

I'd hoped to continue working with Charlie on a permanent basis. That wasn't to be, as it turned out, and it was a very unexpected event that helped bring our arrangement to an end. It was a sunny summer Sunday morning when my mother called to tell me that my father had died suddenly of a heart attack. In the months following his death, CCW let me go in favor of employing my sister, who was in her second year of law school. By that time, of course, they knew there was little chance that I'd become an actual lawyer. The position I'd been filling was one they usually offered to law students they hoped would graduate and pass the bar. Peter Campbell himself let me know that my time was up. He'd been my father's partner for many years, and I think it pained him to have to fire me. He told me he knew about my new career direction and wished me well. I cleaned out my desk and went home to my solitary apartment.

The next day I told Charlie about my greater availability and asked if he was ready for a more permanent, full-time arrangement. He had that same look on his face that he'd had when I first asked him about teaching me the trade. He was sorry, but his was pretty much a one-man shop. What he'd been paying me had come from my father, and that wouldn't be continuing, would it? So, he really couldn't afford to keep me on. And besides, he thought I might be ready to go out on my own.

A lot of what I had worked on with him was insurance fraud. It was mostly work unrelated to CCW, which meant there was no conflict of interest in my doing it while I was employed at CCW. Once I left he'd have more of that than he could handle, and he'd be only too happy to outsource it to me. He'd also refer other requests for that type of work. It was work that I could do remotely, from home, so it worked well with my co-parent status. By that time I'd gotten the training I needed and had received my license. Charlie'd given me a couple of weeks to get my own business set up. When I left his office my head was swimming.

*

"So that's how you became a PI?" I could tell the chief had reached the limit of his investigative curiosity—or maybe his attention span—and I was tired of talking about it.

"Yeah, that's pretty much the whole story," I said. "Look at the time. I guess I've bored you with my personal miseries long enough. See you at the fundraiser." I got up to go. Nailed the trash can with my coffee cup—three pointer!—and headed for the beach.

Later, peddling home, I was annoyed with myself for

having shared too many personal details with O'Donohue. Even more annoyed at myself for having said yes to O'Donohue's fundraiser. What an absolute waste of my time, I thought. I would have to say in all honesty that the chief wasn't one of my favorite Gearhartites. He was a little smarmy, a little too familiar or friendly for someone I didn't know that well. And he was one of those people who stands a little too close, who has a couple of toes inside your personal space—makes you want to take a step back. And, I would add, he seemed a little manipulative, like he knew what he wanted from you and how to get you to do it. Which is why I was sorry I'd told him so much about myself. In spite of all that, I guessed it wouldn't hurt me to give a few hours to his political campaign now that I was practically a local myself. But another thought occurred to me... the chief had checked on my background and now he knew even more about my past—maybe I should return the favor. Who knew what skeletons might be lurking in his closet? Maybe time would tell.

As soon as I got home I remembered the fundraiser. I took out the envelope and RSVP'd before I had a chance to think of an excuse for not going. I hoped I wouldn't hate myself for it.

I woke up a couple of days later remembering O'Donohue's fundraiser that evening. Did I even have anything to wear to an event like that? I was pretty sure it wasn't black tie, but I no longer had a business wardrobe. My present lifestyle didn't require it and, with all the weight I'd lost, I'd given most of my clothes away. I had treated myself to a little Nordy shopping the last time I was in Seattle so I had a nice sport coat and dress shirt, a great pair of jeans and some spiffy loafers. Pretty dressed up for a PI who works at home, so it would have to do.

That evening, showered and shaved, I put on my new duds. I didn't own a tie anymore, but since I was wearing jeans, a tie would have looked out of place anyway. I had bought a trendy belt, and that dressed the whole thing up a little. Then there was the socks dilemma—socks or no socks? In Seattle, it would definitely be no socks, but who knew what the fashion was in Gearhart? I opted for no socks anyway. I checked myself out in the mirror on the back of the bedroom door. I guess I'm not especially vain, because I don't look at myself that much—and now when I did, I was a little surprised with what I saw. In a good way. The weight loss and exercise had definitely paid off. All that running on the beach in the middle of the day had left me with a pretty decent tan. And the new clothes looked good. Who is that dude in the mirror? I asked myself—then went off to waste my good looks getting shitfaced with the Orca Club. I was still committed to being a good boy—but every good boy deserves a break now and then.

With one more glance in the mirror, I checked out the directions the chief gave me and forced myself out of the condo. Okay, I thought, I might as well get on with this, consider it my good deed for the day.

The parking around the Orca Club was pretty well filled up when I got there, and the hall where the cocktail party and fundraiser was being held was easy to find from the noise. The Orcas were just the sponsors of the event, so the attendees went well beyond their membership. I hadn't known there were that many people in Gearhart, and I'm guessing they'd come from far and wide. An interesting crowd with a mix of locals from both sides of the highway (although most of them probably from the west side) and some pretty tony-looking people that I guessed must have come from the cities. I wondered why the chief had felt it necessary to scrape up one more supporter, but maybe he hadn't had any idea who was coming. Or maybe they needed more single men—I could already see that there were a lot of women, talking in little groups together. There had been a time I'd have thought of picking one of them up—and as I thought about it, I realized that time hadn't passed.

I figured there wouldn't be a soul there that I knew. I picked up and stuck on the requisite name tag, then ambled over to one of the no-host bars to see what could be had to drink. I was just paying for my scotch when I felt a tap on my shoulder and turned to see Maddie Jacobs from the Pub & Grub happy hour group grinning at me. It took me a minute to recognize her, since it had been a while since we met. "Fancy meeting you here," she said. We exchanged a couple of sideways compliments about looking nicer than usual before we were joined by a couple I didn't know. Maddie introduced them as her brother and sister-in-law, Curtis and Janelle Jacobs. He was a member of the Orca Club and very excited about the club's support for Chief O's political candidacy. He asked what I did and when I said I was a PI they had all kinds of questions, starting with what there was to investigate in Gearhart. They were clearly disappointed when I told them I worked remotely on insurance fraud. Other people drifted in and out of our little group and I had that same conversation several times, lubricated by several more trips to the bar.

The chief's political fundraiser was a much more enjoyable evening than I'd anticipated. I had a good time talking to Maddie, who seemed perfectly happy to spend the evening talking to me or introducing me to other people she knew. I'm pretty much an extrovert but even so, since I didn't know anyone there but her and the chief, it was nice of her to take me in hand. She laughed at my idiotic comments, and I thought she was fairly amusing, too. Sneaking an occasional look at her, I found her quite nice looking—nearly as tall as I am, curvy, and topped off with lots of blond curls. Not really my type, though, although it's hard to know what that is— probably not Janis or anyone I've met since Janis. Her personality was a little too edgy maybe. Who knows what makes for chemistry? Not me for damn sure.

I couldn't see getting romantically involved with Maddie

but I thought we could be friends. She was one of two women I'd met since I'd been in Gearhart. The other was Officer Terry McConnell of the Gearhart Police Department, whom I'd met the day I had coffee with Chief O'Donohue. Thinking of her in her police uniform, I was pretty sure she wasn't my type either. Not much of a dating pool on the Oregon Coast.

At some point in the evening there was a little presentation by Erik Sandaas that included an ask for contributions and volunteers. Erik Sandaas was tall and fit with Scandinavian coloring—tanned and silver-haired. His coloring was enhanced somewhat by the amount of alcohol he'd consumed, which was apparent by his slightly slurred speech. I doubt that anyone noticed, since most of the attendees were drinking, too, and there wasn't much to eat. He looked like an important person and I was reminded that he was the high mucky-muck of some health-related organization in the area.

When the presentation finished, I looked at my watch, and I was surprised to see how late it was. "Well, I'll be off," I said to Maddie.

"What? You can't be leaving already. We were thinking of going to the Pub & Grub to get something to eat, since the Orcas were a little stingy with the food."

"Sorry, but I've got a lot of work to get to tomorrow, so it's going to be an early morning."

"Oh no, you know what they say—all work and no play makes Henry a dull boy."

"I'm afraid maybe that train has already sailed," I said and made a sad face. Maddie laughed and made one more attempt to lure me to the Pub & Grub. "I want to hear more about how you became a detective," she said.

"Private investigator," I corrected her and then, not wanting to be a spoilsport, agreed to join them.

I figured I should say hello and goodbye to the chief on the way out, since I hadn't spoken to him yet. I had no trouble spotting him, as the crowd had thinned out quite a bit. He was talking with Erik Sandaas. They were standing sort of in a corner, facing away from me as I walked up, deep in conversation. Which made me wonder why the chief wasn't working the room. They didn't hear me and were so intent on their conversation they didn't notice that I had walked up. Sandaas was talking a little too loud, no doubt a result of his alcohol consumption. "Has he quit yet?" the chief asked, to which Sandaas responded, "Not yet, but I think he will. If he doesn't, I'll make it so miserable there for the Black son of a bitch, he will quit. And if not, we'll fire him. I can't afford to have someone working there who... " he saw me and stopped abruptly.

The chief turned and saw me. "Henry, good to see you. Have you met Dr. Erik Sandaas? Our host with the most." He was clearly uncomfortable—that overly-friendly act that covers a multitude of sins—maybe thinking I'd overheard what they were saying. "Erik, Henry here is a private investigator. I'm persuading him to get involved with the campaign." I thought Sandaas looked a little pained. Maybe he didn't like PI's—or maybe he was wondering if I'd overheard his racist talk—or maybe he just had gas.

"Nice to meet you," I said, extending my hand.

He nodded but didn't bother to shake. "I've got to be going," I said to both of them. "Thanks for inviting me."

O'Donohue clasped me by the shoulder, so close that I could smell his expensive cologne. "Hey, I'm really glad you came. Hope you had a good time and met some nice people. I'll walk you to the door." He still had his hand on my shoulder. When we got to the door, I turned to leave, but he tightened his grip. "Say Henry. Do you still have that envelope I gave you the other day—the one with the directions on it? There's some information on it that I need—that is, if you still have it." That seemed odd. I was pretty sure there was nothing on it but the directions and the phone number and email for the RSVP—and he should have had those memorized.

"I don't know for sure," I said. "I'll look and get back to you." He grinned—or did he grimace? "No big deal, but I would like to have it if you can find it," he said—and with that he let go of my shoulder. And I left, wondering what his interest in that envelope could possibly be or if I could even find it.

* * *

I drove carefully to the Pub & Grub, aware of how much I'd already had to drink—not to mention how many drunken Orcas there might be on the roads with me. Fuzzy as I was, I focused in on that conversation I'd just overheard between O'Donohue and Sandaas. I didn't like the sound of it—a couple of good ol' white boys engaged in talking smack about some Black dude. I wondered who they were talking about. There weren't too many Black people in Gearhart or its environs. Someone who worked at Pacific Behavioral Health? A member of the Orca Club? Likely not the latter; more likely the former. Or possibly a member of the campaign staff. I recorded a reminder on my phone to think about this some more when my body and brain were better suited to thinking.

The other thing in my head was my relationship with Maddie. As I've already said, there was no real chemistry there, at least not on my part. But it occurred to me that she might be more interested in me than I was in her. I knew from her conversation that she was single and was looking for "Mr. Right." I didn't think I was going to be him, and I hoped I hadn't made a mistake by agreeing to meet her at the Pub & Grub. I wouldn't have minded having her as a friend, considering how few of those I had in Gearhart, and I didn't want to do anything unfriendly.

Maddie and her brother and sister-in-law were at a table

for four when I walked into the P & G. I had sort of envisioned a larger group. When we ordered I told the server that Maddie and I were together on one ticket. "Well, aren't you sweet?" she said. Mentally I kicked myself, thinking I might be leading her on. "Just want to say thanks for introducing me around at the event tonight." We spent a few minutes critiquing the fundraiser while we waited for our burgers. The opinion of the other three was that it had been a success—and that the chief would be an asset to the state as a senator.

I figured wanting to hear about my career path had just been a ruse to get me to the party after the party, but apparently they had more interest than I'd anticipated. They asked a lot of questions, which I answered as briefly as possible. Later I wondered if maybe Curtis and Janelle had been interviewing me as a potential brother-in-law. I had a sneaking suspicion they had begun to think of me as Maddie's new boyfriend.

"So, we heard the short version of how you became a detective," Janelle launched the grilling. I gave up on correcting the nomenclature—maybe it was only important to me. "There must have been more to it than that. Did you have to get some kind of certification?"

The ensuing conversation was pretty much the same one I'd had with the chief a few days before—except for Janelle's last question. "This is probably too personal," she began, "but do you think your work was responsible for your marriage falling apart?" By that time we could see the staff was getting ready to close up shop for the night, so I was spared having to answer that.

We paid up and headed out. Maddie made me promise to join the happy hour group at the Pub & Grub the next week. I promised I would be there if I could make it. I thanked her for making me feel welcome and gave her a quick hug before I left.

"I'm sure we'll see each other again," Janelle gave me a pat on the shoulder. "Our kids will want to meet you. Aunt Maddie is their favorite." That and the nature of some of their questions related to safety issues and the family-friendliness of the PI business, made me pretty sure I was going to be a disappointment to those three nice people.

Again I drove carefully, although a couple of hours and three Diet Cokes had sobered me up enough not to be a total menace.

When I got home and took off my jacket, I noticed that O'Donohue's envelope was still in my pocket. Again, I wondered why the chief might want it back. It didn't have anything on it but "O'Donohue fundraiser," the directions, the phone number, and the email address—plus a few dirty spots. Maybe the chief thought he had written something else on it. No biggie. But for whatever reason I shoved it in my underwear drawer, and then I sent the chief an email saying that I couldn't find it, that I was pretty sure I'd thrown it away and the trash had already been picked up.

The Inquisition

August/September

"Why do the police want to talk to me?" I felt anxious as Cindy walked with me to the elevator.

"They're talking to everybody here who knew RaeAnne. You know, at first they thought it was suicide, but now they think she might have been murdered."

"Murdered? Holy shit."

"Sargent Gellerman, the cop who's here, is just asking routine questions. You know, like, how did you know RaeAnne. Stuff like that. Nothing to worry about."

I *should* have nothing to worry about. But I felt uneasy as I approached the office where Gellerman was waiting for me. I could only hope he wasn't a racist bigot. Easy to accuse the only Black in town of just about anything that went wrong. Including murder.

I passed Sandaas's office on the way to the conference room. His door was closed. Had Gellerman questioned him? And more to the point, had RaeAnne sent him that letter? Oh God, if only I hadn't seen that letter!

Gellerman stood to greet me as I entered the room, scowling when he looked at me. "Merritt Grace. Is that right?"

"Yes."

"Have a seat please. I'm Detective Sergeant Bruce Gellerman of Gearhart PD." He briefly flashed his badge. "We're investigating the death of RaeAnne MacArthur— talking to folks who knew her to see what you might add to the investigation."

"OK. What do you want to know?"

"I understand you knew Ms. MacArthur."

"Yes. Mostly as a colleague. We're both in the Second

Chance Program here." Why did I say that? Why was I so nervous?

"Second Chance?"

"Yes. It's a state-subsidized program for people who need a second chance to overcome some barrier to getting a job."

"And you were both in Second Chance?"

"Uh, yeah."

"Can you tell me why?"

Damn. Did we really have to go there? "Well, I'd just gotten out of prison. I did some time for dealing drugs."

"Oh?" Sargent Gellerman jotted a note on his pad. "What about Ms. MacArthur?"

"I'm not really sure. You'd have to ask HR about that."

"OK. So you say you knew her from work. Anything else?"

What to say? What did this bastard already know? It's not my place to tell him that RaeAnne went to NA. On the other hand, he likely already knew. And I didn't want to lie.

Gellerman tapped the table with his pencil. "Is this a hard question for you, Grace?"

Damn. I wanted to disappear through the floor. "No sir." With RaeAnne dead, I guessed it didn't make any difference if I told him. I looked directly at his face. "We were in the same NA group. Met on Thursday evenings."

"So, you got to know her through these NA—I gather that's Narcotic Anonymous—meetings."

""Yes. Narcotics Anonymous. And yes, I guess that's where I got to know her. I didn't really know her very well... "

"Did anything ever come up that would lead you to believe she was suicidal?"

"I'm sorry. I'm really not at liberty to share what is discussed at NA meetings. I'm not sure that I should have told you about NA at all."

"So, outside of work and NA, did you have occasion to know Ms. MacArthur?"

Oh, God. "Sometimes we had coffee after the NA meetings."

"Coffee. Yes. And you talked while you drank coffee?"

Was he always this fucking cold? "Yes, we talked."

"From what you talked about over coffee, was there anything that Ms. MacArthur told you that suggested she might be suicidal?" His tone was cool as he glared at me.

"No, nothing."

"Did she ever mention anyone who might be a threat to her? Who might want her dead?"

"No, no one." Oh, God, what about that damned letter? Did RaeAnne ever send it to Dr. Sandaas? Did Gellerman know about it? Was it possible Sandaas was somehow involved? "No, not that I know of."

"OK, Grace. That's all we need for now. Here's my card. Give me a call if you think of anything else."

I put his card in my pocket. "Will do." With that I left the room. My knees were rubber. What did he know? It was bad enough that RaeAnne was dead. Why did I feel so uneasy?

I left work early and headed for home. Over dinner Liz and Val quizzed me. "Are you afraid you're being accused of something?" Val knew just how dangerous it could be to be Black around here. Your innocence had nothing to do with it. Especially if you were a Black man with a prison record. "Do you think you need a lawyer?"

"Not yet. So far Gellerman just asked me some questions about RaeAnne."

"Did you tell him anything?"

"No, not really. I told him I knew RaeAnne from NA. Not sure if I should have, but he probably already knew and I didn't want to lie to him. He gave me the creeps."

Liz pressed me. "So is there anything else you know that you didn't tell him?"

I hadn't yet told them about the letter. It had been so upsetting, and then RaeAnne showed up dead, and then... well

I just hadn't mentioned it. But I needed to tell someone. "Well, there is one thing... " I began. Liz and Val were all ears.

"Maybe you remember, the Saturday before RaeAnne died. She and I took a walk on the beach. She was pretty upset about all kinds of things. She was having financial troubles. And she was lonely. I guess she still wanted me to be her boyfriend. Which, of course, was impossible. She understood—but you know—the curse of being tall, dark and handsome." No one appreciated my feeble attempt at humor.

"Anything else?" Val's face was a picture of concern.

"It gets worse. We left RaeAnne's car at PBH and walked to the beach from their parking lot. When we got back from our walk, RaeAnne couldn't find her car keys. She had a spare set in her desk and asked me to go up and get them for her. I had my key to get in."

"Was that OK?"

"I guess so. I showed the security guard my PBH Employee card. He let me by, no problem. So anyway, when I opened RaeAnne's desk drawer there was a letter at the top. Curiosity got the better of me and when I took it out to look for the keys I looked to see who it was addressed to. You know, if it had been anyone else, I wouldn't have read the letter. But I did!"

"Who? Who was it addressed to?"

"Dr. Sandaas."

"Dr. Sandaas? Isn't he the Medical Director? What on God's green earth was RaeAnne MacArthur writing to *him* about?" Liz was indignant.

"You don't want to know."

"Try us."

"It was a blackmail letter. Said she knew that Dr. Sandaas was overbilling the government and overprescribing painkillers, and she'd keep quiet for a percentage of the take."

"Oh my God! Really! Does anyone else know about the letter?"

"That's the trouble. I don't know. I don't know if she sent it. I don't know if Sandaas received it! I don't know what he did if he did receive it."

"You don't suppose... " Liz's unfinished question hung in the air.

"I guess it's possible. I guess Sandaas could have killed RaeAnne to keep her quiet." I hadn't said those words out loud before. I hadn't really wanted to think them. But there they were.

"Are you going to tell Gellerman about the letter?"

"I'm not sure. I've got to think. This is all happening so fast. What if it is Sandaas? And what if he really was over-billing and over-prescribing? Those are crimes in and of themselves. And what about Marjorie?"

"Marjorie?"

"Marjorie Dawson. The Finance Director. She'd for sure know whatever RaeAnne knew. RaeAnne was small potatoes in that department. Someone—probably Marjorie herself—signed off on her work. Oh my God, do you suppose Marjorie's involved too?"

"Merritt, you need to tell the police about the letter and your suspicions about Sandaas." Ever practical, Liz offered this suggestion.

"I just don't know. I don't know who I can trust."

"Yeah, I totally get that." Val understood in ways that Liz could not.

The next few days at work were uneventful. I was relieved, hoping everything had blown over. No such luck. Early one afternoon Cindy appeared at my desk. "That police guy Gellerman wants to see you again. He's upstairs, same place as last time."

"You're kidding. Does he want to see anyone else?"

Cindy shrugged. "Not that I know of."

"Wow. Well, OK. Do I have to go up now?"

"Yep. He's waiting for you."

"I have a client at 2:00."

"I'll cover for you. Now get going, get this over with."

I hoped my anxiety wasn't evident as I sat down across from Gellerman. "You wanted to see me?"

"Actually yes. Just a few more questions. Can you tell me where you were the night of August 14th?"

"August 14th. What day was that?"

"It was a week ago Tuesday. The day your friend RaeAnne died."

My worst fears were confirmed. I was a suspect. "I guess I was at home. Besides NA meetings I'm at home most every night."

"Can anyone verify that?"

"Well, my sister Val would have been at work. I'm not sure about my other roommate Liz. I can't remember if she was home that night or not."

"So Liz may or may not be able to back up your story."

"That's right. I'll have to ask her. But—why are you asking ME? Am I a suspect?"

"Just following up on a few things, Grace. Do you remember where you were the afternoon of August 13th?"

"August 13th? Let's see. I guess that would have been a Monday. Sure. I was here at work."

"Anything out of the ordinary happen at work that day?"

"Not sure what you mean. No. Not that I can think of." What was he getting at?

"Some folks in finance heard Ms. MacArthur yelling at you that afternoon."

My heart plunged into my stomach. "Oh, yeah?"

"Yeah. They heard her ask you if you planned to kill her. Care to comment?"

OMG. "Well, yeah. RaeAnne did say something like that. But it's not what you think."

"Have I told you what I think?"

"No, I guess not. What do you think?"

"I'm the one who asks the questions around here, not you. So, back to my question. Do you care to comment about the things Ms. MacArthur's colleagues overheard?"

"OK, here goes. The Saturday before RaeAnne died we took a walk on the beach. Afterward, she couldn't find the keys to her car. She asked me to go into the office to get a spare set from her desk drawer."

"So did you? How did you get in?"

"I have a key to the building, so I let myself in. The only person I saw was the security guard."

"Yeah. He told us he saw you that day."

Oh my God. They've talked to the security guard. Who else? I might as well confess right now. No one will believe I'm innocent. Probably best to tell the whole story and be done with it.

"When I went to RaeAnne's desk to get her keys, I saw a letter at the top in the drawer. I know I shouldn't have read it—but I did."

"A letter?"

"Yes. Actually, a blackmail letter. Addressed to Erik Sandaas."

"You're saying this Ms. MacArthur was blackmailing Dr. Sandaas?"

"I'm not saying that. I'm saying that's what I read in the letter. I don't know if she sent the damn letter."

"Whatever. What did the letter say?"

"I can't remember exactly. I read it quickly and I was so shocked by what I read... Something about knowing that Sandaas was prescribing too much pain medication. Also overbilling Medicare and Medicaid."

"How would she know this?"

"From her job in the billing department. She prepared the

invoices. She was low man on the totem pole, but she was certified in medical billing, so she must have known what she was talking about."

"And?"

"And... she said she'd keep things quiet if he gave her a percentage of the take."

"That's it?"

"She'd report him if he didn't."

"You know you're essentially accusing Sandaas of a crime?"

"I'm not making any accusations. Just saying what was in the letter."

"So you say Ms. MacArthur did the medical billing?"

Why are you asking me? "She was an assistant in Medical Billing."

"An assistant."

"Yes."

"So, most likely someone signed off on her work. Someone else would know if Sandaas was actually overbilling. Or over-prescribing."

"I guess so. Probably. Yes, that seems likely. I don't know. I guess Marjorie Dawson would see the bills."

"Marjorie Dawson. The Director of Finance. So... you're saying Marjorie Dawson was also in on this scheme?"

"I'm not saying anything about anything. Or anybody. All I did was read the goddamn letter."

"So back to your argument with Ms. MacArthur the day before she died. I'm guessing it had something to do with this letter?"

"It wasn't really an argument. I just asked her about the letter. I was so shocked the day I saw it, I didn't say anything at the time. I didn't know what to say."

"But you changed your mind the next day. Decided to talk."

"Yeah. I had to say something to her."

"So... you argued about the letter?"

"We didn't exactly argue. I just told her not to send it. Blackmail was illegal. I'd have to report her if she did."

"And?"

"She got pissed. Said she'd get back at me if I talked."

"Get back at you?"

"Yeah. That's what she said."

"What did she mean by that?"

"I guess you'd have to ask her about that."

"Too late for that. But... she knew something you wanted to keep quiet? Like maybe she was blackmailing you, too?"

"What? No! RaeAnne was not blackmailing me!"

"Well, she clearly had something on you. Enough that you wanted to keep her quiet, say?"

"Keep her QUIET? Just a minute here. Are you suggesting that I killed RaeAnne to KEEP HER QUIET?"

"I'm not suggesting anything. I'm just saying that RaeAnne apparently had something on you—something you didn't want anyone to know."

"Even if RaeAnne had something on me, which she did not, there's no way on God's green earth that I would kill her for it. Or kill anyone, for God's sake. We were *just talking*. That's all."

He leafed through his pad. "Well, hopefully, uh, Liz will be able to vouch for you being at home that night. Anything else you want to tell me about your argument with Ms. MacArthur?"

"No. I was just trying to talk her out of blackmailing Dr. Sandaas. She was pissed at me for reading the letter, that's all. I guess maybe we were shouting a little, I don't know. I can't remember for sure. My God, RaeAnne is dead."

"Anything else?"

"Anything else? No! I was upset. I needed to clear my head. I walked out. That's all I know. That's the last time I saw RaeAnne. Damn. We were shouting at each other the last time I saw her. Damn."

"Do you know what happened to the letter?"

"No. I just told her not to send it. I have no idea what happened after that."

"So. If she did send it... if Sandaas did get the blackmail letter... "

"I don't know about Sandaas. I don't know about Marjorie Dawson. I don't know anything about anyone else. I don't know anything more about the goddamn letter. I've told you everything I know! Now can I go?"

"Yes. You're free to go. If you think of anything else that might be of interest you know where to find me."

I stumbled out of the office. The meeting had left me really shaken. Was I a suspect? So easy to accuse the only Black man in town of killing a nice young white woman, regardless of the truth. Racism is all too alive and well. To tell the truth, I was terrified.

That evening I joined Liz at the Pub & Grub. The last thing I wanted to do was sit home alone and stew, and besides, Liz was a good listener. As soon as we got there, I regretted my decision. The regulars were there, rowdier than usual. Driving me nuts. I couldn't even hear myself think, much less anything Liz was saying. I withdrew into the corner of the booth and checked out Facebook while Liz gabbed with everyone.

Ignoring my cues that I did not want to socialize, some woman introduced me to a guy I'd never seen before. Henry something. He decided to be cute—cracked that with a name like Merritt Grace I ought to be a priest. Not the first time I'd heard that—everyone thought they were so original—but this time it was too much. And after the day I'd had I was so paranoid that I was worried he knew something about me. I jumped up. "Liz, I'm outta here." I stalked away to pay my bill.

Much to my surprise, Mister Wise Guy followed me out and apologized as I waited at the counter. Said he knew from personal experience the irritation of being made fun of because of your name. When I asked what was so funny about Henry, he told me his professional name is Justin Case—and that he's a private investigator. No shit. Now that's funny. Then, in a fortuitous lightbulb moment, I realized he might be able to give me some professional advice. Couldn't hurt to ask. Didn't hurt to ask. Before Liz and I left Pub & Grub, I had Justin's card and plans to call him in a few days. For the first time since this nightmare began I felt a tiny glimmer of hope.

What's in a Name?

September

I'd promised Maddie I'd see her and the happy hour gang the next week at the Pub & Grub but it was several weeks before I got back there. I had good intentions but I was trying to make myself toe the line during the week and several of my weekends were taken up with a couple of work trips and another to Seattle to see one of Jenny's soccer games. And I didn't want to give Maddie any more reason to think I was just dying to see her. I'd had a couple of innocuous texts from her, thanking me for the meal at the Pub and urging me to come to the happy hour gathering. Nothing romantic, but maybe intended to establish a closer connection. I liked her but I didn't want to lead her on.

When I walked into the Pub I could see it was a bigger group, a little surprising since it was a weekday. I recognized the people who'd been there before and there were about a half dozen I didn't recognize. I tended to check out the women first, of course. There was an interesting looking woman whom I hadn't seen before, but I assumed she was with the Black guy sitting next to her. I noticed him immediately, and not just because he was the only person of color in the place, maybe in Gearhart for that matter. He was nice looking, nicely dressed, very clean cut. He looked wary—I don't know any other way to put it. I notice things like that. Call it an occupational hazard. I guess I'd have been nervous, too, if I'd been the only Black person in the place. And he could have been worried about people's reactions to his being with a White woman. An interracial couple wouldn't be out of place in Seattle, but maybe it would be in these small towns. They sat a little apart from the rest of the group, in a booth just across. She engaged in the group banter, but he kept his eyes down, looking at messages on his phone, answering anything directed to him with as few words as possible.

Maddie made a place for me next to her and made sure I knew everyone, including the Black guy and his companion. "Hey, Merritt and Liz, I don't think you've met Henry," Maddie yelled over the loud conversation toward the booth and gestured toward me. "Henry Case. He's a detective."

"Private investigator," I corrected her.

"Okay, whatever. Don't take him on at darts if you don't want to lose your shirt. These two are Merritt Grace and Liz Adams. Merritt's an addiction counselor and Liz manages the Above It All kite shop in Seaside." They raised their hands in greeting.

Geez, I thought, this guy's got a quirkier name than I do. "With a name like Merritt Grace I'd expect you to be in religious work," I said. Several people around me laughed, but Merritt didn't. For just a second I saw something like anger, or maybe fear, in his eyes. Then his face closed down as if someone had pulled the shades and he turned away toward his lady friend. What the hell, I thought. Why couldn't I learn to keep my mouth shut? Had I said something racist? Clearly what I'd said was offensive, although I didn't have a clue why. Maybe I shouldn't assume it was racist just because he was Black—maybe that was racist. I didn't want to be the guy who walked into the group and pissed everybody off.

Racist—that made me think of that conversation I'd overheard at the fundraiser between O'Donohue and Sandaas. Merritt Grace was an addictions counselor—what were the chances he worked at Pacific Behavioral Health? Normally I'd think that might be a big leap, but again, how many Black people were there in this neck of the woods?

A few minutes later, Merritt and Liz got up to leave. They were standing at the bar for some time, waiting to pay for their drinks, which gave me an opportunity to catch him before he left. She walked away as I walked up, probably to go to the Ladies. "Hey," I said, touching him lightly on the shoulder, which of course made him jump. "I didn't mean to make fun of your name. I guess that was rude." He was grilling me with those eyes again, probably wondering if he'd have to beat the shit out of me, but he didn't say anything. So, I went on. "It's just that I get so much crap about my own name."

"What, Henry?"

"No, my actual first name is Justin and my professional name is Justin Case."

The corners of his mouth turned up in a slight smile. "And you're a PI? I can see why you get crap about that."

"Yeah, so of course I thought with a name like Merritt Grace you might be in the church business." Why didn't I just shut the fuck up and not keep repeating it?

"Got it. No offense." He looked me in the eye. "You're really a PI? Licensed? That's what you do for a living?"

"Yes, such as it is."

"Maybe we could talk sometime."

"We're talking now. I'll probably be here next weekend—if I haven't pissed off too many people with my big mouth."

He gave me that slightly amused look again. "No, I was thinking of a private conversation. Maybe over a cup of coffee."

He apparently had something that he thought needed the attention of an investigator, probably looking for a freebie. But I wasn't going to compound my previous mistake by shutting him out. "Sure." I reached into my pocket for a card. It was a little dog-eared, as I didn't hand out too many in the course of my work in Gearhart. "Email or text me and let me know when and where.

My schedule's pretty flexible."

"Thanks," he said. He looked at the card and then put it in

his jacket pocket. "I'll keep this handy, just in case."

"Very funny," I said with a mock scowl, but I was very relieved to have fixed whatever problem I'd created. His girlfriend returned then and they left. I wondered if he'd follow through on the coffee.

I went back to the table to finish my beer. Everyone was engaged in a conversation about a local happening, a woman who'd been found dead in her car, apparently from suicide. I wondered how often something like that happened in a small place like this.

I didn't have long to wonder if Merritt Grace would follow up on the coffee. He sent a text the next day with a couple of options for meeting up. I took the one furthest away, thinking this was bound to be a waste of my time. In my reply I suggested that he tell me something about whatever he wanted to talk about, but he said he'd prefer to go into that in person. Three days later I met him at the Daily Grind.

* * *

Merritt was already there when I got to the coffee shop, sitting at the same table where I'd had coffee with Bert O'Donohue. I headed for the counter to order, but he stood up and motioned for me to sit down. "I'll get your coffee. Least I can do," he said. I wasn't going to argue.

"Just black," I said. He stopped and turned around and gave me that amused look, this time with a raised eyebrow. "What?" I said.

"Think about it," he shook his head. I did. I hoped he was joking; surely describing how I drank my coffee couldn't be construed as racist. Maybe I had a lot to learn.

He came back with two large coffees and set mine down in front of me. "Black is beautiful, as ordered."

"Beautiful indeed—thanks," I said. We took a few seconds

to drink our coffee.

"Okay," he dove in, "thanks for agreeing to talk with me about this. Just so you know, some of what I'm gonna say is stuff the other folks at the Pub & Grub don't know about me. I'm not exactly sure why I'm telling you all of this except that I want to ask your advice, and since you're a PI I assume you could find it all out anyway." I nodded, thinking, *if I were that interested.*

"I'm not sure where to start," he went on. "So, I'll just start with when we met. You obviously noticed how I reacted when you made your little joke about my name." He held up his hand when I started to apologize again. "There was a reason for that. I'm actually an ordained Catholic priest—or I was—I guess now I'm what you'd call defrocked. When you said what you did, I was afraid it was because you knew who I was." Geez, I thought, that sounds a little paranoid.

"You're a priest? I never would have guessed that! I was just kidding because of your name. So the woman you come to the Pub & Grub isn't... "

"Liz? No, she's not my girlfriend. Or my wife, for that matter. She's actually my sister-in-law. She's married to my sister Val. But I don't think the happy hour folks know that either."

Okay. She's your sister's wife. Okay, I thought, as I turned that idea over in my mind. No end of surprises today. What next?

I thought I could feel him looking at me to see how I would react to this information. I'm not a homophobe, but I'll be honest. As accustomed and comfortable as I was with being around lesbian couples at that point in my life, I still wasn't used to the new language of marriage equality. "Cool," I said.

"Liz is very cool," he said. "She and Val are two of the most loving, generous people I've ever known. If it weren't for them—" he shrugged and took a sip of his coffee to get his emotions under control. He shook his head. "There's no reason you would know about my being a priest. Not that it's a secret. I guess I'm just a little paranoid about people knowing a lot about my past."

He'd already told me he was an addictions counselor. If he was employed at Pacific Behavioral Health, there was a strong possibility he was indeed the person Sandaas had been referring to in his comment to O'Donohue I'd overheard at the fundraiser.

"Where do you work?" I asked.

"A place called Pacific Behavioral Health. It's a fairly large agency in Seaside." Bingo. Maybe he had something to be paranoid about.

No way I was going to mention that conversation I'd overheard to him, but it was a potentially important fact to file away for future consideration. "So what did you want to meet about?" I asked.

"Where to begin?" He took a sip of coffee and stared out the window. "Where to begin?" He stared out the window again, then looked up at me. "I've let down just about everybody I know. I'd like to build a better life for myself, get back some people's respect—get back my self-respect."

I wasn't sure what he was saying, but it was clear he had a lot on his mind. Maybe more than I could help him with. "I'm here to listen to whatever you'd like to tell me," I offered. He gave me a grateful smile, took another sip of his coffee, and began his story.

Confession is Good for the Soul

September

I'd just told Justin I needed to gain my self respect. I was at once sorry I'd said anything at all and wanting to share my story with him. I sure needed a friend, and maybe he could help me. I took another sip of coffee, looked him in the eye, and decided I would trust him.

"Maybe I ought to fill you in," I started. "You know, something of my background so you'll know who you're dealing with."

Justin nodded. "Whatever you'd like to tell me. Whatever you say will go no further, I promise you that."

I took a deep breath and jumped in. "Did you know I was released from prison a few months ago?"

He looked surprised, but non-judgmental. "No, I didn't know that. Do you want to tell me more?"

"Long story short, while I was still a parish priest I got addicted to drugs. How and why that got started isn't all that important. All through my childhood and teenage years I was on the straight and narrow. But anyway... it happened. At first, my dealer supported my habit. And then he stopped. The only way I could get enough money to support my habit was to become a dealer myself—working for Rafael, the bastard who got me into this in the first place. At first I refused—it was so far from anything I believed in, anything I valued—but then my addiction got the best of me and I agreed."

Justin nodded, silently encouraging me to continue my story.

"Of course Rafael had all the answers. Said that I could deal out of the confessional. Foolproof. I just about threw up when he suggested that, it was so alien to my values. But I was in a deep, deep hole and pretty soon I went along with it. And for a couple of months I did pretty well in my new career as a priest/drug dealer. Oh God. I just hate the sound of that!"

Justin smiled. "It's not the first thing I think of when I see you," he said sincerely. "So what happened?"

"At first I earned enough to pay for my own drugs and fooled myself into believing I was still doing OK as a priest. When I wasn't high I felt guilty as hell and terrified about being caught. I didn't come close to understanding how bad off I was or how much I was hurting myself and others. I just lived for getting high."

"Sounds like a pretty awful time."

"You have no idea. I guess I now believe that God intervened when Tyrone Davis, a teenager in my parish, a good kid, got suspicious. He lived across from the church and spent every day shooting hoops in the field next to his building. He noticed a lot of people pulling up to the church, spending a few minutes there, then leaving. Putting two and two together, he asked one of the men how he could get in the game. He got all the information he needed."

"So you think God intervened when this kid narced on you?"

"Yes, I do. Although at the time, no. That was the farthest thing from my mind. If I thought about it at all, I'd have thought that God had totally abandoned me. Or maybe vice versa. I was a mess."

"That does sound like an awful time."

"Yes, it was. I'll never forget the day Tyrone came into my office to confront me. With a wretched look on his face he told me he thought I was dealing drugs. I wanted to sink through a hole in the floor."

"Wow. I guess so."

"He told me how he'd put the truth together—hating himself for finding out, hating even more having to confront me. But he knew he had no other choice. For a minute I was speechless. Busted. Busted by Tyrone Davis, my parishioner. I knew he was right. I shrugged and admitted that yes, it was true."

"So then what happened?"

"After I had a chance to catch my breath, I told him I was glad he'd busted me. Life had been so damned crazy. It was time to get off the roller coaster. He assured me he hadn't said anything to anyone else. We made a deal. I'd stop then and there and he'd stay quiet. He agreed. After a minute of searching my face, trying to discover just how things had gone so wrong, he turned on his heels and walked out."

"You trusted him to stay quiet?"

"I wasn't sure, but I had no choice. The jig was up. I just wanted to die."

"Did you have anyone you could talk to?" Justin's concern warmed me.

"One person, Father Clement. He was my priest when I was a young boy. I've trusted him my entire life." I thought a minute before continuing. "I came out to him when I knew I was gay."

Justin's head jerked up. "Um... Did you just say you're gay?"

I hoped I hadn't made a mistake in telling him. Did it make any difference? Whatever, I'd let the cat out of the bag for better or for worse. "Uh, yeah, I did just say that."

"So you and Rafael... "

"Uh, yeah."

"I guess that kind of complicated things."

"You could say that."

"So this Father Clement. You went to talk with him?"

"Yeah. I did. He was a tremendous support when I came out. I figured I might as well tell him the rest of the story and hope for the best."

"And... "

"He's such a good person. He cleared his calendar the minute he got my call. The world of hurt in my voice was all too obvious. And when I walked into his office he wrapped me in a hug. I couldn't help myself, I just started to bawl."

"You know, Merritt, you don't have to tell me all of this. I'm happy to listen, and you can trust my confidence, but—I can see this is really deep shit for you."

"Yeah. Yeah, thanks. I... I want to tell you the whole sorry story. Maybe you can help me. I'm pretty sure I can trust you. And I definitely need a friend."

"Well, I don't know how much I can help. But I'm definitely willing to listen. So... what did you tell Father Clement?"

"I poured everything out. Every fuckin' drop. Until then he hadn't known about my using drugs. Or about Rafael, Or about, my God, my dealing out of the confessional. I hated telling him that. Hated it. Hated myself. And yet, he just listened. Disappointment in his eyes. Surprise. But no real judgment."

"You told him you were calling it quits?"

"Yeah. That's the agreement I had with Tyrone. Step one toward earning back my self respect."

"That took some courage I'm guessing."

"Yes and no. I was at the end of my rope. I didn't really have any choice. God knows what might have happened if I hadn't quit then."

"So what happened?"

"Father Clement told me I'd need to turn myself in, to the police. And to the archbishop. I wasn't sure which would be worse."

"What did you think would happen?"

"I had no idea. Archbishop Sartain was famous for being anti-gay. A few years ago, after Washington State legalized same sex marriage, he ordered every parish to petition to repeal the law. Dealing drugs was one thing but being gay...

way worse in his world."

"Did your being gay have to be a part of the story?"

"As it turned out, no. Father Clement said nothing about it, and neither did I. Thank God. I think we both knew things would have been much worse for me if the Archbishop had that little tidbit to deal with."

"So what *did* happen?"

"The next day Father Clement and I went to see the Archbishop. As planned, I confessed only to my drug use and dealing, and to my sincere regret for that behavior. Father Clement spoke up for me."

"And... "

"The Archbishop told me how disappointed he was with me, but he also wanted to help me. I guess I had a good reputation in my parish, and Father Clement's support didn't hurt. And mainly, I guess, he wanted to keep everything quiet. No stain on the church, if you know what I mean. At least I wasn't abusing little boys."

"Well, yeah. The good ole Catholic Church certainly has a lot to answer for in that department. But in any case, you benefited from his need to keep the whole affair under wraps."

"Yeah, I guess so. He told me I'd need to turn myself in to the police, but they'd get a good lawyer for me. He hoped we could avoid a trial. Mostly he wanted to keep the press far, far away."

"I get it. Who cares what happens to you, but let's not get the Church involved. But—I guess that worked out OK for you. So what happened?"

"I stayed in my parish until the court hearing. Stopped using cold turkey, except for one relapse. The church pulled some strings and got me into a good outpatient program. Because of my legal problems, I could only go for a couple weeks. But it helped me through the excruciating first parts of dealing with my addiction."

"That's good."

"Yeah. I lucked out in a lot of ways. The attorney they got for me knew her stuff. She went with me when I turned myself in to the police and then, after I was charged, she worked out a plea deal with the prosecutor. Considering what I'd done, it was better than I could have expected. Based on the amount of coke I'd been dealing, I was facing a Class B felony, punishable by up to ten years in prison. With my plea deal I would agree to a Class C felony with two years in prison. Not something I looked forward to but something I could live with."

"Two years beats ten, for sure."

"The judge agreed to the plea deal and sentenced me to two years at Monroe. My attorney negotiated a delay in my report date to give me time to quietly leave my church. No one in my parish except Tyrone knew the truth and the press never got wind of the case. My parents and sisters were all in another church, so not even anyone in my family knew what was happening."

"That's impressive. Your family must know now."

"Yeah, they do. I'm living with my sister, for God's sake! But the church, no, they never found out. I told my parish that a family emergency necessitated my leaving the church for the time being. They had a nice reception for me with many expressions of gratitude and well wishing following the 11 o'clock mass on my last Sunday there. Tyrone was there. He made it a point of thanking me for turning myself in, promised me he'd keep quiet."

"You believe him?"

"As far as I know he is still the only person in the church who knows anything. He saved my ass, that young kid. I should go back and thank him."

"Yeah, maybe."

"Last but not least, I called Rafael to fill him in on everything. Told him If even one word leaked, he'd take the fall right along with me!"

"How'd that go."

"That asshole. I could almost see his supercilious smile through the phone. Said he knew I'd be back. That everyone always comes back eventually. There it was in a nutshell. It was water rolling off a duck's back. I was nothing to that asshole. Nothing but a quick fuck and a bag of coin. How low could I go?"

I was really relieved to share this with someone, and Justin was a really good listener. And after all of that, I realized I hadn't yet told Justin why I wanted to meet with him.

CHAPTER 13: HENRY
No Good Deed Goes Unpunished

September

Having coffee with Merritt was taking a lot longer than I'd planned. I figured I could give him a half hour in the interest of building goodwill and that would be it. And we'd be on good terms if we ran into each other again. But after all that talk about our respective backgrounds, Merritt and I had already burned up more than an hour of my workday and I still didn't know why we were there. I will say, though, that his story wasn't boring. But it was time to get down to brass tacks and he seemed to be having a hard time getting started. "So, what do you need my advice about?" I prompted him.

"None of what I just told you—that's all background so you'll know who I am and why this might be important."

"Why what might be important?

"Do you know who RaeAnne MacArthur is—was?"

"No—wait," I remembered that she was the woman of the "mysterious death." "She's the woman people were talking about at the Pub & Grub, that the police think committed suicide."

"That's the one, but I'm not sure they really think she committed suicide. Anyway, she was my co-worker at PBH. She was the medical billing assistant, also in the Second Chance program."

"Second Chance?"

"Oh, yeah. I guess I didn't tell you about that. It's a program funded by the state to provide jobs for ex-felons and others who might have trouble finding employment. I got my job through Second Chance and so did RaeAnne. She didn't have a criminal record, just some major challenges with addiction. It's a good program."

"Sounds like it. No, I haven't heard of it. So you were both a part of that program. Hmm... I wonder if that means anything. If she was an addict, maybe she overdosed, accidentally or intentionally... anyway... let's get back to your story."

"The police have questioned me twice about her death. An officer came to the office right after they found her body and talked to everyone who worked with her. It sounded then like the police thought it was suicide. Then a few days later he came back and questioned me again."

"Just you?"

"I'm pretty sure just me. I asked around and couldn't find anyone else who got questioned a second time.

"What was the nature of his questions?"

"He wanted to know where I was the night she died. Could anyone vouch for where I was. He asked a bunch of questions about our relationship, about how we got along."

"So, what did you tell him?"

He took a deep breath. "I was home by myself the night she died. As I told you, I live with my sister, Valerie, and her wife, Liz, who was with me at the tavern the other night. Valerie is a nurse and works nights. When I talked with Gellerman I thought Liz could provide an alibi, but as it turns out she was out of town that night."

"And how did you and what's her name—RaeAnne—get along?"

He exhaled. "We were friends, but we disagreed about some things. I told her the stuff about my past that I just told you and she was holding it over my head. Believe me, nothing serious enough to kill her over, but it pissed me off. She, on the other hand, was into some serious shit at PBH. She'd been there longer than me, so I guess she'd had more time to get into trouble. I called her on her shit, and that pissed her off. Apparently she was blackmailing someone. Not just someone—the medical director of the agency."

That sent a chill up my spine. Eric Sandaas—he was involved in all kinds of bad shit. "She asked me to get her keys out of her desk," he went on, "and when I did I found a blackmail letter she'd written to this guy. I confronted her about it and warned her that I felt obligated to tell someone about it. Then she threatened to tell my former parish about what had really happened with my dealing. We had a major dust-up that got overheard by someone else."

"Hmmm. How long ago was your second visit from the police—and who was it?"

"Some guy named Gellerman. A little over a week ago."

"So, I don't know what the police might be thinking—or what your colleagues may have said about your relationship to this RaeAnne. But assuming you didn't kill her... " I paused.

"Hell, no, I didn't kill her," he said.

"Then I don't think you have anything to worry about."

"Do you know the statistics on wrongful arrest and imprisonment of Black people in the U.S.? Black men in particular?"

"No, I'm sorry, I don't. I do know that Black men are more likely to wind up in prison than in college." Oh God, maybe I shouldn't have said that.

"I guess I'm a two-fer since I wound up in both. But I wasn't wrongfully arrested, to be fair," he said and then went on, "There's some recent research indicating that Black prisoners convicted of murder are much more likely to be innocent than other convicted murderers, and spend longer in prison before exoneration. I don't want to be one of those statistics."

"Why are you talking to me instead of a lawyer?"

"I don't know that I need a lawyer... so far no one's accused me of anything... and I couldn't afford one anyway. And so far all I've paid you is a cup of 'just black' coffee. I thought a PI might know as much as a lawyer about these things. And as it turns out, you're kind of a two-fer yourself."

"Yeah," I said. "I'm not a licensed attorney but I did graduate from law school. That said, I'm not sure how, or if, I can help. Maybe you'll be lucky and you won't hear from the police again. If you don't, it's all good—and if you do, let me know and we'll figure something out." I had no idea what that something might be but it sounded good.

"One more question," I said. "Did you tell the police about the blackmail letter?"

"Yes. It seemed like the smart thing to do. At least it was the honest thing to do, and I figured I couldn't hurt RaeAnne any by telling them."

"What did they say?" I asked. "Did they seem interested?"

"They did seem interested. They said they'd look into it."

"Good," I said. "Let's hope they find it, and maybe that'll be the end of their interest in you."

"Thanks," he said. "I really appreciate this.

Do you mind my asking you how you happened to become a PI?" Okay, I thought. If he'd trusted me with so much of his story, I could trust him with a little of my own. "Sure," I said. "It started with me failing the bar exam."

He nodded. "I understand that's not too uncommon."

"Well, it's uncommon in my family. That pathway was laid down for me since before I was born. And I failed three times— don't know how common that is." I went on to tell him an abbreviated version of how my bar exam failure had led me to where I was now. I finished by saying that where I was now wasn't where I'd planned to be.

"I don't believe there are any 'accidents' or even coincidences, by the way. At least not many," he said. "I'm guessing where you are is where you're supposed to be."

And then he asked me how investigating was different from practicing law. I told him they're a little alike, but that the law with its courtroom drama has that high-wire "sales" component, in litigation at least. That you have to convince a judge and jury that a defendant did or didn't commit a crime. That I wasn't confident I could think on my feet that well. That there are all kinds of law that don't involve courtroom drama, but that my father didn't have much respect for them.

"You say 'didn't.'" he said. "Is your father still living?"

"No, he died some years back. A heart attack."

"I'm sorry." His sympathy seemed genuine.

"Me, too." I said. I was momentarily aware of missing my father. And suddenly tired of talking about that part of my history. "Hey, I've got to get going," I said. "But maybe we can continue this later."

If there was a later, I thought. There was a good chance this guy wouldn't hear from the police again—and that I wouldn't hear from him, unless I ran into him at the Pub & Grub. Not exactly a place to share this kind of personal history. We stood up and shook hands and walked out, headed in different directions.

Later, watching some mindless stuff on TV, I thought about what Merritt had told me. He and I were close in age, had both grown up in Seattle, both had caring families and good educations. And we were both fuck-ups. Or as he had more eloquently put it, he had let down just about everybody he knew and wanted to get back some people's respect—including his own. I knew exactly what he meant—I was in the middle of that journey myself. I guess on the positive side we were both working toward being better people. And that made me more interested in helping him. But I had no clue how to go about doing that, and maybe I wouldn't need to.

There was, of course, the chance that Merritt had killed this woman. Probably not. He didn't seem like a killer to me, but he was a convicted drug dealer. However even if he was innocent there was the statistic about wrongful murder convictions of Black men. And I didn't know—he didn't either—what the police had learned from his colleagues.

Anyone who watches crime shows on TV knows that murder investigations hinge on motive, method, and opportunity. Gellerman probably was leaning hard on motive—he and RaeAnne had been heard arguing by their work colleagues, who apparently had reported the argument in their interviews with the police. As for opportunity, Merritt's alibi was still in question. I didn't know what Gellerman might know or be thinking about method. I began to think about how to have a casual conversation with him. Maybe there would be no need.

But regardless of what did or didn't happen with the police, it appeared that Merritt might be in deeper shit than he was aware of. That was, of course, assuming he actually was the "Black SOB" Sandaas had said he wanted to fire or force to quit—that I'd overheard at the fundraiser. I had no idea what that was about, but it seemed wise to keep it to myself—until or unless there was a reason to divulge it.

* * *

The weekend after my coffee with Merritt I drove to Seattle for Jenny's soccer game. She'd let me know that she was going by "Jen" now and that I should call her that in front of her friends. Her team won and I made the usual fool of myself by yelling too loud—and of course forgetting to call her by her newly abbreviated name "I guess you really can't teach an old dog new tricks," she chided me. Ouch.

I hadn't been back to Seattle for more than two months. I knew I looked better, but even so I was unprepared for people's surprised reactions... people starting with my own family. "Oh my God Dad, you look amazing!" from Jen when I got out of the car in their driveway. More positive comments from Steve and Janis and later from Julia and Mom.

I had a beer with my old law school buddy Larry, the guy I'd first shared my PI career aspirations with. He'd married several years before and was only too happy to get away from his two-year-old twins for a couple of hours. "Hey Buddy, you look great," he greeted me. We ordered and exchanged chit-chat about the Seahawks. "I haven't seen you in a while..." I could tell he was fishing.

"I'm living on the Oregon Coast for a few months. Janis and I still co-own a condo in Gearhart."

"Word on the street is that your family sent you off to rehab. But I see you're still drinking, so that must not be true."

"I guess it is a kind of rehab. I needed to get my life in order, pay more attention to my work and my health. I'm not drinking much usually—but I'm on vacation now."

"Looks like the health part's going well, how's your work?"

"Going well, too."

I asked Larry about his work. He was a successful attorney now, about to make partner in his firm if this year went as well as past years. It occurred to me that he might be someone to ask about Merritt's dilemma. But maybe there was no dilemma.

* * *

I drove off on Sunday afternoon feeling pretty good about myself. When I stopped at the last I-5 rest stop for a pee and a cup of the tasteless coffee the volunteers were serving I looked at my texts and emails. I had one of each from Merritt Grace, both with cryptic messages about dying to have coffee with me very soon. Sounded a little desperate. I wondered if he'd had another visit from Gearhart's finest. I replied to both saying that I could have coffee the next day at the time of his choosing. He picked five-thirty, when he'd be back from work—and suggested we meet at the other tavern in "downtown Gearhart." So much for thinking I wouldn't hear from him again.

CHAPTER 14: MERRITT
In the Valley of Death

September

The next few days were uneventful. After a good meeting with Justin I even talked myself into believing that things had blown over, but no such luck. Gellerman was back again on Friday afternoon. This time he had a woman with him. Officer Terry McConnell. Young, nice looking, but tough. Why was she there? Now what?

Gellerman started things. "So, Grace, just to let you know, we checked out that blackmail story. We haven't seen anything like the letter you described. Sandaas and Marjorie Dawson deny any knowledge of anything it said. We checked the files—just to be on the safe side you know—but nothing. Nada. I don't know what you think you saw in that letter, but from what we can see, there's nothing to it."

Nothing! I know what I saw. What I didn't know was why RaeAnne wrote it. Or if anything in it was true. Or, if it was true, if it was ever mailed. If Sandaas did get it, what had he done with it? And what about Marjorie? If Sandaas had been cooking the books she would have known. Was she in on it? Whatever *it* was. Had they cleaned up the files when he first got the letter? Before the cops even showed up? And, God forbid, had they silenced RaeAnne? Was Sandaas responsible for her death?

"One more thing Mr. Grace." This time it was Officer McConnell. "We found an empty pill bottle on the floor of Ms. MacArthur's car. Nothing surprising about that—if she had killed herself—but here's the thing. There were no fingerprints on the bottle, not even hers. And the label had been removed. Hard to know what to make of that. Any thoughts on that Mr. Grace?"

Any thoughts? What was I supposed to think? "No. I don't know anything about that. I wish I could tell you more. RaeAnne was my friend. Maybe she was murdered. That's all I know. I'm sorry."

McConnell pressed on. "So Grace. You were in prison for the sale of narcotics, is that correct?"

I agreed, yes that was correct. I told them about my crime, my conviction, my time in Monroe. They probably already knew.

"Do you still have contact with, let's see, Rafael Gomez?"

Rafael Gomez? Now that was a surprise. And most definitely not a pleasant one. I hadn't thought about that weasel for years. "Uh, no. I haven't had contact with him since before I went to prison."

"When you knew him he was your supplier, is that accurate?"

"Uh, yes."

"And your boyfriend as well."

"No. Not my boyfriend." Man, they'd really been digging into my past.

"You're sure about that?"

"Yes, I am sure." For a moment I was back with Rafael, higher than a kite, flying on mind-blowing sex. A world away. Jolting back: "Yes, I'm sure."

"OK Grace, that's all for now. Don't leave the area, we may need to be in touch with you again."

I hadn't thought things could get any worse. Wrong. They knew about Rafael. Had they talked to him? Maybe I should find him, see what he told them. And one more thing. After my first meeting with the police I discovered I had no alibi after all. Liz was out of town the night RaeAnne was killed. So much for my alibi. I was a dead man walking.

It was pretty clear, now, that I needed a lawyer. The church had provided one when I was arrested in Seattle, but that was then. The church could care less now. Maybe Justin. He has a law degree, even though he doesn't practice law. I didn't have any other good options and I figured I'd need to get hold of him as soon as possible.

Like a Duck Takes to Water

September

Merritt and I met at the Matrix Bar & Grill—which definitely catered to a younger, trendier crowd. Lots of people and lots of noise. It made me feel old and out of place. But Merritt had sounded a little desperate—and wanted to meet where no one would recognize us. He was sitting in a booth in the back, drinking an iced tea when I got there. He looked more out of place than I felt. When the wait person came I ordered an iced tea—I had to shout it three times before she heard me.

"You don't have to drink tea just because I do. It won't bother me if you have a beer or whatever you want," Merritt said. I told him I hadn't been drinking much since I'd been living in Gearhart and he asked if I had a problem with alcohol.

"Just my weight," I said. He gave me a thumbs up. Then he launched into the reason for our being there. It seemed that Sargent Bruce Gellerman and Officer Terry McConnell together had paid him another visit at the office a couple of days ago. Gellerman started off by saying that they hadn't found the blackmail letter. McConnell wasn't saying much, just giving Merritt the old stink-eye.

Gellerman had poked around a little more, thanked him, and they'd turned to leave. The door was almost closed behind them when it opened again and the two cops had stepped back in. "I just have one more question," McConnell had said. Oh, the old one more question ploy, I thought. Columbo, Monk, and even I had used that little scare tactic. Her question focused on the "method" of the killing. There had been a prescription pill bottle found in RaeAnne's car, which was why the police initially thought she had committed suicide. The label had been removed from the bottle and it had been wiped clean of fingerprints. Not even *her* fingerprints were on the bottle, which was strange. If she'd taken pills out of the bottle why weren't her fingerprints on it? The remaining pills in the bottle were opioids. Their back-and-forth questioning had focused on Merritt's prior narcotics conviction, his relationship with his dealer, and what his current access to opioids might be.

Not surprisingly, the cops had told Merritt not to leave the area. It was obvious to me he was scared shitless. He'd told them he'd served his time and was one hundred percent committed to staying clean in case he ever wanted to serve the church again. Probably everyone had access to opioids if you got right down to it, and he no more than anyone else. He was no longer in touch with his previous distributor and the drug he'd sold hadn't been a prescription opioid. McConnell had made it sound like she believed anyone in the addiction-related field could and would get their hands on any kind of drug they wanted. Clearly she had no use for anyone who used or sold narcotics. They took notes on the conversation, told him they might want to talk to him again, closed their notebooks, and left him to stew.

What was obvious to me was that they didn't really have anything on him that wasn't circumstantial or they would have arrested him already. I wanted to find a way to have a casual, off-the-cuff conversation with one or both of those Gearhart cops to see if I could find out what they were thinking. Were they considering the possibility that Sandaas and Dawson might be defrauding the government? Were they considering Sandaas, or anyone else for that matter, as a person of interest in Rayanne's death? Or were they just following the quick and easy, albeit racist, path of least resistance? I told Merritt I had a couple of ideas for how to proceed, that he should sit tight, and I'd get back to him within two or three days. What was I thinking? I had a ton of my own paid work to do so I'd have to figure out how to fit this in—and I didn't want to get behind again now that things were going so well. And there was always the possibility that Merritt was lying—and, even worse, that he was a murderer.

By this time people had started coming in for dinner and the smell of fried food was filling the air. "Any chance you'd want to stay for a burger? My treat, sort of payment for your time." Merritt said. "Besides, my roommates are vegetarians and sometimes I've just got to have me some beef." I understood that, having lived on Lean Cuisine dinners for several months, and we put in our orders for bacon cheeseburgers, medium rare, with fries and onion rings. He texted his sister to let her know he'd be home later. Then he sighed, shook his head, and asked, "So, what's your story? What brought you here to Gearhart? You know pretty much everything about me, but you haven't said much about yourself."

He'd certainly shared a lot about himself, so it was only fair that I do the same. I could have glossed over my personal history, but for some reason I didn't. I hoped I wouldn't regret it. "The last time we talked, you said something that resonated with me," I started out.

He asked me what that was. "You said you'd let down all the people you cared about. I know what that feels like. It's pretty much my story, too, and why I'm living here," I said.

Our food came then, and we ate and talked with our mouths full, stopping to ask for more iced tea and napkins. "Go on," Merritt said, and I started my story.

I began with my failed marriage, which probably started with marrying a woman I didn't really know or love, and continued on through my bar exam failures that ended my law career and disappointed my parents. I didn't spare the sordid particulars.

* * *

The night after I got my third bar exam failure notice was the beginning of the end of our marriage. I'd spent the after-work hours in that life-changing conversation with Larry. Janis was annoyed because I was late getting home and because I smelled like beer. She had already eaten dinner and Jenny was already in bed. I had decided to get it all out in the open right away. Tell her about the bar exam results and my decision to make a career detour. I was going to play it like this was my karma, what I had been born to do—and therefore very good news. Either I didn't get it quite right, possibly the result of the beers I'd had, or she just wasn't buying it. At first, she just stared at me. Then she sat down on one of the barstools at the island in the kitchen. "Sit down," she said.

I sat. "I don't know what to say, except I'm sorry. I know this probably comes as a shock. Right out of left field."

"Yes and no. I've been afraid you wouldn't pass the bar. And I've been wondering what we would do if you didn't. I've built my whole life plan on your being an attorney, on your being a partner in the firm eventually, and my being married to an attorney. I know that might seem shallow. It's not just about the money either."

"This won't necessarily be that different. I can make a living as an investigator. I can build a whole private investigation firm."

"Don't be naïve. There's a lot of difference between how the world sees attorneys and private investigators. Wait till you tell your dad about this and see how he reacts. I can't imagine what my family will say. Our friends… " She was getting weepy now. "And you've wasted all that time and money on law school. Do you even know what it takes to be a private investigator?" I admitted I didn't know but put forth my guess that law school might be good preparation.

Telling my father was even worse. The next day, I asked if I could take him to lunch. He insisted on taking me to his club where he would have to pay of course. "Heard from the bar?" he asked when we had ordered our drinks. I wondered what he already knew. Turned out he was just fishing—and long story short—once I dove into my conversation about my third exam failure and what I wanted to do with my life there was no lunch. He signed the ticket for the drinks and walked out on me and I walked back to the office by myself. I hadn't even gotten to the part about working with Charlie.

Later in the afternoon my father walked into my office, sat down, and asked what he could do to change my mind. He was coming up to retirement age in a few years. There had been a Case in the title of the law firm since its founding and if I defaulted there wouldn't be any longer. It devastated him not to have that as his legacy.

"Maybe Julia could go to law school," I said. "She's the smart one, the one who should be the heir to your partnership in the firm."

He looked at me like I'd had my first good idea ever. "If I can't change your mind what can I do to help you be successful?"

I told him about my idea of working with Charlie. "Was this Charlie's idea?"

"Absolutely not. Charlie was very skittish about helping me. Said he wouldn't even consider it unless you were the one who asked him. His relationship to CCW is too important to him."

"Do you even know what the requirements are?" he asked.

By this time I could rattle off what I'd learned from my Google research. I emphasized the fact that my years in law school wouldn't go to waste, to which he just rolled his eyes. We ended the conversation with my father saying he'd think about it. A couple of hours later Charlie called sounding all surprised and said he'd just had a call from my Dad. He'd expect me at his office on Monday morning. I'd better be prepared to work my ass off.

*

"So then, how did you wind up in Gearhart?" Merritt asked.

"Too much riotous living after my divorce. I needed to make some improvements in my physical and financial health, and so I came down here where there are fewer opportunities to sin." I wondered if he'd be impressed with my theological vocabulary. All he said was "gotcha."

As I recounted my story I'd expected Merritt to be bored—thinking this was just another rich, White guy's story—but he didn't appear to be. All the time I was talking he was nodding and encouraging me with his liquid brown eyes, so I kept going until I got it all out, the facts and the feelings. I wound up by saying somewhat sarcastically, "Forgive me, Father, for I have sinned," which of course I immediately regretted.

His eyes closed down for a minute, and then he smiled. "I'm not allowed to hear Confession anymore—but if I were, I'd ask you how long it's been since your last one."

I laughed. "Forever, I guess, since I'm not Catholic."

"For a non-Catholic," he said, "you took to it rather well." He sat up straight and cleared his throat. "And if I were allowed to hear Confession—and if you were my parishioner—I would instruct you to go and sin no more. Meaning that you're on a new path, doing the best you can—which is quite well from what I can see—and you should forgive yourself and accept the forgiveness of the ones you love." He made a little sign of the cross in the air. "Sorry, force of habit. Are you any kind of believer?" he asked.

I told him my family was Episcopalian, but that we went to church only on Christmas and Easter and other special occasions.

"Ah, Catholic-lite. Not really what I asked, but it's a start," he said.

160

"Even though I've never been in a Catholic Church, I think I can see you as a priest. Some elusive quality I see in you. I can't quite put my finger on just what it is. Do you think you'll even go back?"

Merritt was thoughtful for a minute. "I'm not sure. For one thing, I can't say for sure that I would be allowed back. But beyond that, I don't know, I'm just not sure whether I fit into the church anymore. I know for sure that I love God and that my relationship with God is essential in my life. But the church—the way it excludes gay people is so wrong. How can I want to be a part of an institution that does not accept who I am? Father Clement is exceptional. He hardly represents the entire church."

I took in the enormity of what he said. "Yeah. I can certainly understand why you might not want to go back."

"It's definitely complicated. On top of everything else is how I desecrated the confessional in my church. That was so wrong. Even if God can forgive me for that I'm not sure I can ever forgive myself."

"So what's next for you?"

"I think I'll take one step at a time. I'll see if there's a church around here where I feel accepted. Work as an addictions counselor for the time being. It's good work, and I'm effective with my clients. Maybe that's enough. At least for now."

We were both quiet for a few minutes, and then we were relieved to lighten the mood by changing the subject to sports. We discussed the Seahawks' prospects until it was time to go.

I insisted on paying the bill. Merritt left while I was waiting to be rung up. That took a few minutes and when I got to my car I could see Merritt walking out of the parking lot and up the road. He was pulling the collar of his jacket up around his ears. It was dark and starting to rain a little—it was September and definitely feeling like fall. I drove up beside him and rolled the window down. "Are you walking?" He said yes, that his roommate had dropped him off and that he'd prefer to walk for the exercise—to work off all that grease we'd just consumed.

"It's probably going to rain harder," I said.

He said that where he lived was probably out of my way, but when I insisted, saying that nothing in Gearhart was that far from anything else, he gave up and got in. He gave me directions and then asked where I lived. When I told him, he said, "I don't live on the fancy side of town like you do." I realized he was embarrassed for me to see where he lived. Railroad Avenue is east of the highway, not as upscale as the west side, but nice enough. A couple of times he suggested that I just let him out at the corner, but by then it was raining like crazy and I kept going.

I understood Merritt's reluctance when I pulled up to his house. It was clearly in need of a lot of TLC. I pulled up in the driveway, or what passed for one, and when I did a woman I took to be Merritt's sister came running out the front door with an umbrella. "Hey Bro! So glad you got a ride home—we were afraid you'd walk." She fairly bubbled. "Hi, I'm Valerie, Merritt's sister. Thanks for bringing him home. I can't believe how hard it's raining. I'm assuming you're Henry?" I nodded, and she reached across with a wet hand to shake mine. "Thanks for talking to him about his little situation, too—we've been really worried."

"Valerie's the shy one," Merritt laughed. He got out. Then his face sobered again. "Thanks for the help and for dinner. I guess I'll hear from you."

I told him I'd be in touch and thanked him for trusting me with his situation—and for listening to my story. I sat in the drive and watched them walk into the well-lighted, if shabby, little house, sharing the umbrella with their arms around each other. Then I drove home to my dark, empty condo on the upscale side of town.

162

* * *

I had never considered myself an introspective person. I'm not sure I'd ever used that word before—or for that matter that I even thought in those terms. But after my second lengthy conversation with Merritt Grace I had a lot of stuff going on in my head. For reasons I couldn't quite name at first I felt like a different person. For one thing, I was surprised at how much better I felt after I told my life story to "Father" Merritt Grace. He had a gift for listening, that was certain. But it wasn't just that... there was something else, too. I had enjoyed our conversations and found that I looked forward to talking to him again. That worried me a little, of course. It finally dawned on me that after all those months of living alone and being separated from my family and friends in Seattle I was just plain lonely. But it was a little more than that. I liked Merritt Grace. He was kind and smart and funny.

Now, before anyone starts thinking anything, it wasn't like that at all. Maybe I had found a friend. It's a pretty well-accepted fact that men aren't especially good at friendship, that they're more likely to have "buddies" or "pals" than friends. I guess the difference could be the depth of conversation between buddies and friends. You probably didn't bare your soul to a buddy the way I had with Merritt. Of course I understood he was more than a potential friend. He was a sort of client—and as a listener, he was a professional. I'd think about this stuff for a while and then let it go and get busy with my work, or

watch something mindless on TV.

Oh, and that question he'd asked me and then let go... was I a believer? I had no idea. My parents weren't religious people. As I'd told Merritt, we went to church on occasion, more for social than for religious reasons. I wondered why he'd asked. I didn't think he was going to suggest I should be "saved" or even start going to church. I was intrigued by how easily he talked about his relationship with God and the church. It didn't make me uncomfortable but I was struck that I would never be able to talk about those things myself.

Not least, I thought about the friendly relationship Merritt appeared to have with his sister. Not that Julia and I didn't care about each other. It was partly thanks to her that I was getting my life together, but I couldn't remember us ever sharing the kind of warmth I'd sensed between the Grace siblings. And their little house might have been on the "wrong" side of the highway but it seemed to be full of light and people who cared about each other.

* * *

The day after I'd had a burger with Merritt and driven him home I woke up with a sense of urgency about helping him with his dilemma. After my run on the beach, shower, and bowl of raisin bran, I called Charlie. He sounded pleased to hear from me. We didn't talk a lot these days, as when he had any referrals he usually just made an email intro if one was necessary. He'd heard I was doing well and he was glad to hear it—yadda yadda. I told him I was looking for a little advice. "Sure," he said. It had been a while since I'd reached out for his help.

I told Charlie about Merritt and his situation. "What're you doing?" Charlie asked, and I knew immediately what he meant. One of the cardinal rules in our profession, he'd told me during the time we'd worked together, was not to get involved professionally with people you knew. And of course, not to work for anyone for free.

"I know, I know," I said.

"Not to mention you could be getting yourself into a dangerous situation—and you don't even carry a gun," he wound up. I hadn't thought of that.

"Here's what I think," he said. "If they've questioned him three times and haven't arrested him, they don't have anything. They're hoping to get something, and they're not getting it. So assuming he didn't kill the woman—and you're pretty sure he didn't—he's probably not in any real danger." He was quiet for a few seconds, but I figured he was still thinking. "And if they do come up with enough to arrest him, whether or not he killed her, he's gonna need a lawyer, not a PI. In which case, you'll want to talk to your sister instead of me." At that point, I jumped in with the stats on Black men arrested for murder. I was surprised to hear him say he knew that, but without stronger evidence they still couldn't arrest him. "My best advice," he concluded, "is leave this alone. Five'll get you ten it won't go any further." I wasn't so sure about that.

After my call with Charlie, I thought about calling Larry but thought better of it, since I didn't want to give the impression that Merritt might need a lawyer because he was guilty of something. Instead I got to work on my insurance fraud cases and my one Carmen San Diego case. I'd think about what Charlie had said and decide what to do about Merritt's situation, if anything at all.

An hour later, I was on hold with the credit card company, working on the CSD case, when another call came and I saw it was Charlie. I was seventh in the queue of callers, so I decided to see what Charlie had to say.

"I suppose you're gonna help this guy anyway," he started off without preamble. I said that possibly I would, that I hadn't decided for sure. "I know you," he said. "and I'm betting you will. So, if you're gonna do it anyway, I might as well give you a little free consult." I said okay, that'd be nice. He asked me to tell him about the cops again, then wanted to know more about the "lady cop." His suggestion was that I try to get information from Officer McConnell about where the case was headed, what they had on Merritt, if anything. He thought I'd have more luck with a woman—the "flirt factor" as he called it. I could tell he'd been thinking about this for the hour since we talked. Good old Charlie—right there in my corner when I needed him. He'd even thought about the possibility of my offering my services to the Gearhart police if they needed help with the case. We talked about whether that was a conflict of interest, since Merritt wasn't a paying client. I thanked him for his suggestion and said I'd work on it. He said he'd let me know if he thought of anything else—and hung up without saying good-bye. Now to figure out how to get some face time with Terry McConnell. Not my idea of fun, and I wasn't even getting paid for this.

But Deliver Us from Evil

September

Was it my imagination or were things at work somehow different following that third interview with Gellerman? Being the only Black employee at PBH I was always on the alert, regularly subjected to microaggressions like people waiting for the next elevator instead of taking the one I was on, but this felt different. Co-workers who were ordinarily friendly avoided my eye. The staff kitchen cleared out when I went in to get a cup of coffee. One time it even looked like there was a staff meeting I hadn't been invited to. I asked Cindy about it. She hemmed and hawed, but finally agreed that yes, ever since the cops had questioned me three times, people were wondering whether I had anything to do with RaeAnne's death. She didn't say anything about Dr. Sandaas or Marjorie Dawson, so if the police had said anything to them about my knowing about the contents of RaeAnne's letter it wasn't evident. Or at least she didn't mention it.

I tried to ride out the storm for a week or so, but more and more it felt like I had to get out of Dodge. If anything, the staff's coldness toward me grew worse. Everyone seemed to be on edge and I was the scapegoat. Besides, the more I thought about Erik Sandaas and the things RaeAnne claimed about him, the less I wanted to have anything to do with Pacific Behavioral Health. Or him. I suspected that he and Marjorie may have had something to do with RaeAnne's death. At the end of the week I turned in my letter of resignation.

Fortunately I'd managed to save a little bit of money and the rent Liz and Val charged me changed from low rent to no rent—at least until I could get back on my feet again. Thank God for those two women.

For a few days I didn't do much except walk on the beach and cook different kinds of vegetarian soup. That *Greens Cookbook* I'd gotten a few months earlier had some amazing recipes. It was good to throw myself into this new endeavor—and I enjoyed cooking for Val and Liz.

Then when Sunday morning rolled around, I decided to go to Mass. It had been a long time since I darkened the doorway of any church. A priest came in to offer the Mass once a week at Monroe, and while that was meaningful, it was hardly the same.

I wondered whether I would be welcomed in a church in this part of the state. In general, the rural coastal communities were more conservative than the larger urban areas. Liz and Val had felt pretty uncomfortable the one time they went to a church. I wondered if it was obvious that they were lesbians, or if it was the fact that they were a mixed race couple, or that new people just weren't typically made to feel welcome. Whatever—once was enough for them.

But I still had a yearning to get back to a church, to experience the Mass within a community of believers. I couldn't hide the fact that I was Black but I could easily pass for straight. Whether I wanted to was another story—it was the way I got through my priesthood at the Church of the Holy Family after all—but it would be refreshing to live this part of my journey with full authenticity. I decided to play it straight, so to speak, at first, and then see what unfolded.

Looking online, I found several Catholic churches along the Oregon Coast with the closest one in Seaside. This was where Val and Liz went the one time they darkened the doorway of a church. Whatever. I decided to give it a try.

I dressed in a white polo shirt, khakis, and a blue blazer. I debated whether to wear a dress shirt and tie, but that was probably too formal for the coast. Entering the church, I went through the familiar and beloved rituals of blessing myself with Holy Water, genuflecting, kneeling in prayer at a pew toward the back of the church before settling into my seat and waiting for the Mass to begin. Several people looked at me with curiosity, many smiled, and one couple reached over the pew in front of me to introduce themselves and shake my hand. So far, so good.

I lost myself in the Mass itself, the sweet familiar liturgy, and felt the sacred moment of God's presence as I participated in the Eucharist. The thought that perhaps I actually could return to the priesthood passed through my mind.

After the service, on my way out, I browsed through some pamphlets that were in a holder in the narthex. One in particular caught my eye.

The Church and Homosexuality

Our Lady of the Coast Catholic Church welcomes sexually active homosexual men and women with the hope and expectation that in due course they will come to see the need to be transformed and live in accordance with biblical revelation and orthodox church teaching.

While we welcome sexually active homosexual men and women, we are unable to affirm their lifestyle, and cannot allow them to volunteer or minister within the church. All those who experience same-sex attraction *and have committed themselves to chastity by refraining from homoerotic sexual practice* are eligible for leadership within the church.

My knees buckled. I had to grab onto the countertop to keep my balance. How could the church say it welcomed gay people while denying them any opportunity to participate in the life of the church? How could the church say it welcomed gay people as long as they were committed to becoming straight? How could the church affirm only those homosexuals who committed themselves to a life of chastity?

I sighed, walked back into the sanctuary for a long look, and said goodbye. Surely not goodbye to God, or to following a lifelong call for offering spiritual leadership, but goodbye to the Catholic Church. I just couldn't continue to pretend to be who the church apparently needed me to be.

Walking down the front steps of the church, tears trickled down my cheeks. This was the final goodbye to what had been a life's dream and mission. And at the same time I felt an enormous weight rise off my shoulders. No longer burdened by the expectations of the church, I could become who I truly was, mature into who I truly wanted to be. And while that wasn't entirely clear in the moment—and might not be for some time—it was a truly liberating feeling.

Tying Up a Few Loose Threads

October

A few days later Justin joined us for dinner. I was still feeling unstrung by my experience with the church—the decision to leave was like cutting away a core of my identity—but it still felt like the right decision and, in any case, for the time being I had even more pressing things on my mind. Hoping for some good news, I prepared the best version of minestrone soup I could muster and over dinner we talked a little bit about my situation. I was disappointed to learn he didn't really have too much to offer. Apparently he was planning to have a conversation with the lady cop, but ethically she probably wouldn't tell him much about the investigation. I didn't hold out a lot of hope for that. So mostly we glossed over my case and, after dinner, played card games. Once I allowed myself to get into it, it was a good, if momentary, diversion.

I found myself thinking a lot about RaeAnne. Who killed her? What were the circumstances? As far as I was concerned, Sandaas was one possibility. Actually, he was at the top of my list. I wondered if the police were investigating him. Maybe not, since they seemed so bent on believing I was guilty. Based on nothing but someone overhearing an argument and the color of my skin.

I decided to go see Peggy Harrison, RaeAnne's counselor at Awakenings. RaeAnne had worked closely with her so she might have some clues. She greeted me warmly. "So, you're Merritt Grace. RaeAnne told me a lot about you. My God, such a tragedy. She was really working hard on her recovery. Do you know if they have any leads?"

I decided against mentioning that I was a prime suspect. "RaeAnne had a lot of good things to say about you. She appreciated talking with you and she tried so hard to stay clean. She was just making it back when... "

"Yeah, I know." She paused for a minute. "I was glad she felt OK about coming back here when she relapsed. That's not an easy decision."

"Yes, I know. I've been there, too."

"Oh?" Peggy seemed surprised to hear this. Good for RaeAnne, not telling Peggy that she'd met me at NA. "So you knew RaeAnne from work?"

Peggy listened quietly while I told her the story of my prison adventures that led me to Second Chance and my meeting with RaeAnne there. "So how are things for you now, at PBH, after RaeAnne's death?" she asked.

"Not great. Actually, I quit a few days ago."

Peggy's raised eyebrows encouraged me to continue.

"Yeah. Things were getting pretty bad there. After RaeAnne died and the police questioned me three times, people started giving me the cold shoulder, looking at me cross-eyed, avoiding me. It was never great there—racial slurs, microaggressions. Several people pretty regularly shunned us Second Chancers. You know, Gearhart isn't the most progressive of all communities."

Peggy laughed out loud at that one. "You got that right."

"But anyway, after RaeAnne's death, it was like people suspected me of killing her. It made working there just about impossible. And then, there was that whole Dr. Sandaas thing."

Peggy looked at me quizzically. "Dr. Sandaas?"

"So I guess RaeAnne never said anything to you about him?"

"No. Something I should know?"

I was disappointed that RaeAnne hadn't said anything. Something that could back up her letter. But I wasn't about to spread rumors. "No, not really."

Peggy briefly paused, then changed the subject. "So, what are you doing now?"

"Nothing much. Clearing my head. Looking for the next opportunity I guess. I'd like to stay here in Gearhart." I didn't tell her that the police had told me not to leave.

"Well, you know... addiction counselors aren't a dime a dozen around here and I'm sure you know how great the need is. Any chance you'd like to work here? We've always got contract positions."

That sounded attractive. If I wasn't going to try to go back to the priesthood I'd need some kind of direction. But I was a long way from ready to make any major decisions. "Thanks Peggy. I think I need a little time off. But I'll keep your offer in mind. For sure."

"Well, just let me know. And meanwhile, thanks for coming in. RaeAnne was a good person. She had a hard life and she was so fond of you. You were a good friend to her."

"She was a good friend to me, too. But you know, I'm wondering. Did RaeAnne ever mention anyone else? Someone who might want to harm her? Anything from her past?"

"I'm sorry, Merritt. You know that I can't share information that RaeAnne told me during our sessions. I wish I could. The police asked me the same thing. I hope they get to the bottom of this."

"Yeah, me too." So the police had been here too. Of course, that made sense. But it felt eerie just the same. "I guess I'll be going now. Thanks for the visit. I'll get back to you about that contract work."

"Good. Thanks again, Merritt. I'm so happy to know you. I can see why RaeAnne spoke so highly of you."

After meeting with Peggy, I called Justin to fill him in— really just to let him know there was nothing of note to share— and that evening I talked at length with Liz and Val. We talked mostly about my case. My decision to leave the church was still too tender to discuss, and my legal problems were so pressing—and increasingly terrifying. It felt like a noose was tightening around my neck. The police were talking with everyone apparently, without turning up any clues. Damn, I wish RaeAnne had said something to Peggy about Sandaas. She could have confirmed the story when she talked with the police. But that hadn't happened.

I made a quick decision. "Liz, can I borrow your car tomorrow? I need to go to Seattle. Just a day trip. Check out a few things."

Liz and Val exchanged glances—I knew they were worried about me—but Liz agreed. "Sure, whatever you need. Just drop me off at work on your way out of town."

There were three stops I wanted to make in Seattle. I called Father Clement to ask if he could make some time for me. He was surprised to hear from me but cleared his calendar for the late afternoon. I wasn't looking forward to that conversation but I had to talk with him about my thoughts about leaving the church. No one answered the second call I made and I decided not to leave a message. Last, but not least, I made plans to have lunch with my parents and Gran-Mo. I really looked forward to seeing them but it wouldn't be an easy visit. I hadn't yet told them anything about the trouble I was in, and even though I was innocent, things were not looking good. I really needed their support. It definitely wasn't time to tell them my thoughts about leaving the church. That would mean coming out to them. No, not right now. One thing at a time.

It was late morning when I arrived in Seattle. Traffic was light and I'd made it in less than four hours, including a brief stop for a bite to eat. Now what? It was too early for the bar scene. I decided to drive over to my old stomping grounds.

Walking around in Seattle's Central District felt like coming home. For one thing, lots of other people looked like me. I didn't stand out like a sore thumb. I briefly wondered whether I really wanted to return to Gearhart, but stored that thought away for another time. I had more pressing matters to attend to.

I checked out the changes at 23rd and Union, the retail center and heart of the African American community in Seattle—some exciting new development was going on—then got up my courage to walk over to my old church. There she was—The Church of the Holy Family. A small sign outside had Father Joseph Radner's name where my name used to be. A flood of emotion overwhelmed me. I had loved serving this parish. Loved the people. Loved the Mass most of all. And then—guilt and shame. How could I have desecrated the sanctity of this church? How could I have so betrayed my parishioners, my superiors, and myself? To say nothing of God. On the other hand, I felt betrayed by the church. My recent experience at the church in Seaside left me feeling so raw. I was definitely conflicted regarding my relationship with the church.

I walked up the church steps, opened the heavy door, and entered. I realized that I still felt at home there. Sunlight beaming through the stained-glass window in the chancel reflected off the pulpit. The place where for several years I'd stood and celebrated the Mass with my parish. I closed my eyes and saw myself there, felt again in my heart my love for sharing the Eucharist with those dear people. I'm not sure how long I remained in that sweet reverie before I opened my eyes to return to the present day. Was I sure that I was making the right decision?

I slowly walked toward the front of the church, genuflected, and knelt in prayer near one of the front pews. I felt the spirit of God filling the room, entering my heart. Reaching into my pocket, I found my rosary beads. They felt familiar as I began reciting the beloved prayers. When I opened my eyes again the sunshine had moved beyond the chancel window. A glance at my watch told me it was time to get going. I left the church with a renewed faith that God was with me, that the mystery of RaeAnne's murder would be resolved, and that a rewarding future in Gearhart was just around the corner. I couldn't wait to talk with Father Clement in a few hours. Hopefully he could help me sort through my confusing feelings.

Before leaving to meet my family for lunch I walked across the street to see if I could find Tyrone. I had him to thank for putting a halt to my dealing—and he had never told a soul, at least as far as I knew. I wanted him to know how grateful I was to him. I walked up to the door of the apartment where he had lived and knocked. A young, harried looking woman with a small child clinging to her leg opened the door. "Are you looking for someone?" she warily asked.

"Does Tyrone Davis still live here? I knew him a few years ago and I'd love to talk with him if possible."

"I don't know anyone named Tyrone. We just moved here a couple of months ago. I don't know who was here before me. I can't help you." And with that she closed the door. I stood in the hallway staring at the door for a minute or so before turning away to leave. "Thanks for everything Tyrone," I softly said. "I hope all is well with you." And with that I left for lunch with my family.

Gran-Mo flung the door wide open when she saw me standing on the porch. "Oh baby, it's so good to see you!" She wrapped me in a gigantic hug. "Lunch is just waiting for you on the stove."

I hadn't been to the family home since I was at Monroe. It felt good to be there. Of course Gran-Mo and my parents had visited me while I was in prison, but it wasn't the same as being right there in the house where I grew up. I was flooded with memories. "I can't wait to dig into some of your famous cooking. You got me started, you know. I'm dabbling in cooking right now—mostly all kinds of great vegetarian soups—but nothing like the soul food that comes out of your kitchen!"

"Vegetarian? Are you vegetarian now? I've got some of my

famous smothered chicken, and I sure hope you'll eat it!"

"Smothered chicken. Oh my God! And mac and cheese?" I added, hopefully.

"Yep. Plus some fried okra, and peach cobbler for dessert. I hope you're hungry boy!"

"Where's Mom and Pop?" I asked.

"I think they're out in the garden. They both came home early from work so as to have as much time with you as possible. We've *missed* you, boy."

"I've missed you, too!" Just saying those words made me realize just how much I HAD missed my family. It had been too long. "I wish I could stay longer today. I just have a day here in Seattle and I've got a lot I need to get done."

"Well you're here now, that's what's important." She called Mom and Pop in from the backyard. "Victor! Gemma! Come on in! Merritt's here." Each gave me a big hug as they came in through the back door. They were clearly happy to see me, but I could see worry on my mother's face.

"You said something you wanted to talk with us about," Mom began, as we took our seats around the dining room table.

Gran-Mo jumped in. "Now let the boy eat before we get to the serious stuff." She walked into the kitchen and returned with platters of food, which she set on the table.

We all folded our hands and prayed together, "Bless us, O Lord, and these thy gifts which we are about to receive from thy bounty. Through Jesus Christ Our Lord, Amen."

It was a familiar ritual, but one we did not practice at Liz and Val's table. I typically offered grace before meals silently, simply repeating the words in my head. It felt good to say it aloud here with my family.

Gran-Mo had indeed outdone herself with the meal. The smothered chicken—tender breast drenched in creamy gravy and topped by bits of fried bacon—was to die for. In my mind

I heard Val warning me not to cook bacon in their house. My two favorite kitchens were certainly different from one another. Although amazing mac and cheese came out of both of them. I felt blessed to have both in my life.

After sopping up the last of the peach cobbler, my mother looked at me and said, "Well?"

"It's a long story," I began. I told them about RaeAnne's murder and how it appeared that I was apparently the primary suspect.

"Do you have a lawyer?" my father asked.

"Not yet. I do have a friend who's a private investigator who's helping me. He has a law degree but never passed the bar so he can't practice law. But he knows quite a bit and has some good contacts."

"I was worried about you moving down to the coast," said my mom. "I know that Liz and Val feel okay living there but it's got to be hard, being one of the few Black people in the area. And a Black man at that. It's different, somehow. Oh, my God, what if you get convicted? Of murder! You read about these things happening all the time. I don't think I could stand it if you were in prison again. And with a murder charge, it wouldn't be in minimum security, I can tell you that." My mother was on the verge of hysteria, her voice getting louder and louder with each word.

Gran-Mo spoke up, "Now everyone just calm down. The boy is innocent and everything is gonna be alright. Before you go," she said looking at me, "we'll pray together." We reached out, held one another's hands, bowed our heads, and closed our eyes. "Heavenly Father," Gran-Mo began, "you know your beloved son, Merritt Grace. You know he is a good man. He has made some mistakes, but he has paid for them. He needs your help now. Please guide him to find the people he needs to help him, and guide the police in Gearhart to find the real murderer. May perpetual light shine upon Merritt's friend

RaeAnne, and may she rest in peace. In the name of the Father, the Son, and the Holy Spirit. Amen."

"Amen," we all repeated. For a minute we were all quiet, then we slowly raised our heads and unclasped our hands. We all felt the import of the moment, as we looked around the table into one another's eyes.

"Thank you, Gran-Mo, for the amazing lunch and for the wonderful prayer. And thank you Mom and Pop for your advice and support. I have to admit to you—I'm scared. But I know I'm innocent. I have good people on my side and I believe that in the long run everything will turn out alright."

"I hope so son," from my Pop.

"Be careful son," from my Mom.

"Come see us again soon," from Gran-Mo.

I left my family feeling hopeful, grateful, and filled. I could not help but compare the loving family I grew up in with the hell that was RaeAnne's childhood. Life just wasn't fair. I took a deep breath and readied myself for the next stop of my day.

Entering Neighbors I scanned the room. There was no guarantee that Rafael would be there, but then I spotted him at the far end of the bar. As handsome as ever. My heart lurched. After all he'd done to me, he still had the power to bewitch. I took a moment to center myself, to pray for strength. "Anyone sitting here?"

"Well, look what the cat dragged in. I knew you'd come back some time. They all do."

"How've you been, Rafael?"

"Well, better than you, from what I hear. Some cops were up here giving me the third degree about you. How did I know you? Were you still working for me? They wouldn't say why they were asking—didn't seem at all interested in me—but it was pretty clear they'd done their homework. Knew more than they were saying. So—what's going on with you anyway?"

"Long story short—a friend of mine was murdered and they

think I did it. Which of course I didn't. But racism is all too alive and well in Gearhart. No more than around here I guess but, you know, it can be unsettling being the only Black face in a sea of white."

"So you came to find me because... "

"I want to know what you told them. They have no evidence against me, but that never stopped anyone bent on prosecuting the nigger. Rafael, I'm really scared."

"Wow. A murder rap. That's big. I knew it was big—but that big? No way. God. Anyway, nothing I told them could be used against you. I told them I hadn't seen you in years, since before you went to prison."

"Good. Good. You know I'm an addictions counselor now. And totally clean."

"No shit. I'm sure you're pulling in the big bucks with that work."

"Enough. I'm earning enough."

Rafael's dark eyes burned into mine. I felt my face flush. "So, Father Grace. Are you sure that all you came for was information? You seem pretty anxious, and if I remember correctly... "

He didn't have to finish his sentence. I remembered all too well the heady pleasure of the cocaine rush, the mind-blowing sex. God it was tempting. I fingered the rosary in my pocket. "Yeah, you do remember correctly. We had some great times. And that was long ago and far away. I've put that life behind me for good. I'm not sure what the future holds but it's not that. No, Rafael, you've given me what I came for today. Some information about the murder investigation and closure with you. We never did have a proper goodbye. So here it is. Goodbye Rafael, I wish you well."

I left Neighbors with a light heart and eager for my meeting with Father Clement. So much to talk with him about. Just the events of today could fill a book.

The sun was close to setting when I approached Father Clement's office. The day in Seattle, especially those tender moments in the church, left me confused. Back in my old stomping grounds, I suddenly wasn't sure what I thought, what I wanted. And then there was the matter of being a murder suspect. I wouldn't be the first innocent Black man to have the book thrown at him. I hoped Father Clement would help me sort things out.

He greeted me warmly when I entered. "Merritt, it's so good to see you. It was wonderful to hear your voice when you called the other day. C'mon in and sit down." I gratefully sank into a deep easy chair. "How've you been, my son? It's been a while. Since you were still at Monroe. From your phone call, I gather there's quite a bit going on."

"You have no idea!" I took a deep breath. "Just give me a minute."

Father Clement's eyes gazed into my soul. "Take all the time you need, Merritt."

"Thanks... I'm not sure where to begin. It's all too much."

"Well, you can start by telling me what you've been doing since you left prison."

"Oh, sure. Of course. Did I tell you that I got certified as a Substance Abuse Specialist while I was at Monroe?"

"Oh? No, I didn't know. That sounds like a good opportunity. Did it work out for you?"

"Yeah, I guess so. After Monroe I got a job as an addictions counselor in Gearhart."

"Gearhart?"

"Yeah. A tiny dot on the map on the Oregon Coast. My sister Val and her wife Liz live there. They told me about this Second Chance program there that helps ex-felons like me get employed. So I applied and, until a few weeks ago, I was working as an addictions counselor at Pacific Behavioral Health."

"A few weeks ago?"

"Yeah. I quit. So here's the thing. A colleague of mine in Second Chance, RaeAnne, was murdered. We were also friends in NA. And now I'm Gearhart PD's prime suspect."

"Whoa! You didn't... "

"What? No, of course not! I didn't kill her! But I feel like I'm being framed. With my prison time and my black skin—I guess that's all it takes to be the guilty party. Oh—did I tell you that Val and I are just about the only Black people in Gearhart?"

Father Clement shook his head and closed his eyes for a moment, taking it all in. After he opened his eyes again I continued.

"To make things even worse, I have reason to believe that Erik Sandaas, the Medical Director of PBH, is cooking the financial books there. Not only that, I'm pretty sure that slimeball is the one who killed RaeAnne! Of course I have no way to prove that. Not yet. But things were getting just too weird for me to stay there. Everybody knows the police suspect me. They shun me even more than they did when my only crime was the color of my skin. That plus my suspicions about Sandaas... well, I just had to get out of there."

Father Clement took a deep breath, absorbing all I'd told him. "Wow. That's a lot for you to carry. What are you doing now?"

"Right now, not very much. Trying to recenter myself. Walking on the beach. Sometimes a little kite-flying. Cooking. I'm becoming quite the cook. It's a lot of fun. Creative and healthy... "

"Have you been going to Mass?"

"I went once, to a church in Gearhart. At first, I loved being there. Participating in the Mass felt like returning home. And the people were friendly enough. After a bad racist experience I'd had a few weeks earlier I was on guard, but people were either indifferent or apparently happy to have me there."

"You said you only went once. Did something happen?"

"After the service I wandered around in the narthex, checking out the literature. I found a pamphlet that stopped me in my tracks. It essentially said that I was OK as a gay person, but unless I was chaste I could not volunteer or serve in the church in any capacity. When I read that I felt like I'd been kicked in the gut. How could I belong to a church where I was not welcome to serve, even as a volunteer? When I walked out it occurred to me that I might just be leaving the church for good."

"How do you feel about that now?"

"I'm really conflicted. I stopped by the Church of the Holy Family earlier this morning. It felt like home. And now... seeing you... " I looked up into his eyes and started to cry. Crying out of grief for RaeAnne's death. Panic about being a murder suspect. Confusion about who I was and wanted to be. The dam finally broke. Father Clement reached out to me, pulled me up out of my chair, and held me in a warm embrace. It reminded me of the time I was so upset when I'd told him about selling drugs. His hugs just wrap you in love.

"Welcome home my son. I'm happy to have you here, and God is as well. Now, what can I do for you?"

"I don't know. I guess I just need help thinking things through. First priority is clearing my name. I haven't been arrested or anything, I just know I'm a suspect. If I could find a way to prove Sandaas did it... "

"Now Merritt, you don't want to accuse anyone based on a hunch. Your own experiences tell you that. Have you told the police about your suspicions?"

"Not exactly. Well, it's a long story. I don't want to get into all of it right now, but you're right. I don't know if it was Sandaas, I just know it wasn't me. A friend of mine in Gearhart, a PI, is helping me poke around. Maybe together we can find something, some way to prove it was Sandaas, or else figure out who did it."

"Well, I wish you well on that. But what about you? Let's assume you get off the hook, and I truly believe that you will. What then? What do you want to do?"

"Maybe we talked about this when I first went to prison. I was so ashamed, not thinking clearly. And I can't remember much from that time. But anyway... what's my status with the church? Am I still a priest?"

"Well, technically, you're on an extended leave of absence. It's longer than most priests take, but then most priests don't wind up in prison."

I winced at that. "No. I guess not. Just me."

"But now I'm wondering—where are you with the Church? Are you still thinking you need to leave?"

"Actually I'm not sure. With all that's happening I just don't know. It's not that I'm not sure about God. I felt His presence during the Mass in Seaside. And then being in my old church this morning felt like home. The sun streaming in the windows—it felt like God streaming in to comfort me. On the other hand, well... after my experience at the church in Seaside... well... maybe the Church just doesn't work for me any more."

Father Clement raised his eyebrows at that one. "Doesn't work?"

"Well, as I told you, I loved the Mass at the church in Seaside, but then it was clear from their literature that I would not be welcome there. Val and Liz also went to that church a couple of times but they didn't really like it either. I'm not sure why. Whether it had to do with not feeling welcome as lesbians or as a racially mixed couple—or for any other reason, I don't know. Then again, there's always the possibility that I still feel so guilty about what I did that I don't feel entitled to go to any church. I don't know. I'm just not sure about the Church anymore."

"Do you miss it?"

"Yes and no. I often spend Sunday morning on the beach. It's incredibly beautiful there. For the most part nature is where I find God these days. The ever-changing sea, the rocks jutting out of the ocean, logs tossed asunder after a major storm." I sat quietly for a moment, reflecting. "You know, Father Clement, I just remembered a powerful experience I had when I first got to Gearhart. I was sitting on the beach, just looking at the enormity of it all, when all of a sudden I felt touched by grace. It was almost like I heard my name. Merritt Grace. Like I merited grace. That was powerful. Especially because I'd just had a particularly offensive racist encounter at the local tennis court. I guess the beach has been my sanctuary ever since."

"Thank you for sharing that memory with me, Merritt. God reveals Himself to people in all kinds of places other than the Church.. But you said that, for you, this morning in the church was particularly meaningful to you?"

"Yes. Sitting there—when I closed my eyes I could see myself as the priest I was when I was there. Celebrating the Mass. Serving my parishioners. I felt myself suffused with God's spirit. It was as profound as my experience at the beach."

"God blesses you with many compelling reminders of His loving presence Merritt."

"Yes. And I am enlivened by His grace. It actually makes me think about possibly returning to the Church. And at the same time, here I am, wondering if I'm going to be sent to prison again, this time for a murder I didn't commit. Father Clement, I'm really scared."

"Merritt, I believe in you. I always have, even when you got lost for a time. I'm so glad you came to see me today. You have a lot to reflect on. I suggest you go back to Gearhart, do everything you can to clear your name, and listen. Listen for the voice of God calling you to the next chapter in your life. Be patient with yourself and with God. He'll make His purpose for you known when the time is right. Meantime, work with your friend to learn the truth of RaeAnne's death. That sounds like your top priority right now."

"Thank you, Father Clement. And now I'd better get going. I have a long drive back home. But before I go, will you pray with me?"

"Of course, my son." We bowed our heads and he placed his hands on my shoulders. "Loving God. Thank you for this man, your beloved child Merritt. Thank you for blessing him with a loving family and warm home, with wisdom and intelligence, and with clear signs of your presence in his life. Be with him in his search—for the killer of his friend RaeAnne and for the next steps in his life. Comfort his fears, strengthen his confidence, fortify his patience, and deepen the clarity of his understanding and discernment. Help him to know that you are always with him, even when his challenges seem insurmountable. In the name of the Father, the Son, and Holy Spirit, Amen." We both crossed ourselves at the closing of his prayer.

"Thank you, Father Clement. You've been a blessing in my life since I was a little boy. I thank God for you."

We embraced, and then I got in the car to head for home. On the drive back I thought about the day—all that had happened. Relief at not being the only Black man in sight. That holy moment in my old church. A beautiful lunch with my family. Not succumbing to Rafael's temptations. I guess I felt good about that. I especially loved my visit with Father Clement. So grateful for his wisdom and his accepting me without judgment. Affirming that God can be found in venues beyond the Church. I'm sure that most of the church hierarchy do not share that belief. Anyway... lots of food for thought. But first things first, can't make any plans until I clear my name. And that means finding RaeAnne's killer. Somehow.

It's a Dirty Job

October

Catching Officer Terry McConnell was just a matter of time and good old-fashioned detective work. On a Tuesday morning I sat in my car a scant block from the Gearhart City Hall where the police station is located, catching up on emails but keeping my eyes trained on the front entrance. About three hours in Officer McConnell exited the building and I came to full attention. She walked across the street to the Daily Grind, and, as soon as she was inside, I made my way over there. Luck was on my side and the place was empty except for the two of us and the barista.

McConnell looked up when I came in. It took her a minute but she finally recognized me. "Hi," she said. "I'm Officer Terry McConnell with the Gearhart Police. We met when you came in to see Chief O'Donahue." I acted like I vaguely remembered. She hadn't ordered yet so I offered to get her coffee. She reminded me that she was a public servant and couldn't accept that. Oh, my—this might not be easy.

I chatted her up while we waited for our coffees. Fortunately she'd ordered some double-fluff thing that took a long time to make. I was going to ask her if she had time to sit and drink them together but—surprise—she asked me first. "Oh sure, I guess I can make time," I said nonchalantly. Sitting across from her, I realized I hadn't really looked at Officer McConnell when we'd met before. If I remembered correctly, she'd been in uniform, never a particularly fetching look. Today, though, she was wearing a khaki skirt, white tee shirt, and navy blazer—much better. She wasn't bad looking—medium height, slender, with long, thick auburn hair piled on top of her head, and big brown eyes behind trendy glasses. She was young, but I guessed that she might be a little older than she looked—still maybe as much as ten years younger than I was.

It must have been a slow morning at work for her because once we sat down she didn't seem in a hurry to get back to it. It was a surprisingly enjoyable conversation and I had to remind myself that I was there with a purpose. Even so, all I wanted from this visit was to establish sufficient rapport for a subsequent conversation. I didn't want to rush in with my questions. Knowing that she also had investigative skills—or so I assumed—I planned to be careful so as not to raise any red flags.

We sat there for the better part of an hour, talking mostly about Gearhart and what a drag it was to live there. Actually, she lived in Tillamook, which she said was as bad as Gearhart. She had wanted to be a police officer for as long as she could remember and she had envisioned herself in a much larger city—Portland, where she'd grown up, or Seattle. But those places hired experienced police officers. For someone without experience, Oregon's smaller cities and rural towns served as starting points for law enforcement careers. One had to be hired by a police department in order to qualify for the state Public Safety Department's police officer training program, which was required for certification. She had completed that recently and done very well with the training she told me proudly.

She asked me what I was doing in Gearhart, and I gave her a much-abbreviated version—needing to get away from the distractions of the big city for a while, yadda yadda. I mentioned that I was divorced and unattached so I could see if there was any reaction, and I thought she definitely registered a little interest. I have to say, I was feeling somewhat guilty about that. Not that I had lied to her about anything yet, but I might be taking advantage of her interest. I hadn't known when I came into the coffee shop that she was single and how this was going to play out, but we had both identified ourselves as single, and there had been a couple of flirtatious moments in our conversation. I should say "what passed for flirtatious" with Officer McConnell. She was a fairly serious woman, very smart and most certainly a feminist. But if she was a straight, healthy, lonely and bored young woman, I may have represented her best opportunity on the Oregon coast for a little diversion or a serious relationship.

The coffee shop was filling up and she said she'd better get back to work. Once she stood up to go she seemed hesitant, like there was something else she wanted to say. I'd been thinking I'd ask for her phone number, so I said I'd walk her across the street. No need to take care of business in front of these nosy townspeople. We were hardly out on the sidewalk when she asked if I'd be interested in having dinner sometime. She was making this so easy I didn't know whether to feel gleeful or guilty—but of course I said that sounded like a fine idea. We settled on the next Friday evening (my suggestion), meeting in Seaside at Nonni's Italian Bistro (her suggestion).

* * *

Friday at seven Nonni's was very crowded and they didn't take reservations, so I waited at the little bar until I could get us a table. Terry (I had made myself quit thinking of her as Officer McConnell) was late, which gave me time to get my name in for the table and start on the bottle of Ripasso I'd ordered before she got there. I almost didn't recognize her. She cleaned up rather well, as the saying goes, and of course that made me feel all the guiltier. She was wearing a nice shortish dress with a flouncy skirt. She wasn't wearing her glasses—contacts I assumed—and she'd done something a lot better with her hair. She apologized for being late, saying that she'd had to change

189

her clothes, this being her day on patrol, which required wearing a uniform.

"Some guys might find the uniform a turn-on," I said.

She gave me that serious look. "I hope you're not one of those."

A couple of racy come-backs floated through my mind, but I let them go in favor of "No, I'm not." She gave me an engaging smile.

It was not a disappointing evening in any way. The incredible chicken piccata, the great wine–and last, but not least, the time spent talking with Terry. We had a lot to talk about considering that we were in similar fields. I heard someone say once that work is sexy, that, for some people, it's the ultimate foreplay. There's definitely something to that— something downright intimate about shared interest and knowledge and a common vernacular. I talked about the private investigating business and some of the cases I'd worked on. Terry really got my work, something I'd never experienced with a woman I was dating—or married to—and listened actively with comments and questions in all the appropriate places. She didn't even turn off when I talked about insurance fraud and said I'd never found it necessary to apply for a concealed-carry permit.

She talked about police work in Gearhart—which, even though it was a little like Andy Griffith's Mayberry, was interesting, too. At least she made it sound a lot more interesting than Chief O'Donohue had. The wine made her somewhat chatty, not to mention a little giggly—which I confess I found rather charming. I asked how it was to work with O'Donahue, and she made the side-to-side gesture with her hand, which I took to mean "not so good." There were things about him she didn't like, she said, but then with his political aspirations he wasn't around very much and left most of the policing to her and Gellerman. When I asked what she didn't like about him, she said that he usually stepped in and took the credit for any good work that she and Gellerman did.

Then she hemmed and hawed but finally said that sometimes he was a little too familiar. She assumed that her youth brought out the fatherliness in older men. Gellerman was a different story, she said; he could be fatherly, too, mostly in a good way. He had been nothing but helpful to her in learning the ropes getting through the training and licensing process. She and Gellerman were sort of opposites, mostly a result of age and where they'd grown up,she assumed. He was old-school while she was more progressive. He'd grown up in this area and had no desire to live anywhere else. She'd grown up in the city and hoped to get enough experience to get out of Gearhart as soon as possible. On the whole, though, they worked together relatively well. She ate dinner with him and his family occasionally, and his wife had been nice to her, too.

"So I've got a personal question," she changed the subject. "Is Justin Case your real name?" She reddened a little, like maybe she was embarrassed to have asked. "I mean, I thought maybe it was like a stage name. It's perfect for someone in your line of work."

I laughed. "Maybe it's my karma," I said. "Maybe my name—which, by the way, is actually Justin Henry Case—set me up for my professional destiny."

"Did your parents think about how those names went together—I mean, did they do it to be funny?" She reddened again. "I'm putting this badly. I don't really mean to be insulting your name."

"No problem. But it's a long story. Justin was my grandfather's name—my mother's father. His last name was Wells and there was nothing funny about Justin Wells. He died about a week before I was born, so my mother really wanted to name me after him. If I'd been a girl I'd have been named Justine."

"Well, that's sweet."

"Yeah, but as they say, no good deed goes unpunished. My parents were smart people, but I guess they didn't have much sense of humor. Somehow, they didn't notice how the names went together—not until the name was on the birth certificate. When they did notice, or someone pointed it out to them, they were smart enough to see it could be a recipe for a lot of bullying down the line."

"Yikes, I guess so. Nobody needs to deal with that."

Fortunately Henry, which was my other grandfather's first name and my middle name, was acceptable. So I've always gone by Henry Case. And whenever I need a first, middle, and last name—J. Henry Case."

"So when did you start using Justin?"

"When I decided to become a PI. I still go by Henry most of the time, but I use Justin professionally."

"Well I think it's very cool."

"Thanks."

* * *

Cool. That wasn't exactly the reaction I'd had from Janis the night I'd told her I'd failed the bar exam for the third time and was planning to be a PI instead of an attorney. In the belief that I might convince her (and maybe myself) that the change in my career plans was meant to be, I blurted out, "and another good thing is I can use my real name. It's just about perfect for a private investigator." And then I remembered that I'd never told her what my real name was. When I did, she wasn't amused. "Justin? Justin Case?! God in heaven, is that a joke? And why have I never known what your real name is? We've been married all this time and you let me think you just had an initial for a first name! You've lied to me about your name— what else have you lied about? Please tell me you're not going to use that name. Justin Case—oh, my God!" And it went downhill from there.

This exchange helped me realize how little Janis and I knew about each other, even after several years of marriage. Why hadn't I ever told her what my real name was? Maybe because the name thing was kind of a big deal—Janis loved my name. When we married, she had personalized stationery made with "Mrs. J. Henry Case" printed on it. She was not a woman who would enjoy being married to someone named Justin Case. She didn't have much sense of humor either, and she was too dignified to pull it off, something she had inherited from her parents.

So "cool" was a refreshing response, so to speak. I liked this woman, especially out of uniform, again so to speak.

Eventually we got around to talking about what I was most interested in. By that time, she was into her second glass of the Ripasso. She mentioned being involved in the investigation of a suspicious death. "Oh, you mean the woman who committed suicide?" I asked. But then she remembered her professional ethics and said she really shouldn't be talking about that case. I said that I was into my second glass of wine and probably wouldn't remember anything she told me. But she didn't budge, so I was a good sport and changed the subject. I'd have to hope I could find a way to get back to that one.

With the Friday night crowd waiting for tables we couldn't sit in the restaurant forever. We drank a couple of quick double espressos to counteract the wine before we left. After I paid for dinner, which I did over Terry's objections, I walked her to her car. "I hope... " I started to say, but she interrupted me. "I hope we can see each other again." I told her that was what I was going to say. She laughed and said she should learn to keep her mouth shut. Then I kissed her, and she didn't exactly do that. I told her I'd be working hard the next few days and going to Seattle the following weekend. She looked disappointed. "But I'm coming home Sunday afternoon. I could be back in time for dinner," I said. She offered to bring dinner to my place, saying that she owed me. I liked having her owe me—I wondered how much she thought she owed me.

Driving home, still enjoying the smell of her subtle floral perfume, I was grateful for the prospect of seeing Terry McConnell again. Of course, it gave me another opportunity to get the information I wanted about what the police thought they had on Merritt. But it was more than that, I liked her. She was an attractive, intelligent woman who clearly liked being with me. And I didn't think she had any ulterior motive. Liking her just served to make me feel guilty, since I did have an ulterior motive. But I liked Merritt, too—in a different way, of course—which was why I was involved with Terry in the first place. I hoped I wasn't about to shoot myself in the foot.

I hadn't dated anyone in a while, and the evening had been very pleasant. Terry was a little on the young side, but not so much younger than I was that it was creepy or anything. I sensed she might be looking for a romantic diversion, if not a relationship. Periodically, I thought about a relationship. Back in Seattle I'd hung out with women friends (yes, sometimes with benefits) and done a little on-line dating, but nothing that led to anything. After a failed marriage that had lacked chemistry (whatever that might be), I was looking for something pretty special. Was there any chance that Terry was it? I didn't know, but I was looking forward to investigating the possibility. If I really liked her, I wouldn't want her to think I'd been using her—even if I had been. And if this was just a short-term diversion, that was okay, too.

I enjoyed the weekend in Seattle, especially spending a little time with Jen, but I was surprised at how eager I was to get back to Gearhart. I wouldn't say I'd come to think of it as home, but I was definitely finding my life there more interesting than I'd anticipated. As I was driving back on Sunday afternoon I found myself looking forward to my evening with Terry. It occurred to me that I should have washed my sheets, although that idea seemed a little presumptuous. But I'd probably make it home a couple of hours before she showed up with dinner, so maybe there was still time. If not, there was always the guest bedroom with its double bed that always had clean sheets—since I was being presumptuous.

It turned out there was plenty of time, as Terry was late getting there. She sent a text to let me know she was waiting on the pizza. She showed up a half-hour later—just as I was finishing making the bed—with the pizza, stuff to make a salad, and two bottles of red wine. She also had a rather large carry-all bag that could have been a purse—or could have been an overnight bag. While she went to the kitchen, I took a tiny hopeful peek inside the bag, which in fairness was open at the top, and saw a wisp of something that could be sexy nightwear. Lucky, lucky me. But then of course I immediately felt guilty. Oh well—I guessed I'd just have to get used to living with guilt.

Terry was appropriately impressed with where I lived, and I promised we could go for a walk on the beach after we ate. We started on the first bottle of wine while she made the salad and warmed the pizza. We made small talk, mostly about what we'd done over the weekend. I wanted to find a way to ask about the RaeAnne case, but then I thought I should wait a while for that—let the wine do its job. I thought about taking a head-on approach, telling her that Merritt was a friend and that he had talked to me about his concerns. I was planning to play it by ear, take that tack if there was no other way onto the subject. And maybe, if I was honest about my friendship with Merritt, there was really no conflict of interest. Not that I'm such a stickler—but life is less complicated if you don't have to remember which version of the truth you've told to whom. Turned out it wasn't necessary.

She brought up the RaeAnne case into her second glass of

wine. She'd had a shitty week at work. She was helping Gellerman with the case of the woman who had committed suicide in Del Rey State Park. Except that they were thinking it was homicide, not suicide. Sometimes it felt like they were in over their heads. It probably should be investigated at a higher level, considering their lack of experience with homicide cases. Gellerman wanted to call in the "Staties," but the chief was adamant about keeping it local. They were getting nowhere fast. She knew she shouldn't be talking to me about it—it was a breach of ethics—but she didn't have anyone else to talk to who would understand. I said I would respect her confidence. She told me that O'Donahue had done a background check on me when I'd first arrived in Gearhart so she figured I was okay. Nice to know I had passed muster, but I was awash in guilt about not being honest with her.

"Is there anything I can do to help?" I asked. "People tell me I'm a good listener."

"I guess considering what I've told you already it doesn't make any difference if I tell you the whole thing," she said. "I told you Bruce and I have different styles... It's never really been a problem until now. This case is complicated and important, and the chief is all over us about getting it wrapped up ASAP so he won't look like a screw-up."

"I'm not asking you to do anything unethical. But if you're going to tell me about it—and maybe I can be helpful if you do—why don't you start at the beginning. How did you, how did the police, discover that the woman's death wasn't suicide? What was the evidence?"

She said that the pill bottle they found in RaeAnne's car had no fingerprints on it, not RaeAnne's or anyone else's. So, with that little mystery they had a suspicious death, which led to an autopsy that showed that there were no opiates in RaeAnne's system. In fact, there was no apparent cause of death. Terry was giving me a meaningful quizzical look—I assumed asking if I knew what that meant. I don't have experience working with homicide, but I do watch a lot of murder shows on TV. I said that it was possible the lovely RaeAnne had been poisoned with a substance that disappeared from her system within a few hours—arsenic being the most probable candidate. She smiled, "Bingo! That's our theory." I asked if they had any idea who might have done it. She said they had a person of interest, but that they were unable to find any hard evidence linking that person to RaeAnne's death, so they hadn't been able to make an arrest. I asked who the person was. I could tell this might be a bridge too far, ethically speaking. But, in for a penny, in for a pound—she took a deep breath and plowed ahead. And (surprise, surprise, surprise) she told me it was one of RaeAnne's co-workers at Pacific Behavioral Health, a man named Merritt Grace.

"Merritt Grace?" I faked surprise.

She asked if I knew him, and when I said yes, she asked how and how well. I told her I had met him in a little group that hung out in the Pub & Grub, that we had learned that we were both from Seattle, and that we had had coffee a couple of times. I said I hadn't known him long, but that I would be very surprised if he was their killer.

"You know he's a priest?" I asked her.

She said she didn't know where I'd gotten that information, that he was an addictions counselor. I didn't enlighten her further. She went on to say that they had questioned him twice—three times if you counted the time they questioned everyone who worked with RaeAnne—but there simply wasn't enough to arrest him. He had a possible motive and no alibi, but that was too weak. She and Gellerman were under a fair amount of pressure from their boss to "get the goods" on Grace and make an arrest. I asked why that was and she said that O'Donahue was running for political office and wanted to look good.

Terry and Gellerman disagreed about whether or not Merritt might be the killer. Gellerman was perfectly willing to agree with Chief O that Grace was guilty. "Detective myopia," I said. She asked if that was actually a thing—she hadn't heard of it. I told her that it's a syndrome that occurs in important criminal cases with lots of pressure to solve in which law enforcement officers lose their objectivity, focusing on one person of interest to the exclusion of others.

"I don't know that there are any other persons of interest," she said. 'Hmm," I said, trying to look thoughtful. "You haven't discovered anyone else who might have had a reason to want her dead?"

She frowned. "Are you defending Grace? I thought you didn't know him that well."

"Just well enough to not see him as a killer."

"Chief O and Bruce both think he did it."

"What do you think?" I asked.

"I don't know. Your opinion of him makes me think we need to look a little further."

"My opinion and the lack of sufficient evidence against him."

"Right. Well, thanks for listening. And I'm really hoping you won't tell Merritt Grace what I've just told you. I know he's your friend, but I'm your friend, too—and I'd really like to keep my job here until I find another one. I hope he's innocent, and I hope there's a way to prove it." And with that, we went on to talk about other things.

After dinner we took our walk on the beach and then came in to finish off the wine and "maybe watch a little Schitt's Creek on Netflix." I was fiddling with the remote when Terry walked out of the bathroom wearing what I'd seen in her bag—a little black lace teddy that was oh so much better than a police uniform. I just let the TV run, silently thanked the laundry gods for the clean sheets, and led her back to the bedroom where the view of the sunset over the beach was even better than from the living room—not that anybody noticed.

The next morning Terry left early for work, after giving me a lingering kiss, patting my cheek, and reminding me that anything personal between us should be strictly confidential. I made the sign of zipping my just-kissed lips. After she left I gave myself a couple of minutes to reflect on the previous evening before I had my run and got to work. This was going in a direction I hadn't anticipated, and once again I was hoping I hadn't shot myself in the foot. Oh well—shooting myself in the foot had never felt so good.

Thanks to my new friendships with Merritt and Terry the shape of my work had changed. I'd need to have a conversation soon with Merritt to catch him up on this new development and see if there was anything additional he could tell me. I expected him to be both worried and relieved; I felt a little like I was betraying him. I had his permission to share with Terry the things he'd shared with me in confidence, although sharing those things with the police probably wouldn't be to his benefit.

With all this Merritt-focused activity I wondered if there would be time to get my paying work done. I'd probably want to have another conversation with Charlie, too, to catch him up on my progress—at least the part that wasn't x-rated.

I started by texting Merritt to see if he could meet me for coffee after work. He texted back that it was his turn to cook dinner at his house, so he had to be home early. Maybe the next morning before work? It would have to be early, 7:30-ish. He suggested we meet at a little restaurant not too far from where he lived, since he didn't have to worry about getting to work. Charlie wasn't picking up so I left a quick voicemail and got on with what my clients were paying me to do.

* * *

The next morning Merritt was having coffee and a pastry when I got to the restaurant. I ordered coffee and caught him up on everything that had happened since the last time I'd seen him—including my conversations with Terry. He raised his eyebrows at that last part.

"Aha, sleeping with the enemy," he said. I'd intentionally left that part out, so I wondered how he knew. I stammered something, probably unintelligible, and he laughed. "Sorry, that was just an expression; I didn't mean it literally." But I knew I was blushing and that I'd been caught. "Hey, man, it's none of my business," he said, holding up his hands. "But I'm extremely grateful you're willing to sacrifice your virtue for my sake." He laughed at his own little joke. I wanted to be jovial, too, but I knew I was still blushing. He punched me in the shoulder and said, "Just say two novenas and go and sin no more—or go and sin all you want." He was definitely enjoying my discomfort a little too much for a priest.

He moved on to ask if I was still committed to helping him. I said yes, that was the reason I was getting involved with Officer McConnell. I had already told her that I knew him well enough to doubt seriously that he could be their killer. Neither Bruce Gellerman nor Terry was a seasoned homicide detective. Not that homicide was my field either, but maybe I could help direct the police investigation toward other possible leads. When Merritt and I parted company I promised to keep him up to date on my progress. And I only felt a little guilty about betraying Terry's confidence.

* * *

On my way back home, I took a little detour and drove to the Del Rey State Park parking lot where the homicide had taken

200

place. There was no yellow crime tape so I didn't know where RaeAnne had been parked when she died. Maybe that wasn't relevant. I sat in the parking lot for a few minutes with the window down, listening to the ocean. Probably one of the last sounds RaeAnne heard before she died. And, I assumed, the voice of her killer. Had the killer actually been there? I wondered. It was still possible to think that RaeAnne might have committed suicide by taking arsenic. But from my research I knew that was a painful way to die and I doubted that was what anyone would choose.

And the mysterious pill bottle on the car floor, with no fingerprints, suggested that someone wanted it to look like suicide when it wasn't. The killer could have given her the bottle with arsenic earlier, telling her it was something else— and then she took it while she was by herself in the car. But the no fingerprints meant she hadn't touched the bottle and that whoever had touched it last must have wiped it clean. It was pretty clear that the killer had been there. I pulled out my phone and recorded these thoughts so I wouldn't forget them. Then I took off for home, to have a run on the beach and then smoke out some fraudsters.

That afternoon, just for the hell of it, I started a little file of information on the RaeAnne MacArthur case so I'd have everything I knew about her life and death and the investigation in one handy electronic place. It's the way I generally approach my "real work" cases and, against Charlie's advice, I'd definitely fallen into the trap of feeling like this case was mine to work on.

I wrote up everything in my notes and memory about the case in an orderly fashion and summarized it with a list of bullet points in chronological order with dates, where I had them. That would provide me with a nice summary whenever my memory needed refreshing. I included details about everything I thought could be relevant, including the discovery of RaeAnne's body, response and crime scene investigation by the police and coroner, results of crime scene investigation/fingerprinting, assumption of suicide to suspicion of murder, what I'd learned from Merritt about Gellerman and McConnell's interviews with PBH execs and staff, G and M's second and third interviews with Merritt, and Merritt's account of the blackmail letter from RaeAnne to Sandaas. Funny, Terry hadn't mentioned the blackmail letter. Probably because it tended to incriminate Sandaas.

I thought I'd captured pretty much everything I knew about the police investigation into the death of RaeAnne MacArthur. Information that had come from the local newspaper, from Merritt Grace, and from Officer Terry McConnell. I read it over several times, hoping to get some new insight into who might have wanted RaeAnne dead and why. I didn't get any new insight but I had lots of thoughts and a few questions:

I could see why Merritt's relationship with RaeAnne raised a red flag with the police. Two co-workers had voluntarily reported overhearing them exchanging angry words, one of those describing the exchange as Merritt making a threat against RaeAnne. When Gellerman asked Merritt about the co-workers' comments without indicating who those were, Merritt had reportedly seemed annoyed that anyone had overheard, let alone reported, the arguments between himself and RaeAnne. He assured officers that none of the discussions had been violent or that he had ever threatened RaeAnne. Maybe he had sounded defensive. When they quoted an unnamed person as having heard him say, "If you go ahead with that I can promise you that something bad will happen to you," he replied that he was simply stating what he thought might happen, not threatening her. That made perfect sense to me, but I could understand why someone might take it as a threat—especially if they had some bias against Black people.

I asked myself why I felt comfortable believing Merritt was

innocent of RaeAnne's murder, believing his account of things. Was it just because I liked him, because we'd shared details about our personal lives with each other? No, there was more to it than that. First of all, I believed he had really cared about RaeAnne, had considered her a friend. And he just didn't seem to me like a man who could kill someone. And finally, his account of finding the letter had been consistent from telling to telling—generally a mark of the truth.

Who else might be a possible person of interest? If I could believe Merritt about the blackmail letter, and I thought I could, that would make Erik Sandaas and Marjorie Dawson bigtime persons of interest in my book. Terry had told me that there were no other persons of interest. So I gathered that if Sandaas and Dawson had been questioned and had both denied Merritt's allegations, there had been no further investigation into their activities or any examination of the organization's files that might have borne out Merritt's accusations. Both executives were highly respected members of the community and Sandaas was a close friend of Chief O'Donohue, all logical reasons why the officers might assume that Grace had concocted the story to protect himself.

So, assuming there was a letter, what could have happened to it? Anyone, including RaeAnne herself, could have removed it or destroyed it. I wondered if RaeAnne had actually sent it to Sandaas.

And finally, I wondered about the investigation itself. A homicide investigation is somewhat beyond the experience of the average cop in a small, quiet town like Gearhart, Oregon. Gellerman had assumed that O'Donohue would call in another agency to handle the case but, for whatever reason, the chief was determined that their little department would handle it themselves. However, with his political aspirations and campaign efforts pending, he was pressuring Gellerman and Terry to get the case solved right away. He'd assigned

Gellerman to be in charge with Terry assisting as needed and with strict orders that they keep him apprised of any developments on a daily basis. Were Gellerman and Terry in over their heads? From what Terry had told me, if the investigation didn't go well they'd get the blame—and if it did go well O'Donohue would take the credit. But apparently, they were under the gun to come up with a suspect and I was afraid that didn't bode well for Merritt.

CHAPTER 19: MERRITT
Good News
from Unexpected Places

October

I just knew in my bones that Sandaas was the killer. The blackmail letter. Doing his best to frame me. If he wasn't the killer there'd be no need to convince the police that I was. Not even his hating Blacks would take him down that road. No, I was convinced it was him. But how to prove it. I decided to ask Cindy Appelbaum to meet me for coffee. I'd liked and trusted her as my supervisor and she always had her ear to the ground at PBH. She might have some clues.

That Saturday morning we met at the Daily Grind. We met in Gearhart because I didn't want anyone from PBH to know we were talking. After getting our coffee – vanilla latte for her, mocha for me, and a couple of pastries to share, we settled into a corner booth.

"Merritt, it's good to see you." The worried frown on Cindy's face spoke volumes. "How've you been?"

"Well, I guess I'm OK. As much as can be expected under the circumstances. I've never been a murder suspect before."

"Do you really think you're a suspect? I know about the rumors and all, but... "

"Cindy. Here's a little *Racism 101* lesson. It's hard to be the only Black ex-con in town without being a suspect. The truth be damned."

Cindy looked stricken. "My God... Merritt... I don't know what to say. How can I help?"

"Thanks Cindy. I very much hope you can help. And thanks for coming all the way here to meet me. On a Saturday morning no less."

"I've been so worried about you ever since you quit. And

when you called you sounded so scared. I'm happy to do whatever I can. But, by the way, I didn't have to come very far to meet you here. I live two blocks away. I just work in Seaside."

"You do? I'm only a few blocks away, too!" At that we both laughed so hard that people began to stare at us. It felt liberating, even as that powerful release communicated just how anxious we both really were. "Yeah. I live on Railroad Avenue, on the other side of the tracks."

"All this time we could have commuted together. But anyway... "

"Yeah, anyway... So, here's the thing. I keep thinking that Sandaas may have been the one who killed RaeAnne."

"What? Sandaas? Are you sure? Why do you think that?"

"Of course I'm not sure. It's just a hunch. But somebody did it. And it wasn't me. And if I'm to ever get off this goddamn hook they've got to find the real killer. Right now they think it's me. They stopped looking. Case closed."

"Wow, Merritt. I don't know. Sandaas? A murderer? No, I don't think so. Well, maybe... There has been some weird stuff going on... "

"Oh, yeah?"

"Well, not about Sandaas as the murderer. But he *has* been placed on administrative leave."

"No shit! Since when? What for?"

"I don't know any details. The top guns have been pretty hush hush. From the little I can gather, I think it has something to do with fraud. Or at least the suspicion of fraud."

"Fraud? When did this happen?"

"Right after you quit. I can't see what one has to do with the other."

"Maybe it does. I might know something."

"Please tell me you're not in this with Sandaas."

"God no. That slime bag? No fuckin' way. But listen to this.

I happen to know that RaeAnne was blackmailing Sandaas."

"RaeAnne? Blackmailing Sandaas? So she wouldn't tell anyone that he was schtupping her?"

"What? RaeAnne and Sandaas? Oh my God! Are you sure?"

"That's the rumor. Who knows?"

"Yeah, well, you never know about that asshole. But no. I don't know anything about any schtupping. Yikes. Actually, the blackmail was about something else.

"What else?"

"Well, I happened to see a letter RaeAnne wrote to Sandaas. I have no idea if she ever mailed it. But anyway... she was accusing him of fraud. Overbilling Medicaid and Medicare. Overprescribing opiates. Said she'd turn him in if he didn't cut her in on the profits."

"Well that could explain... "

"Come to think of it, that letter could also confirm the RaeAnne/Sandaas rumor. She called him Erik, which I thought was strange. Said she hoped that this wouldn't change things. I couldn't figure that one out. But now things seem to be falling into place."

"I need a little more here. You saw a blackmail letter. Sandaas is on administrative leave. You think he may have killed RaeAnne. Help me connect the dots."

"Well of course I don't know anything for sure but... I told the police about the blackmail letter the first time I met with them. They didn't seem particularly interested and the next week they said the files didn't support what RaeAnne said. So I assumed RaeAnne never sent the letter, or was fantasizing, or... God knows what."

"That's interesting. Just before Sandaas was placed on leave a bunch of people were at PBH reviewing files. That's not that unusual, and I didn't think anything of it. But who knows? Maybe they were looking for evidence of fraud."

"So... "

"Just guessing here, but maybe the police wanted to check out the blackmail story you gave them. God knows why they told you nothing panned out. Maybe they were already thinking of you as RaeAnne's killer and didn't want to tell you anything."

"Welcome to my world."

"Anyway, continuing with this theory, the police talked with Sandaas, who denied everything, and then, for whatever reason, the police also talked with the board. Maybe they thought Sandaas sounded suspicious. Maybe just covering their bases. Anyway, maybe the board decided things were serious enough to request an audit. And now Sandaas is on leave. Suggesting guilty as charged. Well, innocent until proven guilty I guess."

"Guilty of fraud. That's a pretty big deal. Not as big as murder. I wonder... would RaeAnne's letter blowing the whistle on the fraud be enough motive for Sandaas to kill her?"

"That's something for the police to look into I guess. If they do."

"Right. If they do. You have no idea how vulnerable I feel, Cindy."

"You're really scared, aren't you?"

"With good reason. Get this, I've been doing some reading. Innocent Black people are seven times more likely to be convicted of murder than innocent white people. Seven times!"

"Oh my God!"

"It gets worse. The race of the victim enters in. Innocent Black people are more likely to be convicted of murder if the murder victim is white. White. Like RaeAnne."

"Merritt. No wonder... "

"And here's the icing on the cake. The odds of being sentenced to death for murder are four times higher if the defendant is Black. The death sentence."

"My God Merritt. Should you get a lawyer?"

"I don't know. I'm not sure of anything right now. I've got a PI friend who's helping me look into things. He studied law. Maybe that's enough for now."

"When you mentioned the death sentence... my hair stood on end. Isn't the death sentence illegal now?"

"In some states, yes. Not here in Oregon. Still legal here in the good ole Beaver State."

We both took a minute to let that sink in.

"So, yeah, Cindy. That's why I'm desperate to find the real killer. Whether it's Sandaas or somebody else."

"Do you trust the police to keep investigating?"

"I'm not sure who to trust anymore. I know when all is said and done, it's up to the police. But right now I feel like I'm walking around with a target on my back. Anything I can do to point the police in the right direction... ""

"I can see how you suspect Sandaas. The blackmail letter, the affair. He could easily get RaeAnne to meet him out in the Del Rey parking lot. I wonder if that's where they regularly met. Oh God, I don't even want to think about it."

"Yeah. Well, it's a theory. One I sure hope the police explore. Meanwhile, I can't just sit still. I'll talk with Justin Case, my PI friend. He's keeping his ears to the ground and he's friends with one of the Gearhart cops, Terry McConnell. Maybe that'll be of some help. Who knows? I'm open to help wherever I can find it."

"Meanwhile you're still out of a job. You could probably come back to PBH, you know, with Sandaas gone. I hope you know just how much I value you and your work."

"Thanks Cindy, but no. That place has been poisoned for me—no pun intended. Besides, I can't really think about working anywhere right now. I need to do whatever I can to clear my name."

"I get it, but when you're ready you can always count on me for an excellent reference. Maybe I should be looking for something else, too. But with Sandaas gone... I don't know. Maybe. As you know, he didn't make PBH an easy place to work."

"Yeah, I never did like that man. And he never liked me. I'm not sure he liked anyone who isn't rich, white, and male. President of the Good Old Boy's Club. Just thinking about him and RaeAnne... "

"Asshole clearly took advantage of her. She was so vulnerable."

"She was easy prey. So pretty, but she was lonely. She wanted our relationship to be more than it was. In some ways I wish it could have been, but no... no. That wasn't possible. I'm wracking my brain. If Sandaas isn't the killer, who is? Who else would have had a motive? Everything I know about the case seems to point to him."

"Well, see what you come up with. You and your friend Justin Case. Is that really his name? Anyway, be sure to involve the police. This is their job."

"I know, I know, I just wish I trusted them. I just keep thinking I'm a dead man walking if I can't find the killer."

"To say 'don't worry' feels pretty empty. But do your best. Hopefully you and your PI friend can turn up some new evidence. And now, I really need to go. It's been so good to see you, Merritt. Keep me posted. Let me know if I can do anything more."

"I will. And you let me know if you learn any more about Sandaas."

"You got it. Bye now. I'm off to walk my two blocks home."

And with that we laughed, hugged one another goodbye, and went our separate ways.

Late the next morning, sitting in the kitchen with my second cup of coffee and staring out at the trees, I heard my phone ring. At first I didn't reach for it—I just wanted to think about things and not talk with anyone—but on the fifth ring, before the voicemail could kick in, I finally answered.

"Hi. Is this Merritt?"

"Yes, who's this?" I brusquely asked.

"It's Peggy Fairchild. From Awakenings."

"Oh, hi Peggy. Sorry to be so rude." I was actually happy to hear her voice. "I've just been thinking about so many things —RaeAnne's murder, my future, a lot of things I guess. But now—to what do I owe the pleasure of hearing from you?"

"I'm calling you about RaeAnne. She named me as the executrix of her will. I knew that but I never thought I'd be pressed into duty quite so quickly. Anyway Merritt, it turns out you are the sole heir to her estate. I guess she didn't have any family and you were her only sober friend. I'm not sure what all is included. Her car, her belongings, her bank account, if she had one."

"My God, Peggy, that's all I need. Me? Sole heir to everything RaeAnne owned? Why me? Why now? What else? The police will pounce on this as my motive to murder RaeAnne. Is this public information?"

"No. Because the value of RaeAnne's assets is relatively low, probate can be avoided and this can all be handled privately."

"What about the police? Can they learn I'm RaeAnne's sole heir?"

"No, not as long as the settlement is private. If it goes to probate all bets are off. But in RaeAnne's case no, the police should not have any way to get this information."

"God I hope not. I'm already their prime suspect. Or at least I think so."

"Well, your information is safe with me. I'd be careful about how many people you tell."

"Right. No need to worry about that, for sure! So now what?"

"Well, most immediately, you need to clear out RaeAnne's apartment. Her rent is up at the end of the month, so it needs to be done by then. If you stop by Awakenings I can give you a copy of the will, the keys to her apartment, and her bank account information. I'm sorry to dump this on you right now. I know you've got other big fish to fry."

"Well, you never know. Maybe there will be something in her belongings that gives me a clue. Although I'm sure the cops have already taken away any items of interest. I'll see if a friend can give me a hand with her stuff." After we agreed on a time I could pick up RaeAnne's things I ended the call. My God! What next?

Closing in on the SOB

October

A few days after I last saw Merritt, I was on hold, as was frequently the case, with either the credit card company or the IRS, deeply engrossed in the work of keeping everyone safe from dreaded insurance fraud, when my phone signaled the arrival of a text message. In the interest of staying awake, I checked it out and saw it was a cryptic message from Merritt: "S is gone." I had no idea what that meant. I texted back, "Sorry, don't understand. Who is S?" The reply was "ES." "I texted again, "Who?" and got "Dr. ES." Ah, Dr. Erik Sandaas (or the Viking, as I'd come to think of him). My curiosity was over the top, of course. Had he run away to Brazil? Died? What did "gone" mean? I figured Merritt was being careful about what he put in writing so I waited until after I got through to whoever it was, got my information, and then called him.

"Fired" was what Merritt said at first, although it turned out that the Viking was actually on administrative leave, an action taken by the PBH Board of Directors. Apparently the rumor that he and Marjorie Dawson were cooking the books had gotten out at PBH. That wasn't surprising, since the police may have questioned others on the staff about the accounting. It hadn't taken long for the word to spread and then the rumor to become the number one topic of conversation at the water cooler and anywhere staff gathered for informal talk. So naturally it had gotten back to the organization's board members, or at least one powerful member, and the board had ordered an official forensic audit—ostensibly for the purpose of clearing their Medical Director and CFO of any taint of wrongdoing. And in the meantime, they were on administrative leave. So not exactly "fired."

"How'd you find this out?" I asked Merritt. He told me he and Cindy, his former boss, had met for coffee at the Daily Grind. He seemed pleased that she'd told him how much she'd appreciated his work and how sorry she was that things had turned out the way they had, even told him she'd hire him back if Sandaas didn't return.

The forensic auditor must have worked fast. It was only the day after our phone conversation when I got the next text from Merritt—"I assume you've heard about S."

I hadn't, but at least this time I knew who "S" was. "No," I texted back, and this time, he called me.

"I thought maybe your lady friend told you," he started off. I told him I hadn't seen Terry for a couple of days, since she'd had the evening shift at work, but I'd be seeing her that night. "Now he's been fired and arrested," he said.

Holy shit! "Arrested for killing RaeAnne?" I asked. No, unfortunately just for the various kinds of fraud. He'd been charged with those but was out on bail walking around. Still, it seemed like a step forward. I'd become somewhat personally invested in pursuing him as the guilty party—and not just because it got Merritt off the hook. I also wanted to help Terry tie up the case—there was that. And I have to admit that I'd come to want justice for RaeAnne. The Viking was a nasty piece of work—an arrogant son of a bitch who took advantage of women in his employ, who promoted addiction when he was supposed to be preventing it, who operated out of a sense of greed rather than a desire to help people. I was glad to hear he'd begun to get what he had coming. But if he was the person who had killed RaeAnne, and I'd become pretty certain he was, I wasn't through with him yet.

* * *

Terry was not as convinced as I was that Erik Sandaas had

killed RaeAnne. Even though there was evidence now that he was guilty of fraud, they had only Merritt's word that she was attempting to blackmail him. And he was missing an alibi for the night she was killed. She and I talked about it over burgers and brews at a tavern in Cannon Beach. His alibi was watertight as far as Gellerman was concerned, and it wouldn't be easy to argue otherwise, since his alibi was Chief O'Donohue himself. I wasn't so sure that was as watertight as they thought, but I didn't have any real reason to think that—just that I thought the chief was a smarmy bastard and that conversation I'd overheard at the fundraiser. Terry said that on the night of RaeAnne's death there had been a campaign meeting at O'Donohue's place, which Sandaas had attended. It had broken up early, way before ten-thirty, the estimated time of RaeAnne's death, but Sandaas said—and the chief had confirmed it—that he and several others had stayed for a couple more hours to watch a game the chief had DVD'd. He'd gone home immediately after, leaving about eleven o'clock, and Mrs. Sandaas indicated that he'd arrived home about eleven-fifteen.

When I said I thought it was just a little too handy that O'Donohue was Sandaas's alibi, Terry asked me why. I said I guessed I just didn't like him, that I was sorry she had to work for such a creepy bastard. She said that he certainly had his faults, but that he wasn't all bad, that he obviously had a good heart.

While we were talking I saw Maddie Jacobs and her sister sitting at a table across the room. I excused myself to go to the gents' and stopped to say "hi" on the way. "Who's your lady friend?" Maddie asked. "I didn't know you were seeing anyone." I thought she looked disappointed. I told her I'd met Terry through work—I had no idea why I said that. Of course when I got back to the table Terry asked me the same question. And I gave her the same answer. What was wrong with me? Was I hedging my bets?

When Terry and I got back to our conversation, I asked why she'd said the chief had a good heart, and she told me a young man had come into the police station a few weeks back looking for the chief. Said the chief and his ex-wife, before their divorce, had been his foster parents. That he was just passing through the area and wanted to pay his respects. He left his name and contact info, which she had passed along to the chief.

Foster parents. O'Donohue sure didn't seem like the fatherly type to me, but maybe the former Mrs. O'Donohue had been the maternal type. Or maybe they weren't actual foster parents—maybe he'd just crashed on their couch for a while. I stuck that little factoid away in my mental file of interesting information. Lately I seemed to be gathering lots of potentially useful, or useless, information in that file.

As we were leaving the tavern we passed Gellerman and his wife at a table near the front. He seemed surprised to see us together and Terry was clearly uncomfortable with the situation. After the requisite introductions, we left quickly. On the way to the car, I asked her if she was embarrassed to be seen with me. She said it was just that she had told Gellerman that Merritt and I were friends and she didn't want him to think she might be telling tales out of school. Gellerman was a stickler for avoiding conflict of interest. She had the right to do what she wanted in her private life of course, but she was probably feeling guilty about how much we'd talked about the case. Small towns—you can't go anywhere without running into people you know!

On the way home I asked if Merritt was still a suspect. "Person of interest," she said. "We don't have anyone else. Merritt's story about Sandaas blackmailing RaeAnne didn't pan out—and anyway Sandaas has a watertight alibi." O'Donohue was still pressing Gellerman to arrest Merritt in the hopes that once in custody he would incriminate himself. So far Gellerman was resisting. I asked why the chief was so sure that Merritt had killed RaeAnne. She said it was Merritt's previous prison term, the threats that co-workers had overheard—and probably the fact that he was Black. She squirmed a little when I asked if the chief was racially biased, but she had to admit that in a town with so little diversity that wasn't uncommon. Then she said that for what it was worth the chief had mentioned that Sandaas was strongly convinced Merritt was the killer. She didn't figure that would carry any weight with me—and she was right. That bastard Sandaas was going to get away with this, and he was getting the police chief to help him.

I'd grown pleasantly accustomed to having Terry come for dinner and then spend the night. At first it wasn't automatically understood, but after a week or so she began bringing an overnight bag that was obviously an overnight bag. Every few days she drew the evening shift at work, which gave us some space in our togetherness. One evening in October I used my time off to catch up with Merritt. I didn't want to go to the Pub & Grub where we would run into the happy hour group, so I picked him up and we drove to the closest McDonald's where there was no one we knew.

After we were seated I told Merritt about the recent conversations I'd had with Terry about the case. He was pretty quiet and I wondered if it concerned him that I was spending time with the "enemy." He hadn't had any more visits from the police, and he seemed relieved about that. After we ate I drove to the Del Rey State Park and parked in the parking lot where RaeAnne had died. We got out and walked around, braving the cold wind coming off the ocean. Being there prompted Merritt to talk about his friendship with RaeAnne and the hole her death left in his life. I hoped he could see me as a friend, someone he could trust, but I didn't know how to say that. So, I just listened.

* * *

Two days later, Merritt texted to let me know he had received a call from Peggy Fairchild at Awakenings telling him she was the executrix of RaeAnne's "estate" and that he was the sole heir to all her meager belongings. He asked if I would be willing to go with him to see the landlord and dispose of RaeAnne's stuff. Of course I was willing.

A New Episode of "Friends"

October

The next day, Saturday, I picked up Merritt at his house and we stopped for coffee and a pastry before heading off to RaeAnne's apartment in Seaside. He was armed with RaeAnne's keys, a copy of her will, and the landlord's phone number. He'd already called the landlord and told him we'd be over to empty out her apartment over the weekend. He said he thought the landlord sounded suspicious, probably because the landlord could tell by his voice that he was Black. I didn't tell him that he was one of the least Black-sounding Black people I knew. Mainly because I figured that was a racist comment, and also because I don't know many Black people that well.

I asked when he wanted to go to the bank. He thought maybe Monday, to get it over with. I told him he'd need a copy of the death certificate, so that might delay the bank visit a few days. I asked about RaeAnne's car and he said it was still impounded by the police. That made sense, of course, since her car was technically the crime scene—and I doubted they would hand over the crime scene to their number one person of interest, assuming he still was.

RaeAnne had lived in a studio apartment in a rundown two-story complex that included maybe a dozen apartments. I was glad to see she was on the ground floor, especially if we would be carrying out any furniture. We were hoping that wouldn't be necessary, as the landlord had said he could probably rent the apartment furnished to the next tenant if there was stuff Merritt didn't want. If necessary we'd have to rent a U-Haul, since most furniture would be too big to fit in my SUV, and that would cut into Merritt's grand inheritance.

I'd say RaeAnne was a minimalist, as the apartment was sparsely furnished, even for a studio. And what there was looked like it had come from Goodwill or the Salvation Army. She'd slept on a twin-size daybed that doubled as a sofa. There was a small coffee table that must have been where she had her meals, and another small table that held a newish, generous-sized flat-screen TV. I guess we all have our priorities. There was no dresser; all her clothes were in the small closet—even her underwear and other folding stuff in a basket on the floor.

The kitchen cabinets held the kind of stuff you'd expect—a few mismatched dishes and glasses, some odd cookware, and a few cans and packages of non-perishable food. The refrigerator was empty, so I guessed the landlord had thrown out the perishable stuff before it could turn green—or maybe she had lived on canned soup.

It was a larger kitchen than you'd expect in a studio and she'd found room for a desk against the only blank wall— probably where most people would have put a table and a couple of chairs. It wasn't a bad-looking desk and it was big enough to be useful, with several drawers. I was just thinking that I wouldn't mind having it myself when Merritt said, "I can use that desk—that and the TV. I'll leave the other furniture if the landlord can use it, and take everything else to Goodwill." We agreed that we could get the desk and TV in my SUV with the back seat down, although we might have to haul the giveaway to Goodwill first.

While we were bagging up the things for Goodwill the landlord showed up. He seemed a little disappointed that we were taking the desk but agreed that we could leave the other furniture. He mentioned that the police had gone through the apartment a few days before. I'd been wondering if there would be anything among the papers in the desk drawers that would give us a clue to who RaeAnne's killer might be, but if there was, probably the police would have found it.

Terry had never mentioned to me their searching RaeAnne's apartment. But of course they would have, and I don't know why it hadn't occurred to me. I'd have to ask Terry if they'd removed anything from those desk drawers. By now I assumed I could trust her to tell me—although why she'd trust me I don't know.

After a quick trip to Goodwill to contribute RaeAnne's meager belongings, Merritt and I came back for the desk and TV. We'd taken everything out of the desk drawers and put it in a grocery bag. That and the other two items just about filled the back of my SUV. I admit to being somewhat spatially challenged and was happy to let Merritt figure out how the big pieces would fit—which he did easily.

The landlord was still there, so we handed him the key. "Hey, aren't you interested in getting the damage deposit back?" he asked. Neither Merritt nor I had thought to ask about a damage deposit. "Oh yeah," Merritt said. "Will you be sending that? If so, you'll need my address." The landlord—I think his name was Bryce something—said there was no need to wait. RaeAnne had paid five hundred dollars—which I thought was a lot for that place—and there was no damage—so he could give Merritt a check on the spot. When he went to get the check, I said to Merritt that he must be the last honest landlord on earth—to which he replied that I should learn to see the good in other people. I guess sniffing out fraud tends to make one negative about humanity.

We drove back to Merritt's place he studyied the check, as if he couldn't believe it was real. "Doesn't seem fair, does it?" he asked. "Me benefitting from her death like this." I reminded him that life isn't fair and that probably she would be happy to know he had the money. He said he would need that and more if he was going to keep her old car running. He wanted to deposit the check ASAP, so we stopped by the bank and he used the cash machine for the deposit.

At Merritt's place I opened the hatch on the SUV and pulled out the desk. It hadn't occurred to us to do anything to secure the drawers, and, as luck would have it, one fell out onto my foot. "Son of a bitch!" I yelled, glad that I was wearing substantial shoes. Landing on my foot had protected that drawer from the concrete driveway, though, so maybe it was lucky. I picked it up to be sure it wasn't damaged. When I did, I scraped my finger on something on the back of the drawer. "Goddam it, this thing's a fucking minefield!" I yelled. I could see that Merritt was biting his lip to keep from laughing. He took the drawer from me and looked at the back of it. "Well fuck me," he said. He held the drawer up so I could see. Secured to the back of it with a piece of duct tape was a key.

We hauled Merritt's inheritance into the house. I grabbed a glass of water before we wrestled the desk and TV upstairs to his room. Merritt ran up to decide where to put the desk and came down laughing, saying he'd forgotten he didn't have a cable hookup up there. He'd either have to get the cable company to come out or just use streaming. Either way, having that TV was going to cost him. We pulled off the duct tape and got the key off the drawer. Of course, we had no idea what it unlocked, so it might not be of any value whatsoever—but it felt like an important find. Merritt asked if I'd be interested in going through the contents of the desk drawers. I was, but right then I wanted to take a nap. "How about this evening?" I asked. Terry, anticipating that I would be tired after my furniture moving gig, had agreed to watch a movie with one of her girlfriends. "Come for dinner," Merritt said. "I'm cooking tonight. This is a vegetarian household, but it's actually pretty good." Oh, shit, I thought. My foot's killing me and now I've got to eat a pound of soybeans. It's true that no good deed goes unpunished. "What kind of wine goes with tofu?" I asked on my way out.

Driving back to my place I thought about the key and what it might unlock. What if neither of us had wanted the desk? That key would still be sitting there—and maybe that wouldn't make any difference in the long run though. I also thought about my life in Gearhart, how it had evolved. There was a woman in my life, whose plans I considered when making my own plans. It had been a long time since I needed to consider someone else's needs or wants on a daily basis. It was inconvenient and at the same time it felt pretty damn good. I had the opportunity to be part of the coastal political and social scene, such as it was. I had people to eat dinner with—nice, interesting people. And I had something to investigate that was bigger and more interesting than insurance fraud. And then it occurred to me that there was some kind of incestuous web binding all these pieces together.

A few short hours later, I was back Chez Merritt with a bottle of red and a bottle of white. I presented these to Val at the door, saying that since I didn't know what went with soybeans I'd brought both, just in case. She and Liz were already drinking, so we opened the red. I really didn't need to be drinking that much. At least I wasn't drinking alone.

Merritt was presiding over the stove, wearing an apron that read "Never Trust a Skinny Cook." Ironic, since Merritt himself is not exactly corpulent. He was drinking seltzer and rolling his eyes at most of what we said. I wandered over and checked out a big plate of no-bake chocolate cookies, the kind with oatmeal and peanut butter like my grandmother used to make. "Don't even think about it," he said when I reached out my hand for a sample.

The dinner was surprisingly good. Plenty of herbs and spices and olive oil could turn beans and groats and vegetables into a tasty meal indeed. My fave was a dish made with farro, butternut squash, beets, and walnuts. Who knew? And afterwards, we were all rewarded for our virtuousness by as many of those cookies as we could eat.

I thought we'd get right to work on the contents of RaeAnne's desk, but as it turned out we didn't get to it at all that evening. "The girls," as Merritt called them, wanted to play cards, and since it was their house, what's a guy to do? We played Hearts, which I'm not sure I'd ever played before, but I caught on and won my share of games.

We did talk about the mysterious key, though, and what it might open. We took turns building ridiculous fantasies about it, which was fun but not too productive. Then Val asked Merritt when he'd be going to the bank to check on RaeAnne's account. I was just about to say that he couldn't do that until he got copies of the death certificate when Liz yelled out, "Bank—what about a safety deposit box? Could that be the key to a safety deposit box?"

We didn't know, but it didn't seem likely that RaeAnne was the safety deposit box type. Even so, it was at least a possibility. And if there was a box, who knew what interesting things might be in it? I reminded Merritt that he'd need to talk with Peggy on Monday about getting a copy of the death certificate. He reminded me that he still wanted me to go to the bank with him. I asked if he thought it would take both of us to carry all the money and treasure home.

"What Merritt doesn't want to say," Val said, "is that if he goes in there by himself, he's likely to scare the tellers half to death. Might not even get what he's entitled to. And—those bank security guards carry guns. Too much shit in the news not to be careful. Your white ass will reassure everybody."

"Jesus," I said, "I'll be sure not to wear a hoodie." She gave me a stern look.

"Okay, I guess you get it Snowflake," she said.

"Yeah, and there's a teller who's got the hots for me—although she's old enough to be my grandmother." That engendered a few tasteless comments and lots of laughing.

Wine and the right company will do that to you.

I drove home carefully, even though it wasn't very far, mindful of how much wine I'd drunk. I'd had fantasies about being arrested by "Officer" McConnell but she wasn't working this evening. I thought about the evening I'd just experienced. I actually couldn't remember when I'd had such a good time without having sex, when I'd laughed so hard or so much.

I'd never had a gay friend before. Oh sure, I knew lots of gay people—you couldn't live in Seattle without knowing gay people—but I'd never been close to any. I wasn't homophobic though, or didn't think I was. And I'd just spent an evening with three gay people as the only straight person in the room and I'd been perfectly comfortable.

I'd never had a Black friend either. Or any other friends of color for that matter. The racial thing caused me some discomfort I'll admit. A lot of the time I felt like I was walking on eggshells when I was around Merritt and Val, thinking I was going to say the wrong thing. But I was feeling less that way every time we were together, so I guess we were building trust—or at least I was. I was beginning to think that if I did say something offensive—some "micro-aggression" to use the word I'd learned from Merritt—he'd just slap me upside the head and we'd go on. As fuzzy as my head was, I knew my life was better for the new people in it. When I got home I texted Terry a couple of heart emojis and fell into bed with my clothes on without waiting for her to answer.

Chapter 22: Merritt
It Once Was Lost

October

With everything that was going on, I was feeling pretty disoriented and more than a little vulnerable. What if the police learned that I was RaeAnne's sole beneficiary? That alone was enough to make me a suspect. To say nothing of race. I was really grateful for Justin's support. With his white face and his natural charm he was an important ally. After I secured RaeAnne's death certificate I asked him to come to the bank with me. He was already pretty well known there and could vouch for me. I just didn't trust that all the certified documents on the planet would trump the bank's mistrust of my Black face.

At the bank a week later we waited in line a few minutes before we finally got to the window. The teller was young, with mouse brown hair and a pale complexion. Her name badge announced her as Trudy. She looked at me with suspicion and at Justin with curiosity. She seemed to be shocked into silence.

After what seemed like an eternity, with everyone behind us shifting to other lines, a grandmotherly teller in the booth next to Trudy looked over at us. "Well, look who's here. It's my boyfriend Henry. Trudy, you take good care of him." I glanced at Justin, who was grinning at the woman. Clearly, I'd made the right choice in asking him to join me. Trudy kind of jerked and asked Justin how she could help him. Justin explained what we needed.

After carefully reviewing RaeAnne's will and death certificate, Trudy trotted off to close RaeAnne's checking account and order a check in my name for the remainder of her assets. RaeAnne had never opened a savings account.

After Trudy returned with the check, I showed her the key

227

we'd found. Did this key, by any chance, go to one of the banks' safe deposit boxes? Examining it, Trudy thought that it might belong to one of the inexpensive boxes the bank offered as an incentive to new customers.

"Would you please see if RaeAnne had one of these safe deposit boxes?" It shouldn't have been necessary to ask. I did not give this woman an *A* for customer service.

Trudy squinted her distrust of me and glanced at Justin. "Please," Justin added, flashing one of his disarming smiles.

"All right." Once again, she trotted off. I couldn't help but think she wished she'd called in sick that day. After several minutes she returned. "Yes, Ms. MacArthur did rent one of our safe deposit boxes just a few weeks ago. That's strange, I wonder why she waited so long. She's been a customer here for nearly a year."

"Well, I don't know about that. And, if you don't mind, I'd like to look through that box."

"Of course."

"I think I'll let you take it from here, Buddy. I've got a million things to do this morning. Thanks for your help, Ma'am." And with that, Justin flashed another smile at his "girlfriend" and headed for the door.

Trudy's eyes followed Justin each step of the way. It was clear she did NOT want to be alone with me. But by that time she had no choice. Her eyes swept the bank, making sure others could come to her rescue if needed. She led me to a small alcove furnished with a chair and a tiny metal table. In a minute she returned with a small safe deposit box. "Here it is, take as long as you need."

I placed the box on the table and sat quietly for a minute, thinking about RaeAnne. Picturing her renting this box just a few weeks ago. Wondering what was going through her mind when she did. Why then? Feeling the import of being RaeAnne's sole heir. Mostly feeling incredibly sad, I guess. This was not going to be easy.

I carefully inserted the key into the lock and turned it. The lock released with a quiet click and the lid shifted slightly upwards. Taking a deep breath, I lifted the lid and peered inside. I didn't know what I expected. RaeAnne had nothing of financial value as far as I knew. Perhaps a few mementos. In fact, the only thing in the box was a large brown envelope. Looking around to be sure I was alone, then quietly saying a prayer for RaeAnne, I unsealed the envelope and withdrew three sheets of paper.

I immediately recognized the first one as the letter I'd found in RaeAnne's desk drawer—the blackmail letter she'd written to Erik Sandaas. A few telltale gray smudges left by a cheap copy machine let me know this was not the original. I could only assume RaeAnne had indeed sent the original to Sandaas. Gellerman told me they'd never found it, but evidently someone had turned the police on to the fact that Sandaas was involved with fraud. He wasn't on administrative leave for his health, that's for sure. Thinking about the rumor about Sandaas and RaeAnne, I looked again at the salutation. *Dear Erik.* Strange way to begin a blackmail letter. And then that curious comment at the end—*I hope this won't get in the way.* It sure looked like Sandaas and RaeAnne had had some kind of relationship. I didn't want to speculate about what it might have been, but I had the feeling I was holding onto an important piece of evidence against Sandaas. He obviously had a motive to keep RaeAnne quiet. My heart began to race.

A second letter, bearing smudges similar to the first, was also a copy. It was dated August 10, four days before RaeAnne was killed.

Daddio

I hope you know how much I love you. Which is why this letter is so hard to write. But I'm in a lot of trouble right now and I have no other choice.

Things could go very bad for you if I went public about everything. You don't want that and I don't want that. So here's the deal. You bring me $50,000 in cash and mums the word. No deal and I sing like a canary. Meet me at our regular spot next Tuesday, and all will be well.

I'm sorry. I do love you.

RaeAnne

My God. *Daddio?* Is that what she called Sandaas? I felt sick. Meet her at their regular spot—with the money. In a flash I saw Sandaas showing up at Del Rey and killing RaeAnne instead of buying her off. He clearly had the motive, the means, and the method.

The third sheet was really just a scrap of paper with a handwritten note. Written to RaeAnne. No date. It was pretty crumpled. I pictured RaeAnne holding it close, reading it over and over, maybe even sleeping with it.

My Dear Rae,

You are the sweetest. I love you so much. I can't wait until we can be together again. Forever. Until then, whenever you're lonely just think of me smothering you with kisses.

Your forever Daddy-O

What a slimeball. Just reading that note made me want to throw up. Daddy-O! Like some kind of father figure. Well, at least the handwriting could provide more evidence.

I carefully placed the letters back in the brown envelope, then sat quietly at the desk for several minutes. My mind was racing. This was all that was needed to convict Sandaas. These letters could get me off the hook! At the same time, I felt incredible pain for RaeAnne. She thought Sandaas had loved her. That they had a future together. What had it cost her emotionally to blackmail him? She must have been in very deep to resort to that. And why did she decide to open the safe deposit box? Did she have some kind of premonition of what was coming? She must have known she was playing with fire.

Once again, I felt guilty for not being a better friend to her. The contents of this envelope answered a lot of questions and stirred up a lot of emotions. It had been quite a morning. I carefully tucked the envelope into my backpack, returned the safe deposit box to Trudy, and left for home.

I called Justin to tell him what I'd found. He was too busy to talk, but he agreed to come to dinner that night. Liz was cooking, and that was always a guarantee of a great meal. Better yet, I couldn't wait to share this incriminating evidence with everyone. Sandaas was toast.

Were Blind, But Now We See

October

Justin showed up at six with a couple bottles of Willamette Valley Pinot Noir. I was learning that Oregon is famous for its Pinot Noir and I was beginning to wish I drank again. With dinner not until seven we had plenty of time to talk about the case. I opened one of the bottles, poured a large glass for Justin, and got myself a glass of seltzer.

Seated at the large dining room table with the dragon kite flying overhead, I showed Justin the contents of the envelope. He carefully examined each sheet. "OK—this one—this is the blackmail letter you saw in RaeAnne's desk?"

"Yes. Well, I'm not sure if I saw this copy or the original, but yes, that's the blackmail letter I was talking about."

"Hmm. And now Sandaas is on administrative leave. Sure makes you wonder if this letter had anything to do with that."

"Yeah. Gellerman told me they'd searched the files and found nothing. But who knows? Cindy thinks maybe the police did know about the fraud and just didn't want to tell me. For whatever reason. She's as much in the dark as I am. Can you get any intel on this from Terry?"

"I can't ask her any direct questions about the case. Anything she lets slip, I'm all ears. So, what else do you have?"

I handed him the letter addressed to Daddio, where RaeAnne instructed Sandaas to bring 50k to Del Rey.

"Hmm, Daddio. That's what she called him? That is so sick! I wonder what she had on him. Just the fraud? Something else? Not that that's not enough, but I like to look in every corner."

"I'm guessing she was planning to go public about their liaison. It can't look good for the married PBH Medical Director to be getting it on with one of the Second Chancers. Especially

233

if he's already on thin ice with the suspicion of fraud. Maybe he was worried that RaeAnne blowing the whistle would be the straw that broke the camel's back and he'd be fired."

"Yeah, maybe. That guy is so slick. You should have seen him and O'Donohue at that fund raiser. Prancing around like good ole' boys, talking shit about you. Two racist pigs. Why would RaeAnne lower herself to get it on with him?"

"Talking shit about me? I don't think you told me about that?"

"Well, I can't be sure they were talking about you, but let's face it. You're one of the few Black faces in Gearhart."

"I am so glad to be out of PBH. That asshole, what was RaeAnne thinking?"

"Who knows? Maybe she believed he'd divorce his wife and marry her. She was so needy for love. I hope she's in a better place now."

"Well, yeah I guess. So anyway—what's that third paper you've got?"

I handed him the handwritten note signed Daddy-O.

"Well this is really interesting," he said after carefully examining the note. "Looks like RaeAnne slept with this it's so rumpled. Or maybe she crumpled it up and threw it away and then retrieved it. Who knows? Whoever sent this note is the mysterious Daddio. Sandaas? Maybe. We can get the handwriting checked out. This note could help the police nab that asshole for once and for all."

"Well, I've got my money on Sandaas. But you're the expert. Let's see where this goes. And now let's interrupt this discussion and eat."

Justin and I quickly set the table while Liz put the finishing touches on dinner. Alfredo made with cashew cream, topped with sauteed mushrooms. I have to say, I was amazed by the variety of delicious vegetarian dishes that came out of our kitchen. Justin poured Pinot Noir for the three of them and we all dug into a sumptuous feast.

"Say Henry, what's happening in your neck of the woods?" Liz and Val both called Justin *Henry*. I guess he preferred it, but I enjoyed calling him *Justin* and he seemed OK with that, too.

"Well, the insurance fraud business is keeping me afloat, but I have to say, I'm really keen on seeing RaeAnne's killer put behind bars. And on getting our friend Merritt here out of the cross hairs."

"Any leads?"

"Well, Merritt just showed me the contents of RaeAnne's safe deposit box. Things sure seem to point to Sandaas as the killer. I want to check out a few things and then give our evidence to the police."

"You're still seeing Terry McConnell?" Liz always wanted to know about everyone's love life.

"As a matter of fact, yes. We see each other a lot. I don't know, it might even be getting a little serious. As terrifying as that sounds when I say it out loud. But—she's quite a woman. Cute as a button, smart as a whip, ambitious, and she seems to like me. Go figure."

"Sounds good to me." Val gave Justin a warm smile.

"Yep. It is good. We don't talk that much about the case, but she does share some tidbits of gossip that come her way. Which I always enjoy."

"Like what, for instance?"

"Well, a few days ago she came in with the news that O'Donohue had been a foster father. I guess interesting enough for her to mention to me because neither of us ever saw him as the parenting type. I don't think he ever had kids of his own and, with his marriage in the rear-view mirror, I don't know, he just seems like a self-serving prick to me."

"Yeah, well I guess maybe his running for the state senate is just the next step on his career ladder. Who knows?"

"Well he was definitely playing the role at that fund raiser Sandaas hosted for him at the Orca club. Walking around glad-handing everyone. I'm still not sure why he invited me to be there. But I was happy enough to be there. Get my name known around town a little bit."

"Yeah, a good opportunity, for sure."

For a few minutes everyone was quiet as we passed the Alfredo around for second helpings. It was so good.

"Say Merritt," Val broke the silence. "Didn't you tell me that RaeAnne had been in foster care?"

"Come to think of it, yeah, she was in foster care. Did I tell you about that? Her father abandoned her and her little brother when they were pretty young. And her mother was so deeply into drug addiction that she couldn't take care of them. She and Luther, I think that's her brother's name, got placed with the same family. But then, if I'm remembering correctly, that family adopted Luther and didn't adopt RaeAnne, forcing RaeAnne to leave. What a horrible thing to do to a young girl. No wonder she was so emotionally needy."

"What happened after she had to leave that family?"

"She got bounced around to a whole bunch of other families I guess. None of them really worked out. She had some traumatic experiences, including being sexually abused by the father in one family. After she got kicked out of the last home, I guess she was sixteen or so, she was sick of the whole drill. Goodbye foster care. She found her mom in the same drug house she'd been in for the past several years. She got hooked on meth, started turning tricks to support herself. The rest is history."

Liz was thoughtful. "My God, I remember now that you mentioned that a few months ago. You just gave us more details now than you did then. Keeping the confidence of the NA group, I guess. Not that it matters now."

Justin spoke up. "This is the first I've heard any of this story.

It fills some of the gaps in RaeAnne's history. No wonder she was so needy, so seductive with Sandaas. She was such easy prey."

"This makes me think. We were talking before about O'Donohue being a foster parent. Wondering how such an asshole could do that. From what Merritt just said, it's pretty clear that not all foster parents are as nurturing as they might be. Maybe that's why O'Donohue wound up divorced and on his own." This time it was Val speaking.

"I didn't remember that RaeAnne had a little brother. Has anyone let him know she was murdered? She apparently didn't have any relationship with him. She left all her assets to Merritt. But he should still know about his sister if we can find him." Liz looked at me. "Do you think you could locate him?"

"I don't know. But I agree, he should know about his sister if there's any way to find him."

"OK. Enough of the somber talk. Who's up for a game of Scrabble?" Liz wanted to lift the mood. She cleared away the dishes while I scooped out heaping bowls of ice cream. Val went for the Scrabble game and Justin poured more wine. The evening ended on a rollicking note with Justin winning two games in a row before he headed for home.

That night as I tried to get to sleep, I kept wondering—had we uncovered yet another important clue?

CHAPTER 24: HENRY
The Plot Stinkens

October

The next morning, after my run on the beach and bowl of Raisin Bran, I sat down with coffee and the file of evidence that Merritt had sent home with me. I looked at the handwritten note again. *Daddio*—I didn't picture Sandaas as a *Daddio*. But if he was, this could be a key piece of evidence. As soon as I could get a handwriting analysis, get this writing compared to whatever sample of Sandass's writing we could get, we'd have the son of a bitch. The thought made me breathe harder. I hoped it wouldn't take too long. Maybe Merritt's former boss Cindy could help us.

I put the letters back in the file. I'd think about RaeAnne's murderer later, after I'd spent a few good hours chasing down some insurance fraudsters for pay. My workload had nearly tripled since I'd been living in Gearhart. I owed that to clean living and lack of distractions I guess. Well, I did have a couple of distractions—Officer Terry and the whole Merritt/RaeAnne business. But all work and no play makes Henry a dull boy, as Maddie Jacobs had said. As usual, I digress.

There was something niggling at the back of my mind, trying to break through my consciousness, that was keeping me from focusing on my work. It wasn't until I closed my eyes for just a teensy little nap that two possibly related factoids came together in my brain... RaeAnne had been abused as a teenager in foster care. Chief O'Donohue and his wife had been foster parents. Coinkydink? Maybe and maybe not. I didn't think it would be too hard to find out. The information would be in her official records with the state, but that would be confidential and maybe impossible to access. So what would be the easiest way? Ask the chief? Nope. Find Mrs. O and ask her? Possibly, but it didn't sound like a very good idea. Terry had mentioned having that young man's name and contact information—he might know something. What ruse could I use to ask Terry for his phone number and email? It was easy.

I texted her and told her I was doing a piece on the chief for the campaign. I thought the foster father angle would be good and wondered if that former foster kid would provide a nice quote. Geez, no wonder I had trouble seeing the good in other people—I was such a liar myself! She texted back that all she had was an email. His name was Jeff Dawson. "Be sure to run anything you write by the chief. He doesn't like to be blindsided." Yeah, yeah—did she think I was an idiot? Nope, just a liar.

I sent Jeff a text, using the same ruse, hoping he wasn't in contact with the chief, or that if he was, he wouldn't share this information with him. But after all, the chief had wanted help with communications for his campaign, so maybe he'd just be pleased.

I had just gotten back to my real work when my phone rang. I didn't recognize the number, so I didn't pick up. If it wasn't spam, they could leave a message. A few seconds later, I heard the little ding that signaled someone had left a voicemail. When I took a break an hour later there was a message from Jeff. He'd be only too happy to talk about his experience with the O'Donohue's as foster parents. I got myself a Diet Coke, just to celebrate, and dialed him up.

He seemed happy to hear from me, which made me feel a little guilty. I didn't even need to ask him anything—he just jumped right in and began telling me what a blessing the O'Donohue's had been in his life. He believed he owed his present success—living in St. Louis, married with a baby on the way, and doing well selling timeshare memberships—to the time he had spent living in their home. He would be forever grateful for Chief O'Donohue's positive influence, for providing him with a strong male role model at a critical point in his life when his own parents were absent. I tried not to gag.

I let him go on for a while before I interrupted to ask what I really wanted to know. "Were there other foster kids there at the same time you were?" He said there were three of them, all boys. He took off on a tale about some high-jinx they'd been involved with and got straightened out by the chief. "That's very inspiring," I said. Then I asked if the name RaeAnne MacArthur rang a bell. "Wow—RaeAnne MacArthur. I haven't heard that name in years." He said RaeAnne had left the O'Donohue home under some kind of a cloud shortly before he had gone there—he hadn't known her personally, but from what he heard she was one bad apple. I told him that she had recently died by homicide, and he said he wasn't surprised. That anyone who couldn't get along with the O'Donohues must have something bad wrong with them. Mrs. O'Donohue, he said, had been something of a cold fish and hadn't related to him or the other foster kids the way the chief had. She actually preferred that they call her Mrs O'Donohue, but in general she was a good sort. The chief was such a warm, caring person that he made up for her lack of motherliness. He tried to be a real father to them, even insisted that they call him "Daddy O."

Bingo! This information was a freaking goldmine—more than I'd anticipated. I couldn't get rid of Jeff fast enough so I could share this with Merritt and get his take on it. But it seemed he could talk all day about the chief's virtues. He even offered to fly to Oregon to speak at a fundraiser or rally if we needed him. I told him thanks, we'd keep that in mind, but not to buy the plane ticket yet.

So, did I feel guilty about lying to Jeff? Hell no. Knowing you're a liar and feeling guilty about it are two different things. What I did feel was anxious about the possibility that he would talk to the chief—and that if he did, he would mention that I had asked about RaeAnne. I asked if he was in contact with

O'Donohue and he said no, that he'd tried to see him when he was in Gearhart and had left his contact information—but that the chief had never contacted him. I hoped it would stay that way.

So now I knew there was a connection between RaeAnne and O'Donohue—that it was possible—no, likely even—that he had been involved with her sexually when she was a teenager. Could that mean she had been blackmailing him, too, or even that he had killed her? It didn't seem too far a stretch. I still thought Sandaas was the more likely candidate. But this complicated our case against him, at least in my mind. I called Merritt and told him what I'd discovered. "No fucking way," was his response. "Shit." I understood what he was feeling. He hated Sandaas and wanted him to be guilty. I had wanted that, too. But it was possible that he wasn't.

It appeared there was no reason to compare a sample of Sandaas's writing to that in the "Daddio" letter. I wished I had a sample of O'Donohue's writing, just to be sure. And then I remembered the envelope in my underwear drawer, just waiting there in among my Tommy Johns to be of service. I pulled it out and looked at it. What I hadn't noticed or thought about before was that it was a cash envelope, one of those the bank gives you. Hmm.

I put the two handwritten pieces on the table side by side. The stuff on the envelope appeared to have been written in haste, and the note to RaeAnne had been written carefully—and based on how it looked, possibly several years earlier. Even so, there was little doubt in my mind they could have been written by the same person. That said, it never hurts to have an expert confirm what the would-be expert thinks—even if it wasn't going to prove that O'Donohue was or wasn't RaeAnne's killer.

Family Ties

October

Until Liz asked me about it, I hadn't thought anything about getting in touch with RaeAnne's brother Luther. He couldn't have had much of a relationship with RaeAnne in the past few years. If he had, RaeAnne would have left her assets, meager though they were, to him instead of to me. Or so it seemed, anyway. But still, he and RaeAnne had been so close when they were young. He'd surely want to know she had died.

Not knowing where or how to begin, I called Peggy for some advice. I was pretty sure RaeAnne had told me it was her caseworker who'd referred her to Awakenings. Maybe Peggy would have some kind of record.

"I can't give you the names of any family members," Peggy said when she called me back an hour later, "but I can give you the name of the person who referred RaeAnne here back in, let's see, 2013. It was a caseworker named Clare Gustafson. She worked in the West Eugene Family Center. I'm guessing that's a part of the Oregon Department of Human Services, although I can't be sure. Here's the number I have for her. That was quite a while ago, I hope the number's still good. Keep me posted, will you? And don't forget Merritt, when you're ready to go to work again we'd love to have you here."

"Thanks Peggy, I appreciate your help. And yes, when I'm ready to work again, you'll be the first to know. But first things first."

The number Peggy gave me was no longer good, but I was eventually able to work my way through the Human Services bureaucracy and locate Ms. Gustafson. Fortunately she was still working for Oregon Child Welfare, now as a supervisor in the West Eugene office. She was too busy to talk when I first reached her, but she agreed to call me back later that afternoon. When we finally connected I introduced myself and asked her if she remembered the name RaeAnne MacArthur.

"Why are you asking?"

"I'm a friend of RaeAnne.We met each other in NA. We'd both struggled with addiction. I believe you were her foster care caseworker. She was killed not long ago and I want to be sure her brother Luther hears about that. I know they were very close at one time. I guess Luther was adopted by a family who wouldn't adopt her and she had to leave that home. Things went south for her after that, and I guess she lost contact with Luther."

"Killed! Oh my God! Things are never easy for any kid who winds up in foster care. Don't get me wrong. We have some great foster families. Some excellent adoptive families for that matter. But for so many kids, there's always the sting of having been taken from their parents' home. But killed. We rarely see that, thank God. So anyway, you say this person's name is RaeAnne MacArthur. It sounds familiar, but I've worked with so many kids. Give me a minute to look her up."

After several minutes she came back to the phone. "OK, I just did a quick review of RaeAnne's record and now I remember her. She definitely struggled when Luther was adopted and she wasn't. Then the family made her leave. That always seemed so cruel to me, but it was out of our hands. She bounced around a few more foster homes before she fell off my radar screen. It was a couple of years before I saw her again. By then, and you already know this so I can discuss it with you, she was struggling with addiction. What a life. She was finally ready to accept help and I referred her to Awakenings. That was the last I heard about her until today when you called. Killed. Oh my God! What happened?"

I gave her a brief sketch of the story, without adding that I was a suspect. Instead, I said "the police are still looking for her murderer. I've got some ideas of my own, but I don't want to go there just now. What I really want is a way to locate Luther. Can you help me with that?"

"I'm afraid that confidentiality won't permit me to give you the name of the family that adopted him. What I will do is call them and ask them to please get in touch with you. I won't give them any details, just that it's important to you to find Luther. And then we'll hope they contact you."

It was the best she could do, so I agreed. "That you Ms. Gustafson, I appreciate any help you can provide."

"You're welcome, Merritt. I'll do my best. And thank you for trying to find Luther. Birth family is really important, even when we sometimes try to pretend otherwise. He deserves to know about his sister. Good luck."

There wasn't much more I could do. I just had to wait and hope that Luther's family called me so I could talk with him. I was eager to see Sandaas arrested for RaeAnne's murder, but Justin was following up on some of the forensic stuff before we took what we found to the police. So for me it was sit around and wait.

Since the police were still holding RaeAnne's car, Liz let me borrow her car to drive up to Long Beach for a few days. The beach there was perfect for kite flying, which I found really soothing somehow. Kind of a meditation. Perfect for the moment. I'd brought a couple of kites with me and managed to get one exceptionally high. I sat down on the beach, planted the string in the sand, watched the kite fly, and thought about the past year.

So much had happened since I'd been here last year with Liz and Val. My kite seemed to enjoy dancing in the wind as the clouds floated by. Not for the first time I found myself wishing that I could fly. Right now I'd love to fly right out of here. Wind up who knows where. Anywhere I wasn't a murder suspect. Anywhere I didn't have to tell someone I didn't even know that his sister had been killed.

Those deep and difficult conversations had been a part of my work as a priest. I loved them. I was good at them. I had a gift for them. I once again wondered whether I would ever again serve as a priest. The role came so naturally to me, and yet I was so wounded by the Church. But still... was that part of my life really over? It would be such a relief to see Sandaas behind bars so I could relax and reflect on my own life again, my life as a free man. Please God.

The day after I returned from Long Beach my cell phone rang. The caller ID showed the name Bowen, Luther's family. I remembered the name now that I saw it, although I couldn't have pulled it out of my brain. I gulped and answered. "Hello, Merritt Grace here."

"Hello Mr. Grace. This is Ginger Bowen. Clare Gustafson asked me to call you. She said you're trying to locate our son Luther."

"Yes, yes Mrs. Bowen. Thank you for calling. I am trying to locate Luther. I was a friend of his sister, RaeAnne. I know they haven't had much contact, but I think he'd want to know that RaeAnne is no longer living."

"RaeAnne is dead? What happened?"

"Mrs. Bowen, I'm sorry, but I don't feel that I'm in a position to go into that with you. I'm sure Luther will share whatever he wants you to know about this."

"Well, she was always a troubled girl. So much like her mom. I guess I'm not too surprised she's dead. Whatever. Well, I'll give you Luther's phone number, if it's still good. We don't have a lot of contact these days. Last we heard he was living in Cannon Beach and calling himself Luke. Luke, like Luther wasn't a good enough name for him. Well anyway, here's his number."

I was shaking with rage at Ginger Bowen's characterization of RaeAnne. After all, she'd kicked RaeAnne out of her house.

Would RaeAnne's life have been better if she'd been adopted by the Bowens and remained with her brother? Impossible to know. But then the question of Luther. Why was he not in regular contact with his adoptive mother? And why did he call himself Luke? I put these thoughts aside. "Thank you Mrs. Bowen, I appreciate your help with this. I wish you a good day." And I hung up. Mission accomplished.

I decided to text Luther instead of calling him on the phone. Give him a chance to think about my request before he has to talk with me. I wrote:

Luke. My name is Merritt Grace. Your sister RaeAnne was a good friend of mine. I know how very much she loved you and how close the two of you were at one time. I'd like to meet with you and talk about what's happened to her. I know she would want that. Please let me know what you think. Thanks.

He immediately texted me back.

How did you find me? And what's happened to RaeAnne? And yes, I want to hear about my sister. Let's meet. Can you come to Cannon Beach?

Within minutes we had a plan to rendezvous the next day at Cannon Beach Pig 'N Pancake. I'll recognize him by his tattoo sleeve. He'll recognize me by my black coffee skin tone. My heart beat a little faster as I anticipated our meeting.

The next morning after I dropped Liz off at the kite shop, I continued down 101 to meet Luke, less than a half hour's drive from Gearhart. How sad that he and RaeAnne hadn't reconnected while they were both here on the coast.

Dominated by Haystack Rock and graced by wide sandy beaches, Cannon Beach is home to upscale shops which contrast with the arcades so prevalent on Seaside's main drag. The town was crawling with tourists. I found the Pig 'N Pancake at the south end of the downtown area. Perched up on a hill, it was in a nice location overlooking an urban wetland. Entering, I scanned the nearly full dining room but saw no one with a full sleeve tattoo—at least as far as I could tell. I was lucky to find a seat at the last empty table—in the back by the window. Nice view. The menu had all kinds of pancakes, but my eye stopped at the Crab Benedict. My God it looked good, and coming from a vegetarian household I was more than ready for a taste of crab. I decided to wait for Luke to order and asked for some coffee to start.

A few minutes later a tall, slender young man, early 20's, entered the main dining area. It had to be Luke. I stood up and waved him over. He greeted me with a wary smile. "You must be Merritt Grace."

I glanced at his tattooed arm. "And you must be Luke Bowen." We laughed, shook hands, and took our seats.

After we ordered—Crab Benedict for me and steak and eggs for Luke—we were both momentarily without words. At least we were going to eat well. Luke finally broke the ice. "So, uh, what's with RaeAnne?" His gaze was again wary. I saw a lot of RaeAnne in his face.

"First, let me thank you for agreeing to meet me. Here I just bounce into your life out of a clear blue sky."

Luke nodded. "It's a nice restaurant. I have to eat. So, what the heck? I might as well meet you here." The concern on his face belied the nonchalance of his words.

"I'll begin with the hardest part of my story." I stopped and took a deep breath. "I'm sorry to tell you that RaeAnne is dead. She was killed about a month ago."

"Killed. Damn. Why was I afraid that's what you were gonna tell me? RaeAnne. She always walked on the wild side. But fuck, I can't believe it. She was a good person—she didn't deserve to die. Damn, damn, damn. How was she killed? Was it an accident—an overdose?"

I had just enough time to tell him RayAnne had been murdered when the waitress brought our order, which now seemed a bit extravagant in the face of all we were talking about. We gratefully let her refill our coffee cups. Luther stared at his plate, took a couple sips of coffee, and began again. "So, how did you know RaeAnne?"

I told him everything—how we were both Second Chancers at PBH, how we became friends at NA, how she had shared her life story with me, how she'd been killed.

"Was she your girlfriend?"

"No, she would have liked to be but that didn't work for me. We were just close friends" I didn't go into any detail. "I know she was lonely. And pretty vulnerable, I guess."

"Oh man, I really regret losing contact with her. Especially now. I kept meaning to look her up. Oh man." He was silent for a moment. "Right up the highway in Seaside. Damn." He took a bite of steak and eggs. "You know, before we went into foster care she was like a mother to me. Our own mother was so fucked up, always loaded, but RaeAnne. She was my rock when I was a little kid."

"She told me."

"After we were at the Bowens things changed. They really liked me but they never took to RaeAnne. I don't know why. Maybe because she was older. Maybe because she still kind of mothered me. Whatever. After a few years the state terminated my mom's parental rights. I guess that made sense, we never saw her. But all of a sudden RaeAnne and I were free for adoption. The Bowens wanted me but not RaeAnne." Luke stopped his story and stared out the window.

"How old were you then?" I already knew these details from RaeAnne, but it was good to hear his version of the story.

"I dunno. Maybe ten or so."

"Did you want to be adopted?"

"Well yeah, I guess. It was a nice house. I liked my mom and dad OK. I hated that they didn't want to adopt RaeAnne, too. By that time she was a teenager. Getting into all kinds of trouble. I'm not sure I would have wanted to adopt her either.

But she was my sister. I was really torn up when they made her leave."

"What did you do?"

"I didn't have much choice. I guess I stuffed away my feelings for RaeAnne and became a Bowen. Luther Bowen."

"Did you ever see RaeAnne after that?"

"A few times. She bounced around from one foster home to another. Got kicked out of most of them I guess. I don't know, I kind of liked the last one she was at. I think their name was O'Donohue. They took in a lot of kids. He was a cop. Big guy. Nice guy. Family man. I don't know why she couldn't get it together to stay there. Pissed me off, to tell you the truth. I thought she just wasn't trying."

O'Donohue. I struggled to maintain my cool. "Well you never know I guess."

"After that, as I said, I lost track of her. I'm quite sure she started using drugs pretty heavily, if she wasn't already. I don't know."

I couldn't wait to tell Justin about RaeAnne being with O'Donohue. But for the time being I had to keep the conversation going. "You said you were pissed with the Bowens for not adopting RaeAnne?"

"Yeah, totally. For a year or so I played the part of the good son. Got along, did OK in school. But when I started high school everything just kinda caught up with me. I started using drugs myself. Me, who swore I'd never use. Skipped school most days. Just about flunked out. John and Ginger always on my case. I'm sure they regretted adopting me."

"How'd you wind up here in Cannon Beach?"

"I lucked out. Chas Arkins, the Voc Ed teacher at my high school, took a liking to me. Can't say why. I guess he saw something in me I couldn't see. He got me started in auto mechanics. I turned out to be pretty good at it and Chas asked a friend of his, Gary Moon, who owns the auto repair here in

Cannon Beach, to take me on. Kind of as an apprentice. I'd have to stay clean of course, and manage my temper. Work hard, you know the drill. The rest, as they say, is history. I've been here a few years now, learning a lot, working hard, making friends."

"And all this time you were just a few miles down the highway from RaeAnne. Man, that's crazy."

"If only I'd known. Fuck. Why didn't I try to find her? I guess it doesn't matter now."

"Do you ever see the Bowens?"

"No. I tell them where I am. Just because, I guess."

"Good that you do. Not sure I would have ever found you otherwise. So... what's with the name Luke? And all the tattoos?"

"My legal name is still Luther, which I hate. I started calling myself Luke in high school, about the same time I started getting these tattoos."

I examined the designs on Luke's arm—mostly an assortment of fire-breathing dragons. "Nice dragons! We've got a large dragon kite hanging over our dining room table where I live. What do dragons mean to you?"

"I dunno, I guess maybe strength. Power." He pointed to a small blossom on the inside of his forearm. "This lotus tattoo here is my favorite. It brought me luck. I met my girlfriend Maria at the Blue Rose Tattoo when I went there to get it. It represents new life. She did a great job, don't you think?"

"Yes, I like it. So, this really is a new life for you here."

"Yeah. Maria and I are living together. Between her work at the Blue Rose and mine at Gary's we do OK. Starting a new life. We're both committed to staying clean. Maybe a beer now and then but no drugs. I've been down that road. I know the damage they can do. And now, RaeAnne... " His voice trailed off.

"Would you like to come to Gearhart to help me scatter her ashes?"

He thought for a moment. "Yes. I think I would. When?"

"No plans now. We'll stay in touch about that. I've got a few other fish to fry before I can get to that. I want to give it my full attention and right now—I can't. But I'll keep you in the loop."

We finished our breakfast, paid up, said our goodbyes, and left. Driving home I was struck by the irony of Luke and RaeAnne living so close together here on the coast without realizing it. So near and yet so far away. Oh RaeAnne, I'm so sorry. I'm doing my best to find your killer, and I think I just may have gotten another clue this morning.

CHAPTER 26: HENRY
Gotcha, You SOB—
Oh, Wait a Minute...
Who Was It Who Dunnit?

October

I'm not a stranger to handwriting analysis, and in the past I've used the services of Emily Woods, a certified expert in forensic document examination in Portland. Forensic document examination, or "FDE" as those of us in the field call it, is all she does. She's trusted by a wide swath of police agencies and PIs, including Charlie and me. I've driven from Seattle to Portland—and now from Gearhart to Portland—a few times when I needed her testimony in a hurry. I have her on speed dial, and the next morning I gave her a call. She agreed to look at my documents for her usual fee and would do it that day if I took her to lunch. We agreed on a time and place to meet. I brushed my teeth, put on my good outfit, grabbed the envelope with the evidence inside, and hit the road for Portland.

Emily's a single woman, a little older than I am. This isn't the first time we've had lunch in the context of work and we both seem to enjoy the work-related conversation. She's nice looking but not my type, whatever that is. It's always worried me a little that she's attracted to me. She made that fairly clear early on and I tried to make it equally clear it wasn't going anywhere. She's been a good sport about it but I think she's still interested. There's almost always a meal when we work together—it makes me nervous but, hey, a guy's gotta eat.

We met at an Italian restaurant in Portland's Pearl district, not far from where Emily works. Over the lasagna special and half a carafe of chianti I told her about what I was investigating. "You're doing this for nothing?" she asked. I told her I was doing it for a friend, that no actual dollars were changing hands. She said she hoped the friendship was worth it considering the time it had taken me to drive to Portland. I think she wanted me to say the drive was worth it to see her but I didn't. I'm a liar, but not that much of a liar.

We walked back to her office and I showed her the two handwritten documents—the "Daddi-o" letter and the cash envelope. She put on a pair of gloves, which made me aware that we'd been handling them without thinking to do that. There was silence while Emily worked, examining the documents with just an occasional "uh huh" coming from her. After a few minutes she turned to me and said that she could certify "unequivocally" that the two pieces had been written by the same person, in spite of the apparent care taken with writing the one and not with the other. She would provide written documentation to that effect—the type that could be used in court if necessary. She assumed I wasn't surprised by this outcome, and she was right. I could see that the writing was pretty much the same—but I'd needed this kind of documentation to take this to the next step, whatever that was going to be.

But here's where the trip to see Emily was worth my time— not to mention her fee and the cost of the lunch. As I was putting the materials back in the envelope she asked if I had had them examined for fingerprints and who had been handling them. I told her that only Merritt and I had touched them since they'd been out of the locked box at the bank. She suggested that I have them examined immediately, before they could be corrupted by additional prints. I asked if there was somewhere in Portland I could go to have them examined without having to wait a long time. She laughed and said that would be a "yes" and a "no." But she would see what she could do. She had friends, too. If the person couldn't see me until the next day, would I be willing to stay in town overnight? Uh oh, I thought.

She made a call on her mobile and left a message for someone named Clint, telling him that she had a friend in town working on a sensitive homicide case who needed his services in a hurry. She ended with "I'll owe you one." I said I'd wait an hour to see if Clint called back but it was only twenty minutes before her phone rang. He was busy the rest of the day but he could see me the next day. I was afraid this meant I'd be obligated to take Emily to dinner but she said she had theater tickets, gave me the name of a cheap hotel near Clint's offices—and a quick peck on the cheek—and walked me to the door. Bullet dodged, crisis averted.

The hotel was cheap and decent. I ordered a burger and a salad from room service and streamed Schitt's Creek while I ate. I tried reaching Merritt to tell him what I'd learned, but I couldn't reach him. If I wasn't mistaken, he'd gone to Cannon Beach that day, so maybe that's where he was when I called. Then I called Jen and Terry and eventually fell asleep.

My appointment with Clint at Rose City Fingerprinting Services was at ten the next morning. I'd looked at their website to check their credentials—not that I thought Emily would send me to anybody but an expert. Clint was former CSI, which impressed me, although to my disappointment he didn't look a thing like Grissom or any of his successors. He seemed in a hurry so I gave him a quick overview of my investigation. He asked what I was looking for specifically. I wasn't sure, so I said to start with whose prints were on the documents.

I sat in a chair outside his office checking email while he worked. After some time he came and got me and we went into a little conference room. There were four sets of prints on the cash envelope and four on the handwritten "Daddi-o" note, a total of five different prints. All five were registered in the national database, which made identification easy. Three of the four on the envelope matched prints on the note. The prints belonged to (in alphabetical order) J. Henry Case,

Merritt Grace, Heather Jacobs, Raeanne MacArthur, and Bertram O'Donohue. My first question was who the hell was Heather Jacobs—and that's because it took a little longer for the really important information to sink in: Raeanne's prints were on the cash envelope that O'Donohue had given me. I could see it was pretty damn clear what that meant—even if I couldn't see yet how to connect the dots.

On the way back to Gearhart, I called Merritt to tell him what I'd discovered at Rose City Fingerprinting. He was surprised to hear that news, then he told me what he'd discovered from talking with Luke Bowen the day before. Wow—when it rains, it pours, as they say. I wanted to talk with him in person and see if together we could figure out what our next steps should be. It was clear to me that I had come to the point where I was obligated to turn any evidence I had over to the police. But since I'd be telling Terry that I suspected her boss of being RaeAnne's killer, I wanted to have tied up as many loose ends as possible, to be able to present her with a plausible scenario. And I felt I owed Merritt the courtesy of involving him in any decision about the information before I gave it to the cops.

It was evening by the time I got to Merritt's house. All three of them were there, just finishing dinner. Fortunately there were a few leftovers because I hadn't taken time all day to eat and I was starving. I was quite pleased to see that there was a big plate of those no-bake chocolate oatmeal cookies for dessert. We ate those and drank coffee while we discussed everything Merritt and I had learned in the past two days. The big discovery was RaeAnne's connection to O'Donohue. And we all had the same question: Who the hell was Heather Jacobs? But the more important question was what was the order of events that would account for the overlapping fingerprints?

As much as he hated to let Sandaas off the hook, Merritt had to admit O'Donohue was the more likely murderer. Actually, he was relieved that there was evidence of anyone's guilt but his own. But who was Heather Jacobs? With the guidance of the blackmail letter, we constructed several possible scenarios based on the money in a cash envelope and a meeting between RaeAnne and Daddi-O'Donohue at "their regular spot." There was no evidence that RaeAnne had a large amount of cash; it certainly wasn't in the bank account she'd left to Merritt. The fact that O'Donohue had a cash envelope with her prints on it suggested that he had given it to her and then taken it back—we assumed with the money in it—most likely after he'd poisoned her and she'd lost consciousness. That's how both their prints got on the envelope. It was obvious how mine got there.

Someone brought up how many bills it would take to make fifty thousand dollars—five hundred if they were hundreds. We did a little Google research to be sure that the hundred-dollar bill is indeed the largest denomination in use and to find out how thick five hundred of those would be—a whole lot thicker than would fit in one cash envelope. We were scratching our heads over this when Val jumped up and yelled, "I've got it! Who else would have had to touch a cash envelope?!" We looked at her, not getting it. Then Merritt said, "Of course—the teller. Heather Jacobs must be a bank teller."

"I wonder where that scumbag O'Donohue banks?" I asked.

I was certain that the police should be able to take it from there. When I said as much to Merritt I could tell the thought made him nervous. "How do you plan to go about doing that?" he asked. I said that I would meet with Terry and present her with the evidence. I didn't think she would try to protect O'Donohue. Maybe Gellerman would, but how could he in the face of such compelling evidence?

"Maybe we should find Heather first," Merritt said.

"I think we're way past the point of doing the job of the police," I said. "But maybe Terry will find Heather and get the

257

evidence from the bank before she talks to Gellerman." Merrittt looked skeptical but he didn't object any further.

As soon as I got home I called Terry and told her I needed to talk to her as soon as possible, that I had something important to tell her. She responded with, "I have something to tell you, too." I wondered if she had discovered what I'd discovered. I asked about breakfast the next morning. She said that would be too late, that she really wanted to see me, and that if I was game she'd be at my place within an hour. That would give me time to shower away the road dust and tidy up—of course I was game. We hadn't seen each other for several days, victims of our busy lives.

Just shy of an hour later Terry arrived with her overnight bag and a nice bottle of Oregon pinot noir. I got out the glasses. "What's up?" she asked. I'd given some thought to how I wanted to lay this out for her. I'd decided that rather than spring it on her with "Guess who killed RaeAnne?" I'd tell my story step by step, so she could guess the ending before I got there. She got the meaning of the overlapping fingerprints right away. And I have to say she didn't even seem that surprised. "That bastard. That creepy son of a bitch," she said. Always a lady.

She knew she'd need to present this to Gellerman in the most compelling way possible, so it was she who suggested looking for Heather Jacobs before talking to Gellerman. I thought that was a little cavalier of her, considering that such actions could cost her her job.

Looking at O'Donohue's bank account would usually require a warrant, and that would be tricky, since the warrant would need a judge's signature and a judge would expect O'Donohue to authorize such a request. But even having the testimony of a bank teller would be enough for now.

One nice thing about small towns is that people know a lot about other people. Terry knew, for example, that O'Donohue banked at the Bank of America in Seaside. We drove there together the next morning, stopping for an Egg McMuffin on the way. I waited in the car while Terry went into the bank. I'd been waiting for a long time, just finishing my cold coffee after a little nap, when she opened the door and got in. "Bingo," she said.

There'd been some confusion at first because Heather Jacobs was now Heather Lockwood, having gotten married six weeks before. She'd shown Terry her giant rock of an engagement ring and started to talk about her wedding when Terry interrupted by pulling out her badge and telling her she was there on police business. The new Mrs. Lockwood almost wet her pants at the sight of the badge—which meant that she wanted to do everything possible to be helpful. She backed off somewhat when she discovered who the target of the investigation was, but in the end she did confirm that she had helped O'Donohue with the original transaction.

But Terry had it wrong she said; he'd only taken out ten thousand. Even that had been enough to be memorable. Then, wanting to be super-helpful, she offered the tidbit that he had replaced the money a few days later. No, she couldn't remember if he had brought it back in the original envelope.

Terry drove me back home in silence. Before I got out at my place she asked, "I guess I need to give you credit for the investigative work when I talk to Gellerman?" I didn't see how she could take credit for it except for the Heather Jacobs/Lockwood part—since she hadn't been authorized to investigate on her own. But she'd done more than Gellerman had to solve this murder, even if she'd been talking out of school by sharing information with me—and I'd be damned if I wanted to see Gellerman get credit for solving a case he'd barely touched. "Yeah, you can give me credit for it. You can tell him I was working with you. If he has a fit, tell him you suspected O'Donohue and you didn't know how he was going to react to that since he's so loyal to him.

"Maybe it won't make any difference anyway," she said. "Remember, I told you I had something to tell you?" Oh shit, I'd totally forgotten. I asked what it was.

"I have an interview for a job in the Seattle Police Department," she said proudly. "They have several openings. If I get one of those I won't have to worry about what Bruce thinks. That's why I felt okay about talking to Ms. Lockwood this morning."

"If you get one of those I'm going to miss you like crazy—but I'm going to be very proud of you," I told her.

"And you do get to Seattle once in a while, don't you?" she asked. Maybe more often now, I thought.

As it turned out, Gellerman didn't take a lot of convincing about his boss's guilt. I guess Terry must have done a good job of laying out the evidence. And he must have been impressed with the expert handwriting and fingerprint documentation—thank you Emily Wood. Gellerman knew the limitations of his authority, and he went straight to the Oregon State Police with the evidence, which they believed was sufficient to arrest O'Donohue.

After the arrest there was no difficulty obtaining a warrant for his bank accounts, which showed that he had withdrawn ten thousand dollars from savings in cash the day that RaeAnne was killed and made a cash deposit for the same amount three days later. At first O'Donohue denied everything, claiming innocence. He continued to plead not guilty, saying that he had planned to buy a new car with the cash withdrawal and had changed his mind three days later. When faced with the blackmail letter, he pointed to the difference between the fifty thousand demand and the ten-thousand dollar withdrawal as proof of his innocence. Although we couldn't explain that one, it didn't really matter.

An interview with the most unmotherly Mrs. O'Donohue in Eugene revealed that one reason for the O'Donohues' divorce had been her suspicions about his relationships with the teenage girls they fostered, RaeAnne in particular. The case against Chief Daddi-O was strong, if not altogether airtight.

Case solved—Merritt off the hook. A lot had happened to me in the context of that experience—new friendships, a new romance, a broadening of my professional experience. I'd begun to feel like a Gearhart local. But for a few days after the case was wrapped up things seemed awfully quiet and I experienced a new restlessness. My professional focus was back on insurance fraud, and there was a lot of it since I'd let it go somewhat the last few weeks in favor of the murder investigation. I didn't want to get behind again, so I was making myself keep my nose to the wheel. I didn't hate my bread-and-butter work, but I'd learned that it's more palatable if there's a little something else to spice things up.

At first Terry was still around. When she got the job with the Seattle Police Department she gave Gellerman her notice, but was planning to help him hire and train her replacement before leaving. I'd called my old friend in human resources in the SPD and put in a good word for her. She wasn't totally pleased when I told her, but she was ecstatic when she got the job. We both believed she would have gotten it without any help from me. We still saw each other, but we weren't really naïve enough to think a long-distance relationship was going to work for us.

Merritt was incredibly grateful for my help in proving his innocence. I was hopeful our friendship would last beyond this utilitarian phase. But right now he was working on his work life and I was working on mine. He'd let me know he hoped I'd attend a little memorial he was planning for RaeAnne on the beach. Since he'd gotten in touch with her brother and his girlfriend he had more new friends to keep him company. Ouch—I really felt like I might be jealous.

Maybe my time in Gearhart was up and I should think

about moving back to Seattle. After all, I'd just come to Gearhart for a month, and that had been more than six months ago. I'd accomplished most if not all of what I'd come here for. My physique and finances were in much better shape, not to mention my self-esteem. Terry would be gone, and my prospects for finding someone else to date in Gearhart weren't that great. The holidays and the winter storms were coming.

But then, after a while, things picked up again. I joined the Pub & Grub happy hour gang at least a couple of times a week and a very cute second-grade teacher named Amanda showed up one evening. I was thinking about asking her out, but then Terry came for a weekend visit—when it rains, it pours.

With O'Donohue behind bars and awaiting trial, Gellerman was acting police chief, hoping to get the job permanently. He called one morning to see if I'd meet him at the Daily Grind for coffee. I wondered if he wanted to kick my ass for interfering in the RaeAnne case. I was surprised when it turned out he wanted to thank me for my help. Terry had of course let him know of my involvement. He was chattier than usual, taking the time to catch me up on where the case stood.

And then the biggest surprise of all. There was an occasional need, he said, for the services of a PI. The Gearhart Police Department used the services of a firm in Portland—but they had signed an annual contract and the year was almost up. Would I be interested in bidding for the contract? Of course I would. There wasn't that much work, he reiterated, but one never knew, did one? Maybe RaeAnne's death was just the beginning of an upward trend in crime on the coast.

On the way out I noticed that the "For Sale" sign was still in the coffee shop window. If my work expanded anymore I'd need an associate—and that would mean an office. Maybe I'd call the owner, just to see how much.

Celebration of Life

November

On a clear, sunny Saturday afternoon a couple of weeks after Luke and I met at Cannon Beach, a small group gathered on the beach at Del Rey State Park. Justin and I had given our evidence to Gellerman a couple of weeks earlier. The mystery of RaeAnne's death finally resolved, it was now time to celebrate her life and scatter her ashes. Liz, Val, and I had debated at length about the best location for this to happen. Even though Del Rey was the park where RaeAnne had been killed, it had also been her favorite place along the coast. We finally agreed that a cleansing ritual could both purify the site of her murder and offer a healing closure to her life. Once we decided, it seemed just right.

As the group assembled, we sat in a circle on quilts we had spread out on the beach. Luke and his girlfriend Maria arrived shortly after Liz, Val, and I got there. It was the first time I'd seen Maria and I was impressed by her gentle countenance. With her tan colored skin and long, shining black hair she had the appearance of being Native American or Latina. Or perhaps a mix. She had a single blue rose tattoo on the outside of her left forearm. I immediately took a liking to her and felt grateful for Luke to have this lovely woman in his life.

We began our ritual soon after Peggy and Justin arrived. We initially sat in silence, relishing the warmth of the sun, the crashing of the waves, and our own private thoughts about RaeAnne. I then offered a prayer and invited people to speak, sharing anything they'd like to say. I was pleasantly surprised when Maria removed an Indian flute from the colorful cloth bag she had slung over her shoulder. She glanced at me for permission to play. I nodded my assent. For the next few minutes we were mesmerized by haunting, soulful tones that carried us to our deepest places. I could feel RaeAnne's presence and I knew we had chosen well when we decided to come here.

Luke was the first to speak after Maria put her flute away. "I haven't seen my sister in several years. I'm really sorry about that. She was like a mother to me when I was little. Our real mom—well, let's just say she couldn't be a mom. But RaeAnne—she always made sure I had something to eat, clean clothes, and that I got off to school on time. Stuff like that. Then I got adopted and she didn't. I'm still pissed—sorry—still unhappy about that." He paused a moment, looking out at the ocean. "After that we lost track of each other. We both got into drugs, like our mom. Runs in the family I guess. I was lucky to get clean."

He gazed fondly at Maria. "This beautiful woman helped me find my way out." A loving look passed between them. "I know nada about my mom now. My birth mom, that is, not the adoptive one. Even if she's still alive." He shrugged. "And, of course, we all know what happened to RaeAnne."

A sob escaped him as he struggled to continue. "I want to thank you, Peggy, for helping my sister as much as you could." A few tears trickled down his face. "And thank you, Merritt. For being her friend. Perhaps her only real friend." He sighed. "Thanks for finding me. For telling me about RaeAnne. For including me in this day." He stood and looked toward the sky. "Sis—I hope we meet again, next time in a better place." Maria squeezed his hand as he sat back down. "That's all for me. Thanks."

Peggy spoke next, sharing her memories of RaeAnne. Her courage in the face of the trauma that filled her life. Her heart. Her hopefulness that things could get better. Her love for her brother. "RaeAnne was doing well. She had a good job. She was beginning to heal from the wounds life had inflicted on her.

And then—this. It's hard to accept. I'm sorry, RaeAnne. I'm sorry you never got to fully live your life. I'm sorry you never knew just how beautiful you really were." She looked at me and nodded. "Thank you."

I was the last to speak. Of the seven of us gathered, only Luke, Peggy, and I had known RaeAnne. I simply talked about my friend. How much she meant to me. How I appreciated our talks, our walks on the beach. How I admired her resilience. How much I missed her now.

After the sharing we processed to the area in the parking lot where RaeAnne had lost her life. I took a cedar smudge stick out of my backpack and lit it. Maria played her flute softly as I spoke. "May the smoke from this cedar cleanse this area, remove any dark energies that still remain, and attract healing spirits to revitalize and renew this beautiful space. May the healing smoke of this cedar reach our beloved RaeAnne, wherever she may be, protect her from any darkness and let her know how deeply and well she is loved and missed." We passed the cedar stick from one to the next, each of us waving it to circulate the smoke, each of us silently praying in our own way for cleansing, healing, and love." Ending the prayer, I made a sign of the cross.

Returning to the quilts on the beach, it was time to scatter RaeAnne's ashes. I poured a portion of them into a wooden bowl I had brought with me for the occasion. Luke would take the remainder with him to disperse at sea. He and Maria planned to rent a boat at the marina in Warrenton for a family-only ceremony the following day.

With the wooden bowl resting on the quilt in front of her, Val removed eight fabric squares from her bag. They were remnants of materials she had used in quilts she had created over the years. One by one, each of us placed a small quantity of ash into one of the fabric squares, searched for a place on the beach that felt just right, and silently buried our share of the ashes in the sand. After we had all returned to the circle, one fabric square remained. This we filled with ash and tied into a tiny pouch. We fastened the pouch to the tail of a beautiful butterfly kite provided by Liz. I took the kite, ran down the beach, and watched RaeAnne's ashes rise to the heavens as the kite began to soar. I took a small knife, cut the kite string, and watched as the butterfly carrying RaeAnne's ashes disappeared from sight. "Goodbye, RaeAnne. May you know God and be blessed in His presence. I will miss you."

Our scattering ritual complete, it was time for another ritual to begin—eating. Reminiscent of the loaves and fishes, an abundance of food—more than enough for a small army— soon appeared on the quilts. True to form, Justin contributed two bottles of wine and some sparkling cider to the feast. Even as many of us were just getting to know one another, the conversation easily flowed as we enjoyed our picnic. In truth, none of us had known RaeAnne well enough to share many stories about her, but simply coming together to celebrate her life was sufficient to create a sense of family in our small gathering. Lots of talk, lots of laughter, some walking on the beach, some wading a few steps into the chill Pacific Ocean. Our celebration of RaeAnne's life ended with Maria again playing on her flute. It had been a beautiful day, and after an extended group hug we left the beach sated with gratitude for all we had shared.

Walking up to the parking lot, I turned one more time to gaze out at the ocean, to wish RaeAnne well. I was satisfied that I had done well by her with our ceremony, and I again sensed her presence. Almost like she was thanking me for the day. It had been a long time since I'd led any ritual, and today's was a far cry from anything you'd find in a traditional Catholic funeral. I felt a small twinge—of guilt? of confusion?—with this realization, but for the most part I felt profoundly satisfied with the ceremony that we had created together to celebrate

RaeAnne's life. I was particularly grateful for Maria's deeply spiritual music and presence. I hoped and expected that she and I could become good friends. I was also aware that even though the ritual had onot followed the Catholic liturgy, I had felt God's presence. I had again felt that deep spiritual calling that initially led me to the priesthood. I knew that I needed to again respond to that calling—whether or not it was as a priest. There was much that I needed to think and pray about.

I caught up with Peggy just as she was driving off. "Hey, Peggy. Do you have a minute?"

"Sure, Merritt. What's up?"

"Remember when you asked me to let you know if I wanted to come work at Awakenings?"

Peggy smiled. "I do remember that, Merritt."

"Well, I'm ready. I'd like to do some addiction counseling again."

"Come see me on Monday and we'll start the paperwork. And Merritt, thank you again for including me today. It was a beautiful experience from start to finish. You're going to make some incredible contributions at Awakenings. I can't wait to see how this all unfolds."

"Thanks Peggy. I'm eager to find out, too. See you Monday."

* * *

I looked around to see who was left. The wind was whipping up and it was cold, so everyone had scattered quickly. Just Val and Liz, who were waiting in the car for me, and Justin, who was sitting in his SUV, talking on his phone. He hung up, and I signaled to Val and Liz that I was going to go talk to him and then knocked on his window. "Hey," he said. He looked startled and a little dazed. "Great memorial. I think RaeAnne would be pleased."

"Thanks," I said. "Thanks for being here. And again, thanks

for everything you did to help. It means a lot."

"No problem. I'm glad things turned out the way they did. I mean, I'm sorry about RaeAnne, but I'm glad you're off the hook. And this was my first murder investigation—broadened my resume."

Huh. I'd been wondering what our relationship was. Was I just a *pro bono* client, or were we friends? I guess we would see—I had no way of asking. But I could use a friend in Gearhart, if I was going to stay here. I figured Justin could, too, although I didn't know what his plans were. "Hey," I said, "if you're around this next week, my other sister'll be in town, and if you want to you could join us for another feast and some five-handed card games."

"Sure—that'd be great!" His enthusiasm said a lot. "You have another sister? How did I miss that?"

"Yeah, Vicky. She and Val are twins. She's the straight one. She lives in Portland, but she's interested in moving to the coast if she can find a job."

"Well I'll look forward to meeting her next week. I'll bring the wine."

"Thanks," I said. "I'll text you and let you know which night. I gotta go—Liz and Val are waiting.

"Hey, before you go—"

"Yes?"

"You can be the first to know. That phone call—I'm the new proud owner of the Daily Grind—looks like I may be staying here a while longer."

ACKNOWLEDGMENTS

Writing this book has been an exercise in joy. The authors gratefully acknowledge the many friends who have contributed to the experience. Thanks to our "pandemic writing group" whose prompts led to the emergence of Justin Case and Merritt Grace; to Rebecca Morris, Lynne Gaertner-Johnson, Jeff VanGilder, and Peter Leander, who served as readers, critics, advisors, and editors; to Maria, our designer; and to Justin and Merritt, whose personalities are extensions of our own.

We couldn't have pursued this adventure without the love and support of our husbands and life partners, David Kile and Atit Marmer. Nor would this creative adventure have been the same without the inspiration of the amazing Oregon coast, where the four of us have spent many happy days.

Pat and Nancy lovingly toast their forty-year friendship that has brought them together as colleagues, traveling companions, and writing partners.

Made in United States
Troutdale, OR
04/22/2025

30838813R00149